STORM IN A D CUP

STORM IN A D CUP

Book Three of
The Husband Diet series

Nancy Barone

An Aria Book

ISBN (PB): 9781803287713
ISBN (E): 9781803287690

Typeset by Siliconchips Services Ltd UK

Printed and bound in Great Britain by
CPI Group (UK) Ltd, Croydon CR0 4YY

MIX
Paper | Supporting
responsible forestry
FSC® C171272

Head of Zeus Ltd
5–8 Hardwick Street
London EC1R 4RG

WWW.HEADOFZEUS.COM

To my family and friends near and far.

I

Italian Playboys

Castellino, Tuscany, five years later

'**C**iao, bella, *want a rrride?*'

I ignored the slowing Ferrari that had materialized next to me on the deserted Tuscan country lane as I trudged up the last hill leading home from the village.

The countryside around Castellino, in the province of Siena, the place we had chosen to be our home almost eight years ago, could not have been more idyllic. It was a vast, bucolic setting of endless patchwork hills of greens, yellows and russets that chased to the horizon, brushed by squiggles of tall cypress trees that ran single file, now purpling under the dome of a magenta sky.

'Flat tire? Come, come!'

'No, thank you,' I said without turning to acknowledge my molester.

'Come on, Eri-ha! It's a long way up from Castellino to your home…'

Oh God, the last thing I needed was to be ambushed by

Leonardo Cortini, the local playboy. With long, wavy sun-streaked hair and blue eyes, he was sort of good-looking-ish, in a savage, old-world, long-nosed noble family kind of way. The kind of looks that come from money and confidence. And, alas, regular visits to tanning salons. He regularly catered to the needs of lonely and/or bored women down in the Val d'Orcia.

Personally, I was neither lonely nor bored, so I couldn't understand why he was wasting a single moment of his time with me, a happily remarried mother of two. Because if Prince Charming ever existed, it was no doubt my husband Julian Foxham, the former principal at my children's school in Boston. Not that that was why we'd met. Oh no. It had to happen in the most embarrassing of ways.

My brother from another mother, Paul Belhomme, had been in the hospital with a broken leg, so I'd volunteered to bring him a change of pajamas and other essentials from his home. Only on the way, I'd had to stop at a restaurant for a quick pee. In the ladies' room, as I was washing my hands, a giant spider had somehow ended up inside my trousers, sending me into a flurry of blood-curdling screams.

At that, a man had burst in, alarmed by the ruckus, only to find me bouncing from wall to wall trying to get the dreaded thing off me. And when that hadn't worked, I'd grabbed the man, begging him to pull my trousers off. And kill the beast. When he was satisfied that I wasn't a total whack job trying to frame him for indecent acts in public, he'd proceeded to comply to my extraordinary request.

Only my zipper was stuck and he'd had to wrench my trousers off me as I continued to scream, my arms and legs flailing in every direction. By the time we were done, I'd realized that, in my panicked frenzy, I'd ripped his shirt open too.

When he'd offered to take me to lunch, I'd refused, for several reasons. One, Paul was waiting for me; two, I couldn't bear to look my rescuer in the eye after he'd seen all of my wobbliest bits; and three…? In all honesty, I struggled to find any other reason why I shouldn't have seen him again. And yet, I'd let that train pass, while thinking about him day after day. And night after night, actually. Until I came face to face with him at a meeting with my kids' principal. Meaning that he *was* my kids' principal who had called me in for, as he'd said, a simple 'chinwag'. Just so you know, when your kids' principal calls you in, it's *never* for a simple chinwag. There is always trouble lurking behind that call.

Of course it had to be the day that I had a stinking cold and looked like shit, wearing my worst suit that smelled like mothballs because I hadn't had a chance to pick up my dry cleaning. And of course, he had to go and recognize me, what with the gazillion parents he meets on a daily basis. My daughter, only eight at the time, had mentioned at school that things weren't going very well at home, as my husband Ira and I were divorcing. That had caught my principal's attention, so he'd decided we should meet. You know, just to make sure I wasn't starving them or something.

Patient, kind and gorgeous, he was the dream of many women in and outside the school and later in the town of Castellino where we'd moved to seven years ago, dethroning Leonardo Cortini as the Number-One Hunk. Not that Leonardo did anything for me, physically.

And what was it with this Leonardo guy anyway? At least a couple of times a year he tried it on with me whenever our paths crossed. He simply couldn't take *no* for an answer. I was probably one of the few married women in the province who hadn't slept with him.

Even when I was a young love-starved girl in Boston, I'd have steered clear of this guy whose ego was the size of a cathedral and who thought he was the best thing in Tuscany since Chianti wine.

Not to brag, but if you were married to the gorgeous former baseball star Julian Foxham (subsequently my kids' principal, personal savior and now full-time novelist), Leonardo Cortini wouldn't be your type either. And I, Erica Cantelli, a forty-three-year-old housewife who was always battling to keep the pounds off, was nowhere near Leonardo's (nor my hunky husband's, I would soon find out) type.

So I still had no idea why the Tuscan playboy wanted to play with me on this warm, perfect, early-summer afternoon here among the impossibly romantic and picturesque Tuscan hills dotted with cypresses and olive groves. I wasn't warm, or romantic (maybe a little picturesque) nor Tuscan. So why was he even looking my way?

'Come on, I give you a rrride, Eri-ha…' Leonardo drawled as he came to a full stop, blocking my path.

I bared my teeth at him (old habits died hard) and shook my head, pushing my stubborn handlebars as if they were the ears of a donkey that refused to budge. He laughed, and I threw him my famous hairy eyeball, but he didn't seem fazed.

'So yourrr 'usband's out of town again, *si*?'

It was the *again* that annoyed me. Otherwise I wouldn't have given him the time of day, or been suddenly defensive

4

about the fact that, yes, Julian *was* out of town again to meet his agent Terry Peterson in New York. They were apparently planning the longest book tour in history. (If that sounds even remotely familiar to you, then you know the story of my life. Because it just keeps getting harder, being happy. If you don't know much about me, then you're in for one helluva ride.) Meaning that he was away most of the time.

But when he *was* home, he entertained the guests of our exclusive holiday rentals that, thanks to Julian's connections, had lately become the secret haven for the jet set – stars who needed extreme privacy, like the lovely Lara Stanic, a Serbian gymnast whom Julian used to date, albeit for a month. She was currently seeing someone but was afraid he was cheating on her (familiar territory for me) so we'd often have a chat and she'd let me read his text messages and ask me what I thought. The guy was nuts about her. Who wouldn't be? Lara was so down to earth, a real woman despite her fame. I loved her. I didn't see how anyone couldn't. Which brought a question to mind.

'Why did you leave her?' I asked Julian.

He looked at me in alarm, like I was going to start one of my interrogations, but then he shrugged. 'I didn't. We mutually agreed that some people are meant to be just friends. Lara's a great gal.'

'Absolutely. I love her,' I agreed. Trouble was that I couldn't understand why he didn't. 'And she's absolutely gorgeous.'

'Yes, just as much on the inside, if not more,' he agreed. And I still didn't get it. What could I possibly have that she didn't? I mean, come on, between you and me, I'm a normal-ish-looking gal with unruly hair and a few curves that sometimes seem too many, depending on what mood I wake up in the morning. But Lara? I've seen her first thing out of bed and let me tell you she is gorgeous, especially without make-up.

And as I still lived outside of the Beautiful People Alliance, I often asked myself why two gorgeous and nice people who'd slept together, and decided to see more of each other, could let the relationship die. I mean, if the sex (cringe of jealousy) was great and conversation was brilliant, what could possibly go wrong in a relationship? What was it that constituted that special ingredient that you just couldn't pluck out of thin air?

'Only you could ask a question like that,' Julian said with a chuckle. 'When will you stop thinking it's just about two bodies?'

'Huh? It's not?'

He caressed my cheek with his index, his eyes shining. 'Of course not. It's about communion. The kind that lasts beyond everything else. *Our* kind of communion, Erica.'

Communion? Sure, Julian and I got along great, but what made him not look elsewhere in the times when we didn't? Even you would wonder at it. I mean, he had plenty of choices, if our guests and his army of ex-flames visiting were anything to go by, including Polly Parker, a tap dancer, and Moira Mahoney, owner of at least a dozen fashion magazines and still 'very fond' of my husband. 'Hang on to him, Erica,' she'd warned me with a wink. 'Watch out for the vultures.' Meaning, first of all, her.

Don't get me wrong. I know he loves me and all, but when I see all these classy women from his past sitting at my dinner table, all so cultured and glamorous and classy, all oh-so-put-together, I can't help but wonder... why me? Why did he choose me, and not, say, the Nobel Prize winner? Why not the gold medalist? Why not the eminent surgeon? What could I possibly have that they don't? It's a question I have always asked myself and have yet to find an answer to. And it is the only fly in my champagne. I mean my lack of confidence is. Because God knows Julian has never given me a reason to doubt him or his love for me. So yes, it was all on me, and I would have to solve my issues on my own.

Sometimes I wondered how Julian managed to remain so down-to-earth with all the fame and connections. And his talent? Both Julian's reader fans and baseball fans were waiting with bated breath. But I, his wife of five years, was allowed nowhere near the book – or even his study, for that matter, until it was finished.

That was the only thing I never liked about Julian being a writer. And the fact that to him running A Taste of Tuscany had become secondary. Not that he ever refused to collaborate or anything, but he was away a lot of the time, and although it had started out as *my* dream, I always hoped it could be his, too.

But, day by day, he'd carved his own parallel life outside our family routine, delegating his own chores on the property to our employees while concentrating more and more on his own craft. Which was his right, of course. But why did that make me feel excluded from his life? Weren't couples supposed to have a sense of communion?

This had been a huge problem for us in the past. But I'd ultimately learned my lesson a few years ago when I was crazy jealous of his gorgeous publicist. After a rocky road that almost led to our big fat Italian break-up, we swore we'd never do *that* again, had managed to patch things up and soldiered on.

And despite all his sermons about beauty only being skin deep, yada yada, I still found it hard to believe that, in Julian's loving eyes, my personality actually compensated for my looks.

Don't get me wrong – I'm not that ugly. At least I don't think so. I'm just rather non-modelesque. Tall, I'm tall, and I could do with losing some weight. My curly brownish hair is always all over the place and I'm so insecure – and conscious of it – that I can sometimes come across as arrogant. But Julian knows that inside I'm pure mush.

'Ah, Ameri-han men – no passion and verrry ambitious!' Leonardo concluded for me. 'Eri-ha, be *my* woman and I treat you like a queen!'

Which I found very hard to believe, judging by his reputation. Leonardo Cortini lured the ladies, 'loved' them (as much as a misogynist could) and then left them hanging for all the time it took to make yet another full lap of the female population inhabiting the entire province of Siena, from the Val d'Orcia to Le Crete.

I can assure you it would take even Leonardo Cortini quite a while to exhaust the area, all the while, mind you, keeping telephone contact with his previous victims, promising to return. And when he completed the rounds (and got his ass kicked by some angry husbands in the process) he *did* return, just in time to find the damsel in distress oh-so-grateful that he actually had kept his promise. Of course he would. Where else was he going to go? Because Leonardo Cortini had never, get this, been outside of Italy, can you believe it? With all his money and his fast cars, he never actually *traveled* anywhere.

Can you imagine actually sitting home and waiting for someone like that to call you on a Friday night? Come to think of it, that was beginning to sound like *my* relationship with Julian, minus the other women.

Because I knew lots of women who had their claws into married men and when someone began sniffing around, I kept a close (but silent) eye on my own guy. You wouldn't believe the stuff I had to put up with even in broad daylight. Endless (and that's a mouthful for a population of barely five thousand people) females parading themselves for Julian's benefit at the market, on parents' night or even in the piazza during our Sunday morning cappuccino.

Even the waiter at Nando's, our favorite café, gave him the coy smile. From the morning when we went into town to run our errands, be it to get fresh milk (we had chickens for eggs but as far as farm animals were concerned I drew the line at cows) to our weekend strolls through the streets of Castellino or Cortona or Anghiari, we were always admired. Well, he was admired and I was envied.

Just to prove to you that I'm not imagining it, whenever we went to a shop or an eatery, I'd try to get the attention of the person at the counter, but they would ignore me. Until Julian walked in to see what was keeping me. And instantly the people in charge, mainly women, would turn to him, eager to please.

OK, I know he's a heart-stopper, but are there really no other good-looking men available that they have to prey on mine? I worked hard to find him, ladies, and at the end of a twelve-year slog, karma finally decided to cut me some slack. So please leave my guy alone and go get your own, thank you very much. Why do people not behave themselves or remember their place?

Like this idiot following me home now, getting a clear, unobstructed view of my oversized derrière.

'My husband will be back very soon,' I bit off as Leonardo got out of his car, now towering over me.

'Come home with me for *aperitivi*. I make you fantastic *bruschette*! And then, we'll see what happens, *sì*?' said the Big Bad Wolf to not-so-little old me as, with a sudden yank, he hefted my bike out of my hands. If this was his seduction technique, I wondered how he managed to pull anything more than a muscle. Again I gave him my world-famous hairy eyeball.

'Uh, no, thanks,' I assured him.

That's when, smiling his expensive, fake-tanned smile, he put his hand on my arm. And I realized that we were in the middle of the infinite green and yellow countryside, where there were no proper main roads, let alone traffic whatsoever, particularly at this time of year. The wheat was still maturing in the fields, gently swaying, green over hill and dale, and so were the olives in their vast groves, and the grapes still clung lovingly to their vines. Nothing was ready to be reaped, much less me.

In the golden rays of the sinking sun, and the russet reflections reverberating from the fields, I looked at him and, despite my big, strong body, trembled with apprehension. He was much bigger than me. I swallowed, trying to gauge the seriousness of his intentions by the glint in his eye. And let me tell you – it wasn't looking good.

'Come on, Eri-ha,' he whispered, now running his index finger up my arm. 'I trrreat you verrry good.'

OhGodohGodohGod. I tried to catch my breath, to get some oxygen into my system to prepare for a damn good fight. If I struck out, I'd escalate this thing to a new level, which is something you don't want to do, right? You hope the guy calms down. That is, if you can't outrun him. Outrun a guy in a Ferrari? I tried to swallow but it wasn't working. I could barely breathe.

'She already *has* someone treating her good,' came my neighbor's voice, thank you God, from out of the blue.

Marco, big, tall, cute in a very boyish, wholesome farmer way, and good as gold. I sagged in relief, so deep had my terror been that I hadn't heard him coming. Marco and his wife Renata lived a mile down the road and had adopted us from Day One when we had arrived totally clueless and with a container full of furniture, home design magazines and a whole lot of dreams. Besides our real estate agents and notary public, they had been the first people we'd met in Castellino.

Renata is tiny and blonde, with big blue eyes and big breasts, which is pretty much a man magnet around here. When we're out and about, I see the way men check her out. She may be slight, but she's a rebel packed with strength, determination, oodles of mischief, irreverence and talent. She is the best cook in the area and works hard to raise her kids. And like me, she couldn't care less about appearances.

They had arrived one morning, the entire family, with a basket full of goodies such as homemade bread, cakes and cookies, along with fresh jams and Nutella. And a thermos full of espresso coffee and endless chatter. How could you not instantly fall in love with them? And soon thereafter we became like family, sharing our weaknesses and secrets, seeing each other out through thick and thin. And the best part was that Julian and Marco had become like brothers, too.

Marco would give Julian advice on running the farm, and Julian would give Marco tips on how and where to invest their savings. There was a very strong bond between us that, outside Paul and my aunts, I had found nowhere else.

Marco stepped out of his faded blue Fiat Nuova Strada pickup and strode to my side, facing Leonardo with his fists clenching at his sides, sheer murder in his eyes, although Marco had never, in the seven years I'd known him, hurt a fly. 'Get lost,' he spit out. 'She has her family and friends. You are neither. Now get into your car before I run you over, and you have no idea how happily I would do that.'

'*Calmati, mi-ha te la mangio*. Calm down, I won't eat her,' Leonardo said and Marco turned to snarl at him as he loaded my bike onto his pickup. Poor Marco was ready to put up his dukes for his crazy American neighbor who still had to learn the unspoken laws of female survival in Italy.

'Now, or I'm getting in my car,' Marco ordered.

And Cortini obeyed. I watched as he scowled, got into his Ferrari and gassed it for all he was worth, disappearing over the hill in a cloud of dust.

'Are you OK, sweetie?' Marco asked, touching my elbow.

'Yes, thanks. Just a bit shaken, I guess.'

'Well, try not to be out on your own without anyone else being around.'

'But this is a safe place,' I argued. 'Nothing ever happens here.'

'*He* happened, isn't that enough for you?'

Of course, Marco was right. All you needed was one scumbag to ruin everything.

And all this because I'd gone into town after a sudden hankering for a piece of ready-made *Panforte*, too lazy to bake it myself. This wasn't the first time my gluttony had got me into trouble. Screw my old bike – next time I was taking the Jeep. Or baking something myself.

'If you care about your marriage at all, I suggest you stay away from that *pezzo di mota*. He's only trouble,' Marco growled as the pickup plowed through the colorful countryside still tinged with the light of the setting sun.

It really *was* beautiful. If only Julian had been there to see it. But at the moment Julian was very far from all this. I decided I wasn't going to tell him about Leonardo. He'd have a fit and probably go down to his house down by the river and sock him one himself. He was like that, Julian. Protective and territorial, probably due to the memories of our life in Boston, where my ex-husband Ira was constantly on my tracks and Julian always on the alert.

'He sure *looks* like trouble,' I said to Marco. 'Is there any truth to his reputation? That he attacked a woman once?'

Marco gave me a sidelong glance and my suspicions were confirmed. 'Yes. And he and Renata were officially engaged many years ago.'

'Ah.' So that was it. She had bedded the monster. Or vice versa.

'*Ah* is right. He left her waiting at the altar, the *bastardo*.'

'Now I understand why you hate him.'

'Everybody hates him.'

'I wonder why he doesn't move away, then?'

Again Marco cast me a sidelong glance as we reached the bottom of the hill where my driveway began its squiggly drunk's doodle, with giant, deep green cypresses piercing the magenta sky like sentinels on either side. 'Because he owns half the town, that's why.'

I looked over at Marco's face in the rapidly darkening sky. '*Owns*?'

'Yes. The *villa comunale*? He owns that, gardens and all. The secondary school building? His family owns that, too. Remember the school had to move premises last year?'

'Yeah?'

'That was because he upped their rent so high, just to make them leave the premises.'

'Geez…'

'And the public library? They pay rent to *him*. The list is endless – the banks, the post office and all the buildings around the town square. Why do you think it's called Piazza Cortini?'

Seven years of living here and I hadn't made the connection. 'What are they, rich and famous as the Medici?'

Marco snorted. 'Worse, if you can imagine that at all. Every medieval building you see has the Cortini coat of arms on it.'

'What, the one with the hawk and lilies with the chipped eggs?' To me the two white spheres below the hawk looked like eggs, but obviously my mind wasn't as filthy as someone else's who'd spray-painted a penis in on every single plate bearing the coat of arms. The perpetrator, someone who obviously hated the family, was on a mission.

After the phallus addendum had been dutifully (and quickly) whited out, said perpetrator decided to do a more thorough job and chip off the plaster balls completely.

'Actually, the Cortini family were very intimate with the Medici family centuries ago. And today Leonardo is the only heir to the Cortini dynasty, one of the oldest and richest families in the Val d'Orcia.'

I turned to look at Marco in surprise as he negotiated the twists and turns up the hill. 'Wow.'

'Half the Val d'Orcia is in the hands of a *stronzo*.'

I got the message. *Stronzo* is the word I'd have used to describe my ex-husband Ira through and through. (And still use, whenever my mind – rarely – strays that way.)

'Didn't you mention to Renata you're on your own tonight?' Marco asked.

I nodded. What else was new? Now that the kids were older and my B&B, A Taste Of Tuscany, practically ran itself it seemed to me I had more time for myself. *By myself*.

'Maddy's sleeping over at Angelica's and Warren stayed in Siena this weekend.'

Warren is my twenty-year-old son who looks so much like my dad. Ever since we got here, his hair has gone lighter and his eyes brighter. He is a happy-go-lucky boy with a love for sports and his friends, particularly his girlfriend. Nothing can shake him. I guess he'd done all the family drama when he was a kid and was now all the stronger for it. You could tell him that his pants were on fire and he'd still have to ponder over it before he panicked. Which was a good thing, considering he could have turned out like his father, my first husband.

In his first year of college, normally, Warren would return

from his flat in Siena, loaded with his laundry and empty Tupperware food containers that I dutifully filled up for him every week, like a good Italian *mamma*. And when he did come back, he spent all his time with his girlfriend and study-buddy (although how much studying they get done is debatable) Stefania, who, you guessed it, practically shared his digs with him.

Rumor had it she actually had her own place, like everyone else, but Warren's was way nicer, so she had decided to sublet hers and sponge off Warren. I mean off us. They preferred Siena, which was, at least by Italian standards, a larger city. And now they hardly ever came back to Castellino, too wrapped up in their romance. I only hoped that Warren would soon develop a similar love for his books.

But all in all so far, if you didn't count his goo-goo eyes for his girlfriend Stefania, raising my son had been a piece of cake. He'd always, well almost always, been collaborative and helpful. Always a great kid. Brave. Loyal, even to his own detriment. Remind you of any other fool?

Maddy and her BFF Angelica, on the other hand, were always holed up in her room or at Angelica's house near the piazza, the safest place I could think of. They couldn't make a single move without the entire village knowing what they were up to. And the rare times Maddy was at home, she'd chat with Angelica on her cell phone or send texts. I swear I'd never seen anyone type so fast. The next generation would have two very well-developed thumbs. When I pointed out how it was still important to read an actual book, or watch the news, my former little angel-fairy would roll her eyes and groan, 'Mom, get yourself a life and stop badgering me.' And she said that quite a lot, lately.

Where oh where had my beautiful angel of yesteryear gone? The sweet little princess and frequent hug-dispenser who always said, 'Yes, please, thank you', and, best of all, 'I love you, Mommy'?

'Where the hell did she get her temper from?' I'd ask myself loud enough for Julian to hear, hoping he'd have an answer.

He'd step into the kitchen, smile at me and in his good old Liverpudlian accent he'd reply, 'I haven't the faintest idea, luv.'

I always blamed Marcy. She's my dead mother's twin sister who had passed herself off as my real mom from my birth for thirty-five years, leaving me in the dark as to why she preferred my siblings Judy and Vince, her own biological children. But hey, that's a story for another time.

Once that family mystery had been solved, my life had improved overnight. No longer did I question myself as to the reasons for this palpable preference of my siblings over me. I got it. She was my mother's twin who married my father. She'd been in love with him before he even married my mom. So in the end when my real mom died, Marcy had got what she wanted. Except for the excess baggage, i.e. me, and she never missed a chance to show me how she felt about me intruding on her happiness. Although she and my mom were identical twins, I didn't look anything like them. But my mother's three other sisters, my aunts Maria, Monica and Martina, assured me I had my mother's personality.

Well, sort of. I was still me, unfortunately. And now I was beginning to see traces of my Marcy in my daughter Maddy. Not physically, because while Maddy is tall and has light hair and green eyes, Marcy is a petite and glamorous (fake) brunette who loves her eye make-up as much as Cleopatra did. Always bejeweled and dressed in the latest (and highest) fashion, she can usually be found either lounging or lunching. Or fashion shopping, usually with Judy who was practically her mini-me in so many ways.

If on one hand it annoyed me that Marcy's uncontrolled narcissism had rubbed off on my daughter, on the other I was also grateful that my own painful, gut-wrenching insecurity hadn't penetrated my daughter's soul. And that she hadn't inherited my tendency to pile up the pounds. Oh, how I wished my kids really were Julian's biological children.

He certainly spoiled them like they were really his own. And when they were late, it was Julian who did all the pacing, the checking of our cell phones to make sure we had a proper signal. You'd think he really was their father instead of their (albeit very zealous) ex-principal turned my partner and subsequent husband. Legally, they were Foxhams because after our marriage Julian had adopted them, much to Ira's indifference.

Luckily, I hadn't heard from Ira for years. After trying to financially ruin us by stealing the kids' college funds, he had a baby with Maxine Moore (his then-secretary slash lover slash mother of his third – as far as I know, child). Once he came out of the loony bin for crooks, she continued to give him the cold shoulder until he stopped calling her.

Rumor (OK, my friend Paul) had it he had done time for tax evasion and hooked up with younger ladies in Vegas who systematically drained him of his winnings. Ira had always been a cheat. Cards, marriage – you name it, you got it. He simply couldn't stay committed to one decision.

'Erica?' Marco said, jolting me out of my family musings. 'Why don't you come over to dinner tonight? Renata has a pheasant in the oven and we haven't seen you forever.'

Renata. She and I were very similar, only she was amazing. She ran the family *agriturismo*, a restaurant where they grew their own livestock and vegetables which they served on a delicious menu. She was a wonderful cook and had taught me loads of recipes while I taught her how to make cheesecake and some Sicilian recipes like *arancini*, these big, sinfully tasty rice balls filled with meat. Just thinking about them made my mouth water.

She easily had the best food in the province of Siena if you didn't count Alberto Veronesi, owner of the Degustibus restaurant (whom I steer clear from for the gazillion reasons you will remember if you've been on this crazy band wagon with me from the start). If you haven't, well, you've missed out on all the fun.

I always recommended Renata's restaurant to my guests. Which was why I was tempted to go and spend my otherwise empty evening with them. But even after all these years I'd never actually been there for dinner on my own.

Normally when Julian was away I considered it my duty to hold the fort, make sure everything was under control and catch up on my ironing or cleaning. Or preferably my grooming and my numerous Netflix series. So now going over there on my own without Julian felt awkward.

'I don't know,' I said. 'I'm not really up for it. I think I'll catch up on my sleep.'

'Come on, Erica. It'll be a relaxing evening. Some good Chianti, some *sugo alla lepre*…'

'You had me at the pheasant,' I said with a grin. 'OK, I'm in.'

He dropped me and my bike off at my front door and I turned to wave. 'Thanks, Marco!'

'I'll stop by tomorrow to fix that,' he called as he pulled out.

'Oh, that's OK. Julian will be home tomorrow.'

With a grin and a wave he drove off. What a wholesome guy. I wondered how Renata could have been in love with such a *stronzo* like Leonardo.

2

The End

I was piling my freshly decorated cupcakes into my favorite food-traveler basket, our five-year-old Jack Russell Sookie slack-jawed in the hope of a crumb or two, when Maddy and Angelica sauntered in and reached for the goods.

'No more than one each. These are for Renata. There's some cake in the pantry if you want,' I said, so proud to be able to say that I'd had time to bake. Because ever since we'd uprooted from Boston our life had literally slowed down. No more rushing down the highway to work, no more speeding tickets, no more feeling sorry for myself and the bad marriage I literally ran from (well, OK – *Ira* ran. I simply let him).

'Are you going out?' Maddy asked me in surprise as she downed the last of her milk.

'I was going to dinner at Renata's as you said you were sleeping at Angelica's, but if you've changed your mind, I'd much rather stay in with you two.'

They eyed each other, the words *as if* written in bold

letters across their foreheads. Maddy was the first to recover from my offer. 'Uh, no thanks. Angelica's mom's like, due any minute.'

'Oh? OK, then,' I conceded, a little crushed. 'Don't forget your keys.'

She rolled her eyes. 'When have I ever forgotten my keys?'

'Got your toothbrush?'

'Yes,' she huffed.

'Right. Well, call me when you need a ride back tomorrow. And say hi to your mom for me, Angelica, will you?'

'Sure. Bye, Mrs. Foxham.' Angelica smiled sweetly as I turned to go down into the cellar to retrieve a crate of our own wine while making a mental note to keep a closer eye on those two.

Call it motherly instinct, call it that I am Mrs. Suspicion by nature, but I had a feeling they were up to something. I made a mental note to keep my eyes even more peeled than usual.

Now, which bottles to bring? *Vino della Tenuta Cantelli*, the labels read. Could you believe it? If years ago while sipping Chianti with Ira in Boston and talking Tuscany, someone had told me I'd have a vineyard bearing my own surname, I'd have laughed and told them that things like that only happened in the movies. Well, after a few big bumps in the road two years ago, so far my personal movie was a success. I looked around our house with great satisfaction.

Built in local stone, it had three stories, a paddock, two swimming pools (one for us and one for our guests) and a tennis court. With his own money and before we married, Julian had separately bought the adjoining acres and the four ruins, which we had painstakingly renovated, respecting the

Tuscan style, and rented out to jet-setters from around the world.

So you can see how it had then been a no-brainer leaving my job as hotel manager of the luxurious Farthington Hotel in Boston. When my cheating and IRS-scamming first husband Ira ditched me, I upped sticks and took Maddy and Warren to Castellino. Luckily I had drummed up the nerve to ask Julian to come with us, despite the fact that I'd turned down his first marriage proposal with the promise that I'd consider it while we lived together in sin for the first year. But it didn't take me long to stop being afraid and succumb to my dreams.

Everything – Julian in my life, and our subsequent move to Italy – had happened so suddenly, when the bad days had been piling up faster than I could count them and the only friendly face was my kids' gorgeous and incredibly kind principal. I deserved this now. I'd earned it.

I stopped at Maddy's bedroom door that was open for once. Because the walls were frescoed, posters were prohibited, so she had a cork board propped up on her desk, just like Julian had for his writing ideas, only hers was plastered with images she had taken of herself, lips pursed, eyebrow cocked (that was one thing she got from me) and hair tousled.

Yes, at almost sixteen, she was a beauty. All I could do was hope that her self-obsession would soon pass – as my Nonna Silvia had hoped while watching her own daughter Marcy preen in the mirror – and that it wasn't genetic because otherwise we were screwed for life. But that was nothing compared to my real fear. She was too impatient to become an adult and already acted like she knew everything about the way the world turns, and especially men, whom she seems to prefer over boys her age. I've seen her stop to flirt with the more pleasant-looking members of our staff and people in the village. Lesser men would seriously take advantage of her naivety. That, mixed with her newly found worldliness was a recipe for disaster. I definitely owed my first grey hairs to my daughter.

The fear that she'd turn out like her grandmother had driven us to be extra careful and strict, as Maddy was very popular and overly confident of her looks and artistic aptitude. At least that was the message she was sending out. Only I knew that her best friend Angelica's more mature looks made Maddy feel like a little girl in comparison.

Angelica had a shapelier figure, a throaty laugh and that look in her eyes that Maddy, who was at least a year behind in the curves department, didn't have yet. One day Maddy wanted to be a fashion designer. The next she wanted to be a model slash actress. And for a while she wanted us to call her Madeleine Silvia (my grandmother's name). No surname.

For me, being a mother was my constant worry. No wonder I'd aged since we got here. At least that's what I thought. Every morning there was some new line on my face. Not that I minded the aging process. Until I saw the younger ladies flirting with Julian (who was almost forty-six but didn't look a day over thirty-six, which meant that he looked at least seven years younger than me). But I'm learning to accept myself and every part of me. Which doesn't mean that I've stopped my bouts of self-improvement. And still…

I wished I was twenty again. But then I'd remember

what my life was like at twenty, if you could call it a life, practically dragging my misery along through the years. I was relieved to be here in Tuscany with the kids, far away from Marcy and my super-slim sister Judy who visited every year – which was fine with me as long as they didn't stay more than a couple of weeks, time during which they both piled their silly notions into Maddy – not that she needed any persuasion – about the latest trends in make-up, couture and hair.

And Warren – at twenty he was passionately in love with 'his Stefania', whose mother once told me she couldn't think of a better future husband for her daughter, which made my alarm bells ring every time he brought her home to stay with us.

I was not Stefania's biggest fan, simply because she was a real sponger, and a kiss-ass. In front of the family she would listen enthusiastically and nod her head to our conversations, saying, 'I absolutely agree with you, Mrs. Foxham', or, 'You are so right, Mrs. Foxham.'

But – and here's the thing – whenever Warren and I got a moment to catch up on things alone (the family hardly ever saw him without Stefania anymore), she would come in only to stand there and shake her head at him as if saying, *You're not actually listening to your mother, are you?*

Just so we're clear here: I'm happy to see that my son is in love, but it worries me to see the way his very *will* is nullified by her mere presence. I'd like my son to mature and go off into the world, but with his own opinions that don't have to necessarily reflect hers. I want him to be a thinking man, not a doormat.

And then behind my back (I know because Maddy

heard her once) she'd say to Warren, 'Your mother's an overbearing control freak.'

So what if I was controlling? I was controlling, as one does, *my* household, not hers. Unless she was considering taking over for me? I wouldn't be surprised. Once she even came into the kitchen while I was giving Maddy a piece of my mind about not washing up properly and actually stood by my side, folded her arms like me and glared at Maddy as if she was majorly disappointed that *her* mothering skills hadn't sunk into my daughter's brain. You get the picture. With Stefania, it was a 'Keep your friends close and your enemies closer' kind of thing. And yes, I would have to keep an eye on her. My son is such a wonderful person, but clueless regarding the wiles of some women.

At the moment Maddy didn't have a boyfriend at the *liceo artistico* – the art school in Castellino she attended, or anywhere else (so I was told), but a posse of guys from other schools were constantly texting her and trying to impress her. She got dozens of WhatsApp messages every hour, and her SMS inbox was crammed with all sorts of messages inviting her out on dates. But Maddy only ever said, 'Have you seen his teeth? Ewh!' or, 'Oh my God he's, like, such a junkie!' To my knowledge she neither doted on nor dated (my rule for now was no dating) anyone in particular.

Which was fine by me. I was in no particular hurry to start worrying about date nights and ohmygod – contraception even? I have no idea how all the mothers around the world coped with their own private fears about raising a teenage girl, but ladies, I salute you. You mothers are my heroines.

And Julian, you might ask? What's he up to these days? He was the same old Julian. Nothing short of a bomb falling onto our house could shake him. He was patient and spoke in his usual deep, low Liverpudlian voice that made him sound like John Lennon. After seven years together, five of which as husband and wife, Julian had proven to be my rock. So when he'd sauntered into the kitchen two years ago announcing that he wanted to seriously kick-start his writing career, we were all thrilled for him. After a rocky start, we're OK now.

'So, how are things?' Renata asked as she dished up her culinary miracles of the evening to her eldest, twins Chiara and Graziano, who were still little. I loved that she had managed to get them to taste and eat everything from a young age. My two were and still are so fussy.

'Yeah, we're great, thanks,' I assured her, swinging my eyes to Marco, wondering if he'd mentioned my encounter with Leonardo Cortini to her, or if that name was taboo in their home. Renata and Marco were like the bulwark of marriage in my eyes. Nothing could drag them apart. Just sitting in their presence filled the room with ease and family warmth. Which was a bit lacking in the Foxham household, seeing that lately it was just Maddy and me, and she was not exactly my biggest fan. There would be time to talk in private.

After dinner with my friends, I drove home late that evening in a squiggly if not drunken line (there was only a narrow dirt road leading back home so no risk in running anybody over or smashing into a telephone pole) and parked my Fiat 500 L outside the front. Julian was due in time for breakfast and the kids not until the next day at dinnertime.

Funny how life revolved around food in Tuscany, and especially in our household.

The telephone rang as I was getting ready for bed. It was one a.m. so it had to be my sister Judy. She had no idea what time zones were and regularly called at one a.m. Funny, when I was living in Boston just ten minutes away from her she never wanted to know, just like my stepmother Marcy. Now she was all *Sis here and Sis there*. Go figure.

When we were kids, she was constantly getting into trouble, spending late nights out with boys that you wouldn't exactly want to be taking home to your mother. Slim and attractive, Judy went through life assuming that the world owed her a living, and that she didn't have to study or learn a skill or anything at all, because one day, just like her own mother, she would meet a man of means who would support her so she wouldn't have to go out and earn her own crust of bread. But she's my sister and I love the hell out of her and am fiercely protective (albeit also critical) of her.

She was a regular Madame Bovary who was never happy, convinced that the grass was always greener on the other side, that other women's lives were more romantic and caring than her own (a blatant lie) and that one day she would be happy simply because it was her destiny to be so. The fact that she had jeopardized her marriage with her personal trainer was merely a coincidence. And if her husband Steve hadn't come home earlier that day, he would've been none the wiser. Because nothing was ever her fault.

'Hey – you alone?' she hissed as if not to wake anyone up despite the ringing of my phone.

'Yes. Julian's in Los Angeles at the moment.'

'Again? Well, you can hardly blame the guy. A hunk like that cooped up on a *farm*?'

Here we go again, on and on about how great my husband was and why did I ever drag him to Italy? I yawned.

'I won't keep you if you're gonna be like that,' she snapped.

'Be like what?' I countered. She had a temper worse than mine.

She huffed. 'I can't talk anyway. I'm packing. Marcy wants to see a bit of the world.'

As long as it wasn't Milan. Every year they did this to me. They flew to Milan, called to say they just wanted to swing by (Milan is an hour's flight from here) and ended up staying two weeks. Not that I didn't love them or anything, but if, individually, they were a handful, together they were deadly. They'd talk fashion twenty-four seven and gossip about all the stars as if they knew them personally. And beg Julian, who did, for juicy tidbits of gossip.

'Marcy wants to celebrate her birthday and be there by next week.'

'There, where?' I asked, a deadly suspicion burning its way up from my stomach to my throat. It couldn't be. Not again, please God.

'At your place, of course. She's finally convinced the whole tribe to come and see you guys. Even Vince and Sandra are coming with Vito and Michael.' (Need I mention my brother's obsession with *The Godfather*, Parts One, Two and Three?) 'Vince checked your website and saw there are no bookings for two weeks.'

Two weeks? *Those* two weeks? Not again! Marcy did this

to me two years ago! We had already booked for France, but had to cancel because of her. She couldn't possibly be doing this again, could she? Surely, not even she would go that far?

'But – but…' I faltered.

'Ah, don't tell *me*,' Judy said. 'I'm missing out on two weeks of my gym classes, you know.'

If my sister's past was anything to go by, gym class meant everything to her. If she was missing out on two weeks with a possible new trainer/lover, I could miss out on our own holidays, according to her twisted logic.

'If you have issues, call Mom and tell her.'

Son of a gun – she did it again! And so smoothly, too! 'Right. Let me know your arrival details and I'll come pick you guys up at the airport.'

'Bring two vans. The aunts are coming as well.'

Now *that*, on the contrary, was very good news. My aunts Maria, Monica and Martina were loads of fun. Everything went well when they were around. The three of them co-owned a successful restaurant called Le Tre Donne. The fact that Marcy hadn't been invited into the joint venture spoke worlds on its own. They didn't get along. Or rather, Marcy didn't get along with them.

The truth is that Marcy was jealous of the attention my aunts gave my dad, who is a fine man in every way. Tall and dark-haired, he has these amazingly piercing dark eyes that shine with mischief. He's always impeccably coiffed and dressed, whether in a suit or his golfing gear.

In fairness, after my own mother died and he married Marcy, if it hadn't been for my grandmother Silvia and my aunts chipping in to help with the daily chores, we'd have developed lice and scurvy, to say the least.

But Marcy was not grateful in the least. If anything, she called them nosy and interfering. They were all so beautiful, sharp-witted and extremely classy and had a soft spot for Maddy and Warren. They were also crazy about Julian who, in turn, spoiled them rotten. It would be great to see them again.

My brother Vince, who acted like Vito Corleone, was an overbearing, know-it-all husband who turned into a little lamb in Marcy's presence (he adored her and treated her like the matriarch of his family – God knows how he'd come to that conclusion). His poor wife Sandra, whom he'd fallen out of love with years ago, simply bore with him, presumably because he was a great dad. He loved Vito and Michael.

'Is Steve coming too?' I asked. Steve being my sister Judy's husband and the only sane person in the family.

The only non-Italian member of the family was a true-blood American guy whom she'd cheated on more times than anyone could count. He'd thrown her out once and taken her back almost immediately. The scare had been tremendous, so for a while she was on her best behavior. She'd always been a bit of a floozie, Judy. But her kids – Jake, Jamie and Tony – were real darlings.

'Steve? That would be a yes. He never lets me out of his sight since I... well, you know...'

'Ah yes, I remember, the Face Eater,' I recalled, meaning Judy's not-so-little tryst.

'Do you have to keep saying that? It's gross.'

'Gross? If I recall, you weren't complaining back then.'

'Erica…'

'I'm sorry – you're right. I don't want to be judgmental like Marcy.'

Judy snorted. 'She's gotten even worse. Now she drinks more than ever, and poor old Dad has a tough time controlling her.'

'Oh, great, can't wait.'

'Erica? My two cents? Just ignore her. That's how I get through the day.'

'I guess. OK, then, see you guys soon…'

'Bye, Erica…'

Thinking of all the fun things the Cantelli/Foxham clan could do together if Marcy didn't ruin everything at least once a day, I fluffed up my pillow and shifted to my ready-for-sleep, face-down frog-like position when the phone rang again. Judy must have forgotten to tell me something.

'Hello?'

Silence.

'Hello?' I repeated. We had crap connection sometimes.

'Hello? Is this that holiday place?' said a woman in an American accent who, if I may add, didn't sound awfully bright.

'Yes, this is A Taste of Tuscany. How may I help you?'

'I need to speak to Julian.' No 'May I?', no question mark, no please.

I cleared my throat. 'I'm sorry, Mr. Foxham isn't available at the moment. May I take a message?'

Dead silence.

'Hello? May I ask who's calling, please?'

'Never mind,' the voice said. A voice I'd heard before. 'I'll call his cell phone.' And with that, the line went dead.

Now *you* try to get to sleep after a call like that.

Eventually I did drop off, but woke up to the sound of the phone again, groaning as my fingers grasped the dreaded thing. I wondered if it was that American woman again, and how she'd managed to get Julian's cell phone number of which, by the way, he was extremely secretive.

'H'llo?' I rasped. At least I think it was me. Jesus, no more Chianti after ten. And no more *tagliatelle al sugo di lepre*, either. I just couldn't stomach that wild food anymore.

'*Signora Cantelli?*' came an unfamiliar voice. A man, this time, and Italian.

'*Sì?*'

'Mr. Julian Foxham's wife?' the voice persisted.

'Yes?' I sat up, instantly awake. 'Who is this?'

'I'm sorry, *Signora*. There's been an accident.'

'What?'

'*Il Signor* Foxham... he didn't make it to the hospital. I'm sorry.'

I reached out, feeling for Julian's warm, strong body, finding the bed empty. But that was OK because he wasn't supposed to be back until the morning. Somebody was just playing a prank, that was all.

'Is this a joke? Who is this?' I said, thinking that none of this was actually happening.

'You're dreaming. Wake up,' I said to myself. 'Come on, wake up, dammit!'

'*Signora Cantelli?*' continued the voice. 'I'm sending you a squad car.' *To identify the body, of course*. What else for?

I kept smacking myself in the head but couldn't wake up, like those nightmares you somehow, masochistically cling to, so you have one helluva story to tell over breakfast the next morning. 'Where... did it happen?'

'Just outside Cortona...'

Cortona? 'Impossible. What was he doing in Cortona? He's away on business.' Apart from the fact that we didn't know anybody in Cortona. Did we?

'He was on his way to see... someone.'

'Who?'

'A... friend.'

As if it mattered. I tried to think of who the friend could be. But we knew the same people. And then, like giant psychedelic pink and purple mushrooms taking over your brain-space, the words formed in the few cells I had left. Julian had a lover. And he had been going to see her. In the middle of the night. So much for his bloody meetings with his agent. So much for the loyal husband bit. *Now* I understood his restless attitude, his listless behavior. My husband of seven years had finally tired of me and wanted out. The other shoe had finally dropped.

And now he was gone. *Gone.*

'*Signora Cantelli?*'

The man had been babbling on and on and I hadn't got a single word of it. 'Oh, yes, sorry.'

My husband, my beautiful, kind husband had gone without even saying goodbye. And then it was like being at the bottom of a well, or maybe even the ocean, I don't know. There were too many things, it suddenly hit me, that I didn't know.

'Who is she? Tell me!' I screamed, my voice sounding muffled, echoey, like I was crying from said bottom of the ocean, and after a confused moment of silence, the line went dead. 'Tell me!'

'Sweetheart,' came a voice from above the ocean, and I flapped my arms as if they were fins, trying to make my way back to the surface. 'Wake up, sweetie, you're having a bad dream.'

I opened my eyes, relieved it was only a nightmare. But it wasn't, because the bed was still empty. I hadn't dreamed it at all. Julian really was dead.

'Julian!' I cried at the top of my lungs, my throat dry and my heart a big black swinging demolition ball in my chest. 'Julian, come back!'

'I'm just here, sweetie,' came his voice, followed by his beautiful head as it poked around the corner of the door to the en suite bathroom. He returned with a glass of water and sat down on the bed next to me as I gulped it down in one snap of my neck and threw myself up into his arms, squashing his midsection, trying to explain.

'You had died!' I managed before I broke down into a new fit of tears. 'In a car crash on the way to your lover's house!'

Julian put his arms around me and moaned, 'Again? Serves me right then, doesn't it?'

'It's not funny, you know,' I argued, trying to shake off the dreadful feeling of tragedy that still clung to me like a pair of soaking pajamas.

But then his face split into a grin, and it was like the sun had come out in the middle of the night. 'Honey, when are you going to get it that I'm not going anywhere? And that I drive very carefully.'

'But you *cheated* on me...'

He sighed. 'Only in your worst nightmares. But you know I love you and you only. And I wouldn't cheat on you for all the women in the world. Not ever. OK?'

I nodded fiercely, refusing to let go of him. Boy, if this kept up I'd have to fly my former shrink, Dr. Denholm, over in a jiffy. Maybe even take him up as a permanent resident here at A Taste of Tuscany. Crap, was this what my life was becoming? I had a wonderful husband, a loving family, a business that I actually liked. And I'd never looked and felt happier or healthier.

On the *outside*. But on the inside, it was pure chaos. My mind was going for a hike every night. But luckily it returned before I woke up in the morning. How did people – OK, I mean *me* – have such bad dreams and actually manage to keep a hold on their (my) sanity?

The truth was that, after years of marriage to this wonderful, sexy man, I was so happy I was terrified. All I needed was one glitch and my whole world would cave in. All I needed was one of my loved ones to be in an accident or become ill and goodnight Vienna. That was our life down the toilet. Did I really need all that drama, all that *tragedy*, in my life? What the heck was wrong with me?

Smarten up, a demon-voice inside me would then say. *Can't you see he's cheating on you – left, right and center? Do you really think that such a good-looking guy is going to stay faithful to you?*

Of course I do, I'd answer the mean voice, and then I'd be OK for a while.

Until I got those foreboding feelings, you know, when you are positively certain that some tragedy is going to strike?

Nonsense, I'd try to reassure myself. *Nothing bad is going to happen. Just shut up and enjoy your life, you lucky idiot. Julian loves you and that's that.*

And I really believed he did. Until another woman would land like a bomb on our home (only I didn't know that yet), and my nightmare would come true.

My brain was a one-woman band with multiple personalities. One day I'd be so confident about everything and the next I wasn't even sure of my rock-solid skills, like cooking, painting and my business sense.

'Erica...?' Julian said.

I looked up, my arms still wrapped tight around him. 'Yeah?'

'Can you let go, sweetie? I've just got in and I'm breaking my neck for a pee.'

'Oh. Sorry.' I leaned back in bed, pulling the covers all the way up to my chin despite the fact it was May. *Crisis averted. I can now relax.*

But just as I was getting back to sleep Julian's cell phone rang. Two a.m. What the hell?

'Can you get that?' he called from the bathroom. 'It's probably Terry – he's worse than your sister with time zones.'

I groaned and rolled over to his side of the bed and night table. 'Hello?'

Silence again.

Now this time I was awake and Julian was here, safe and sound. Unless... Maddy? Warren? Alarm bells started ringing. I expected to hear Angelica's mom or Stefania saying something had happened, but no one spoke.

'Hello?' I said, louder, sitting up.

More silence, and then a click.

'Who is it?' Julian asked, padding back into the bedroom to take off his clothes.

I shrugged. 'They hung up.'

Now if I were a suspicious wife and Julian a sleazeball, we'd have a real problem on our hands. But Julian was not the cheating kind. With him, thankfully, I was on safe ground. For once. Or so I thought.

3

Mission Impossible

The first thing I felt when I woke up the next morning was a wet, sticky sensation, like the guy in *The Godfather* who finds his dead horse's head in his bed. Yeah, sorry, that's sick, but it's also *exactly* how I felt.

My period, biblically late, had made its appearance with a vengeance. That was my body lately. I'd have dry spells and then, just like that, *woosh* – the Nile would flood. I jumped to my feet, not daring to look back at the mess I'd made of our bed.

'Are you all right?' Julian asked from behind the bathroom door. I quickly washed and emerged, finding him sitting on the bed, wide awake now.

'Sorry – had a little accident. I have to change the sheets.'

He looked at me and shook his head before reaching into the linen closet for the burgundy sheets, the ones I always put on the bed during my period. It was kind of a signal that sex was off the agenda during those days. He knew the code. Burgundy meant no sex. So why was he shaking his head like that?

'Why are you shaking your head like that?'

'I was kind of hoping you weren't going to get it this month.'

'That would be cruel if I were on menopause alert,' I objected as I billowed the sheets out before me. 'Heck, I'm only forty-three, Julian.'

'Erica – do I have to spell it out to you? I was hoping you'd get pregnant,' he whispered as he caught the sheet and tucked it under the mattress on his side. I giggled at his joke, but he didn't join in. Was he serious?

'Are you serious?'

Julian plumped his pillow inside its new pillowcase and looked at me with an expression I'd never seen before, and nodded, his eyes studying me.

I swallowed. 'Please tell me you're still asleep and sleep-talking, or rather, that I am and this is just a silly dream?'

'No dream, Erica. I'd like a child. Wouldn't you?'

We'd never discussed this in seven years and he wanted a child *now*? 'Like I said, I'm already forty-three, Julian,' I said, backtracking, as if apologizing. Apologizing for what, I wondered – not being an automatic baby dispenser?

I let myself fall onto our now burgundy bed with all my weight, which was still quite noticeable. I had gained ten kilos in seven years, and at eighty-five kilos, I was anything but slender, and I was absolutely fine with that. But how the heck was I going to face another pregnancy? I looked up and wished I hadn't because Julian was getting down on his knees by the bed, taking my hands and searching my face.

'Don't say anything, honey. Just promise me you'll give it a thought.'

Give it a thought? I was so shocked I couldn't think of anything *else*. Did he have any idea of what he was asking me?

'Do you promise?' he repeated.

Was he serious? And why after all these years? It just didn't make sense. He'd been by our side, supported us and – oh. Self-sacrifice and all that. Maybe now he thought it was payback time. Gosh, was that the way it worked in healthy relationships?

'It'll be great, you'll see. Raising her will be a dream.'

I swallowed. 'Her?'

He grinned. 'I've always wanted a little girl.'

'A girl...'

'But I'll be just as happy with a boy, of course. And you?'

Oh, Dear God, kill me now, please? 'I've... got to go the bathroom again,' I said, sliding off the bed. *And possibly smash my head against the mirror a few times.* What planet did my adorable husband live on? I could already picture myself expanding until I resembled the hot air balloon Julian had bought me a ride in upon our arrival in idyllic Tuscany. He'd made all my dreams come true. Was it now time to pay the happiness bill and return the favor?

'How was having Andrea so late in your marriage?' I blurted out to Renata as we were lunching under my pergola the next day.

She snorted. 'Why, are you thinking of having another kid?'

When I didn't answer she almost choked on her fish *cacciucco* stew. I whacked her on the back.

'Why didn't you tell me you and Julian were having problems?' she wheezed before gulping down a glass of San Pellegrino water.

I stopped in mid-bite. 'What? What are you talking about?'

Renata cleared her throat and stared back at me, her eyes watering.

'Here, a baby at this age is usually a fixer-upper. So what's going on?'

I shrugged, inwardly panicking at the news. Was that why Julian wanted a baby? To fix a problem I wasn't even *aware* of? Impossible. I'd know if there was a problem. Right?

'Nothing's going on. Just… Julian wants one.'

'*Oyoy*,' Renata sighed. The typical Tuscan, *something is wrong* sigh. 'Not good.'

'Shut up,' I said, cutting away furiously at my *carpaccio* and rocket lettuce. 'Julian and I are fine.'

'Are you sure?' she insisted, not taking her eyes off me.

I rolled my eyes. 'Of course I'm sure.'

'Hmmm, I don't know. That's pretty sudden, isn't it? Why don't you ask him?'

'Ask him why he wants a kid? It's obvious.'

'He could've had one all this time. Why now?'

My sentiments exactly. 'Because we're finally settled? We've had a rough start,' I reminded her. The second year we were here, we had *quasi* zero guests, and it would have been none at all if it hadn't been for my Matera Brainstormers, a group of international writers who booked a week with us every summer. And with my panicking and wacky plans, I'd almost lost him. Perhaps he thought that now, everything else being on an even keel, it was time for another baby. He had the right to want one of his own blood, of course. I knew and understood that. But I wasn't sure I wanted to go through that entire ordeal all over again.

'True, you are all nice and settled now. Maybe Julian's looking at the fact that Warren's already flown the nest, and that in two years' time so will Maddy. Maybe it's his way of keeping things interesting at home.'

I crossed my arms in front of my chest. 'Thanks for that.'

Renata laughed. 'I didn't mean it that way, Erica. All I meant is that when a man wants a baby so late, there's usually a good reason. But it's up to you to discover what that reason is.'

'And there was me thinking that with all my financial problems solved, that it would be smooth sailing from now on.'

'Ha,' Renata shot back. 'There is never smooth sailing when you're married.'

'Good thing you live far away in that little peaceful bubble of yours,' Judy said to me the next evening as I sat on the floor next to the bureau, knees drawn up under my chin. One more pound and I wouldn't be able to sit like that anymore. I know that for a fact because once I'd pigged out at a restaurant and suddenly my stomach was in the way. It had taken me three months of practically fasting before I returned from The Point of No Return. Boy, had that been close. Not that it wasn't in the way now, but I could still keep it at bay by squishing my thighs up against it and wrapping my arms around my knees real tight. Enough. I'm OK with being big, but not when my body starts to feel different.

'Are you listening to me?' Judy asked as she exhaled cigarette smoke, and I could almost see her sprawled on her king-sized bed. 'It's pure hell here. Marcy's drinking like a sponge again and not talking to Dad, nor Sandra to Vince, nor Vince to Marcy. So I have to do messages for the important stuff. I can't wait to see it all come to the fore when we get there...'

'Thanks for that.' I sigh, resigned.

What else was new? That was the Cantelli family for you, in all its dysfunctional Italian glory. Boy, was I glad I was on the other side of the ocean, at least for now. Hopefully by the time they got here it would all blow over.

'So how *is* living in paradise?' my sister Judy asked. 'You looked really good in those pictures you sent, by the way. I never got a chance to tell you that.' For trim-slim Judy to tell me I looked good could only mean one of two things – either it was true (which it wasn't) or she needed a favor.

'Thanks. I feel great,' I lied, then thought, what the hell. 'I'm so happy I'm terrified,' I whispered.

I heard her exhale. 'Why?'

I shrugged, as if she could see me. 'I dunno. I just keep waiting for this bomb to drop.' There was no way I was telling Judy about Julian's request for a child, not yet, anyway. And it was true – I was so terrified. Even during the day I'd catch myself dreading losing it all, either through Julian's abandoning me for another woman, or his death, which would have been, if I'd have any say in it, only minutes apart. Was our life just too perfect? Nothing bad ever happened. We were living what you'd call a life of domestic bliss. Yet this baby thing really was bugging me. Why now?

Judy inhaled deeply and I could almost see the smoke.

'I thought you'd quit, after all you put Steve through,' I said, meaning her *quasi*-divorce over her gym instructor, or The Face Eater, as I'd dubbed him seven years ago.

Judy exhaled. 'Oh, get real,' she said. 'I learned to cook, didn't I? And that's still one more thing than *Marcy* ever did. Anyway, I'm glad for you that everything is perfect, although I don't believe it ever lasts because really all men care about are looks. So keep fit or you'll *lose* him.'

To hell with anybody's feelings. That was Judy for you – blunt, tactless and inconsistent. Hadn't she just said I looked good?

'Actually, Julian and I are trying to get pregnant,' I blurted out.

Whoa. Where had that come from? I'd told Julian I'd *think* about it. And now my mouth had suddenly decided – without even consulting me – that I wanted me to become a mother for the third time?

Silence on the other end. I waited, wondering how long it was going to take her to enter her usual routine of lectures about keeping a figure. Because, unlike Renata, Judy never questioned the deeper whys and wherefores. She didn't disappoint me, of course.

'Oh, Erica, what the hell *for*?' she gasped, and I could almost see her eyebrows shoot into her hairline with what could only be described as disgust at the thought of a levitating me. 'You already have two – why the hell do you want another one?' Judy had three herself, but her second was a twin birth so she'd got shafted, in her opinion. But if you look at it figure-wise, she only had to get fat twice for three children. So far I'd gotten fat three times for two. It figured, didn't it?

'Erica,' Judy continued. 'If you were still, say, in your thirties and didn't have any, I'd understand, but I just don't get why you want to put yourself through all that again.'

'Uh, because Julian wants a child of his own?' That would have been the perfect moment for any woman to question the reason behind a man's wishes. As per her character, Judy let the moment pass.

'So what?' she said flatly. 'Tell him to get a surrogate. You don't want to totally blimp out again, do you?' Then she gasped. 'Did you say yes?'

'Er – not exactly.'

'Well put him out of his misery and tell him if he wants a baby to look around somewhere else! You already gave. Unless—'

'Unless what?'

'Are you guys in a rut?'

Oh my God, was it really true then, that a baby this late in a marriage is usually a fixer-upper situation? Judy was the man expert. If she confirmed Renata's opinion then it had to be right. We were in a rut and Julian thought that the only way out was having a kid? What ever happened to working on things? And why were things cooling between us? Although we'd been married for five years, we'd been together for seven, so we were still technically subject to the Seven Year Itch.

True, we hadn't had sex in quite a while because we were always so busy. But it wasn't the first time it had (or rather, hadn't) happened. The kids alone had soaked up three-quarters of our marriage when they were younger and – *oh*. OK. I think I got it now. I needed to focus more on my wonderful, fantastic husband. Do more for him. Get the sex rolling again. Be ever-attractive, sexy, beautiful.

But the mirror told me I was going to have one helluva time doing that, and that months of munching on rice cakes and lettuce was not going to make me look anything like Angelina Jolie.

4

A Family Affair

One week later, we were on day three of my family's stay and having a lazy lunch under the wisteria-laden pergola. Thinking back now, I could put it all down to the excessive heat, maybe even the scirocco breeze that is known to have driven people to murder in the past. But we all knew the truth. Even in Arctic temperatures, Marcy managed to damage relationships. Per se, she wasn't really that bad once you got to know her. Once we'd cleared our past of all those cobwebs, we'd become quite close, even if I was in my late thirties at the time. All we had to do was understand that it was the booze talking whenever she hurt your feelings. She had a drinking problem that was getting worse and worse, but she would never admit to it.

After berating her three lovely sisters who, for my sake, chose to ignore her, Marcy came up with one of her outrageous (but not out of the ordinary) comments about my cooking. Dad made the big mistake of snorting and saying something under his breath, something that he never did. I can't remember all the details but it went something like this:

'Edward, what are you muttering about?'

'Nothing, dear.'

'Nothing? You've been like this for months now. Will you please tell me why you are never happy?'

Dad stared at her for a long moment before he said, '*I'm* never happy? Jesus Christ, Marcy – if anyone here is always complaining, it's you. Just leave everybody alone. And stop ruining everything.'

That alone shocked us all, because Dad never raised his voice. He was the mildest man in creation. And Marcy wasn't used to anyone talking back at her. It earned him a smile but also a silent admonishment from my eldest aunt Maria who could smell trouble a mile off, especially where Marcy was concerned.

'Me?' Marcy said in drunken horror. 'You didn't even want to come out here in the first place! I had to drag you!'

Julian glanced at me but I was too busy keeping my eyes downcast and praying Marcy wouldn't be there when I reopened them.

'OK, Marcy,' Julian said softly. Even though she lived on the other side of the ocean her outbursts were legendary to him. 'Come and help me dish up dessert now?'

That's when she turned to me. *Me*. I hadn't even *breathed*. 'Dessert? When are you going to understand that I don't eat dessert? How do you think I manage to fit into my clothes, by having dessert after every meal like you?'

I shot a quick glance around the table. Besides Julian, no one seemed to have heard a word. So she continued, in a louder voice. 'If you'd only listened to Ira instead of complaining about what a bad husband he was you wouldn't be on your second marriage, with all due respect to Julian here.'

'I never complained to you about Ira,' I countered, always flammable but still wary of an argument in front of the entire family. 'Never. I always kept my problems to myself.' And before I could stop myself, I added, 'Besides, you'd be the last person I'd turn to.'

Marcy looked at me with rounded eyes. 'What's that supposed to mean?'

I snorted. 'That if it weren't for Nonna Silvia who raised us I'd be a basket case.'

My maternal grandmother Silvia had left Tuscany for Boston to give her daughters a new start in life after she was widowed. She'd sold her farmhouse near San Gimignano to buy a shop with an apartment above. She sold imported goods from Italy and had rapidly established herself in the area as an honest and capable businesswoman, earning the respect of everyone. Her daughters – Maria, Monica and Martina – followed in her footsteps, working in the shop and eventually opening their own restaurant called Le Tre Donne (the three women) while Marcella (Marcy) the black sheep of the family, preferred to dedicate her entire life to fawning over the inconsolable widower of her dead twin Emanuela (my real mother, nicknamed Manu).

Only there was one huge fly in Marcy's champagne, i.e. Manu's little orphan (me). If she wanted Edoardo (my dad) she would have to agree to be a loving (ha) mother to me. Marcy had wanted him so badly she had agreed, but soon after she had Judy and Vince who absorbed her completely. Let's say I was lucky that we had Nonna Silvia taking care of us for as long as she lived.

'You *are* a basket case!' Marcy assured me. 'Look at yourself! You lost Ira because you couldn't take care of him, or yourself. He had to blackmail you into surgery so you could fit through the door!' (Surgery that never happened as he'd dropped his phone on my gurney minutes before my stomach bypass. When it had beeped with a message from his lover, you can imagine my reaction. Let's just say it involved escaping the hospital buck naked and a police car chase with a female cop who understood where I was coming from.)

Julian cleared his throat, but Marcy interrupted him. 'And now that you're married to a sex symbol who's on all major chat shows you *still* don't take care of yourself! Look at you in that bland green sundress, ponytail and your flip-flops. *Flip-flops* – where do you think you are, the beach? Do you want to lose him to some Hollywood movie star or something?'

Julian coughed. 'Uh, actually, Marcy, I like the way my wife looks very much.'

I beamed at him and he squeezed my hand. 'Now,' he continued. 'Who wants dessert?'

There was a collective 'me' as I cleared the dishes, eyeing Marcy who sat back in her sloshed stupor, barely able to sit upright, let alone help.

'I hope it's not one of Erica's fat-bomb cakes,' she muttered to anyone who would listen.

But Maddy was too young and inexperienced in the Cantelli affairs to know any better. 'I like Mom's cakes, Nana.'

Marcy snorted. 'Well then watch out you don't explode like your mother. And don't call me Nana.'

'Why not?' Dad suddenly barked and I flinched at the unfamiliar sound of his raised voice. It was like he'd finally found a backbone from under the table. Good for him. 'They are your grandchildren. You've got seven of them.'

'And God knows how many more,' Judy added. Everyone, me included, stared at her.

Dead silence. 'What's that supposed to mean?' Vince suddenly demanded.

Marcy waved her glass around, the martini sloshing around the sides. 'I don't need to be reminded of my grand-children with all the babysitting I've done in my life—' (at that Judy, Vince, Sandra and I snorted. Steve, who was too polite, and Julian, who hadn't been around early enough back then, sat in silence) '—it's a wonder they don't call *me* Mom.'

'No one *dares* call you Mom,' Judy snapped, then turned to me. 'What is it she said whenever we asked her to babysit?'

'Children belong to their parents, not their grandparents,' I answered. I knew the spiel by heart.

'I don't recall *your* mother ever saying that to you when she used to watch them while you slept your afternoons away,' Dad said, glaring at Marcy who shot him an injured look. 'What?' he said. 'I'm not allowed to say the truth? If it wasn't for poor old Silvia, bless her soul in heaven, and your sisters here, we'd all be dead by now.'

'Yeah, and what a great job she and my marvelous sisters have done!' Marcy spat. 'My eldest daughter's a fat loser, my youngest is a slut who sleeps around—' (at that Steve turned beet red and excused himself) '—and my only son has had more affairs than I can count.'

Sandra blanched and turned to Vince. 'They *know*?' she squeaked.

Vince swallowed and dared a quick glance around the table. 'Let's go upstairs, honey. I think I've heard enough.'

'But I haven't!' Sandra snapped.

I put my head in my hands again.

'Slut?' Judy cried in disbelief. 'At least I didn't abandon my baby!'

And then my head shot up again to stare at Judy, then at Marcy. I thought that was a secret Marcy had revealed only to me, in a sign of truce years ago. 'You knew?' I asked my sister.

'Of course I knew. You thought you were the only bearer of her secrets? She can't keep a secret any more than she can hold her booze.'

'Abandon?' Vince whispered, wide-eyed and sitting back down and even Sandra seemed to have forgotten her own little drama. 'What's she talking about, Ma?'

'About the fact that your angelic and celestial mother had a baby before she married Dad. In England,' Judy sneered. 'She left him on the steps of a church, for Christ's sake! Anyone beat that if you can!'

Julian's head snapped up and he stared at Marcy. Really hard. It must have hit home because that was what had happened to him too before Maggie and Tom adopted him. I squeezed his hand, my eyes swinging to poor old Dad who sat pale and still. Shit. Everyone seemed to know but him.

'Dad?' I whispered. 'Are you OK?'

'Edoardo?' Zia Martina asked, placing her hand on his, which Marcy readily slapped away.

He didn't flinch but stared ahead for a long time as if he hadn't heard or felt any of it. Or as if he had a gazillion times. I held my breath, waiting for him to say something, and everyone at the table froze.

'Dad?' I nudged him gently, my heart skipping a beat.

'Edoardo?' Julian echoed me.

Dad turned to us with a sweet, sweet smile. 'Yes? I'm fine, thanks. Marcy, I think you have quite a few apologies to make before you leave this table. Julian, please pour me another glass of that fantastic wine you and my lovely daughter make. Would you mind?'

Julian stared at him at length, then nodded.

I took advantage of that beat and left the table for barely thirty seconds, almost missing the grand finale. I wish I had.

'She's so bloody obese!'

'Marcy,' I heard Julian say. 'With all due respect I think you've had too much to drink. Now why don't you go upstairs and lie down for a while?'

'I don't want to lie down,' she snarled.

'Of course she doesn't,' Judy snapped. 'She's been horizontal all her life. And not always alone.'

Marcy crossed her arms and glared at her. 'Look who's talking, Mother Teresa of Calcutta.'

I packed the dessert trolley with my home-made *tiramisù*, blueberry cheesecake and Sicilian *cannoli*, Tuscan *cantuccini* and *castagnaccio*, along with a fresh pot of espresso coffee and some Vin Santo, a sweet dessert wine, hoping that all this sweetness would counteract all the bitterness at the table. It usually worked for me.

'Yeah, well at least I had the decency to sleep with guys my age,' I heard Judy say.

'What?' I said as I returned with the dessert tray. I could feel my ears getting hot, and I can tell you the situation was getting way out of hand even for someone as confrontational as me.

Had Marcy had an affair while she was married to my dad as well? And with a younger man?

'Oh, you don't know about her toy boy?' Judy said.

'Toy boy?' I squeaked.

'Yeah,' Judy said. 'A kid from your school, too.'

I froze, my voice struggling out of my mouth. 'Who?'

'That cute Italian dropout, remember the one who used to take the older girls behind the supermarket? What was his name? Tony – Tony Esposito.'

Not just the older girls. He'd taken me, too, but no one needed to know that. Because it had been an absolute disaster of an attempt at being like everybody else. The minute he'd put his hand up my shirt, I'd pushed him away and run all the way down the alley, my heart beating like it would crush my ribs.

I turned to Marcy, barely breathing. 'You slept with a *kid*?'

'He wasn't a kid. He was eighteen.'

'And you were, what, forty-something?' I countered, rapidly calculating the age difference.

I looked around at my family, from my parents to my siblings and their families to my aunts to my own children. I thought that I'd managed to drag the children away from all that Cantelli drama by moving to the other side of the world. I thought I'd also protected myself, but it was obvious to me that Dad and Marcy were at the end of the line. Vince and Sandra, ditto. Judy and Steve, ditto as well.

As I thanked my lucky stars for my healthy relationship with Julian, I couldn't help but wonder. Why was it so hard to stay together? Was it a Cantelli trait? Ira had almost driven me to insanity slash depression. I should be supportive of them, not melancholic. Still, when I look back and remember our childhood, I saw the signs, loud and painful.

My aunts, who constantly turned down marriage proposals from all of Little Italy, seemed to be the only ones who, besides Julian and myself, were happy. How did they manage to not be lonely?

'OK, everybody pipe down now, please, and enjoy your desserts. We've had enough drama for today,' Julian said. 'And then I suggest you all go to your rooms and calm down for the rest of the afternoon. It's too hot to do anything anyway.'

'Marcy – apologize to Erica and Julian,' Dad said softly.

'It doesn't matter,' I said hastily. I just wanted to get this lunch over without any bloodshed.

'Yes, it does, sweetheart,' he assured me. 'Marcy?'

But Marcy just glared at him and took another sip of her wine.

'Please,' I whispered. 'It's OK. I'm OK.'

At that point, Zia Maria turned to me. She was the oldest of my aunts, but also the spunkiest. She took care of everything domestic, like cooking and cleaning. After my nonna's death, it was she who had taken the reins of running our household, seeing that Marcy was only capable of napping all day long while the laundry basket exploded and the fridge got emptier and emptier every day. Zia Maria was, for all intents and purposes, our mother-in-charge and we all loved her fiercely for taking care of us so selflessly.

'Of course you're OK, sweetie,' she reassured me. 'Because you are like your mother Emanuela. You've got guts and you are strong. You have all her best traits and she had all of Nonna Silvia's. You're a winning combination.'

Marcy snorted and lifted her empty glass. 'Yeah, Manu was a real concentrate of virtue.'

'Do *not*... even *try* to soil your sister's reputation,' Zia Maria warned her.

'You shut up!' Marcy slurred. 'You frustrated tramp, trying to steal my husband from me with all your casseroles!'

'I'm not going to listen to any more of this,' Dad said, looking up from the table to me. 'Sweetheart, forgive me, but I'm taking Marcy home. I'm so sorry that we've ruined everything, and so soon. Just when I thought we'd be able to make it to a week.'

'Oh, Dad, no, please...'

'Edoardo, don't worry,' Maria said. 'You stay and enjoy your daughter's family. 'We'll go.'

'No, please don't,' my father begged her. 'You and your sisters work so hard, you deserve a break...'

'It's fine. We can always come back on our own some other time.'

'Of course,' I assured her. 'Anytime you want, the door is always open to you guys...'

'Oh, but *I* have to literally beg to be invited,' Marcy snapped.

Why oh why did my family have to drag their baggage all the way across the ocean? Couldn't they just bring sunscreen and flip-flops like every other traveler? No, of course not, we had to flog every family issue of the last fifty years, from my aunts' role in our lives to my weight, to Judy's infidelity – but never, ever, Marcy's flaws. As if she was some fragile, glass princess who was never to be held accountable for her mistakes. Normal admin in the Cantelli household. They say Italian families are particularly solid, but you wouldn't say that looking at mine.

So just like that, the whole band – all fourteen of them – had come and gone, just like they'd come from next door and not over the Atlantic Ocean. And in the space of three days. Thank you, Marcy, for turning our family into a circus.

'Thanks for your support, honey,' I said to Julian as we later loaded the dishwasher.

He shook his head. 'Your family never ceases to amaze me.'

I snorted. 'That was nothing. You should've seen Marcy at Maddy's christening.'

'Yeah?'

'After her sixth gin and tonic, she climbed up onto the table and accused all of her sisters of having an affair with my dad – simultaneously.'

'Jesus.'

'Yeah. I'm going to have to do something about her drinking. It's way out of hand – more than I thought.'

'Honey,' he said, hugging me. 'You are not your stepmother's keeper. She's an adult and has to learn to take care of herself. Or if not, she has plenty of people to lean on. You live on the other side of the Atlantic and have got your hands full enough as it is, yes?'

I frowned. He was right – I was the least qualified in any

case to deal with her, what with our stormy past. Needless to say Marcy had shattered three couples including her own marriage in the space of five minutes and in less than two hours each had boarded a different plane back home. What should've been two weeks of hell was concentrated in three days. One needs to always look for the silver lining.

A week later I called my dad's cell phone to make sure he hadn't suddenly lost his cool and murdered her. 'Hey, Dad, how are you?'

A long, long sigh. 'I swear to you, Erica, your mother is killing me. After forty-three years she still drives me crazy. She's going to die an old selfish woman. And even if she lived to be a hundred years old, she will never be like my Manu.'

Just the thought of my real mother made me smile. When I didn't burst into tears.

'Dad…' I faltered. This was the very first time I'd ever heard him complain about Marcy. I always thought he was happy to be her slave, valet, et cetera. How the hell was I supposed to know he was suffering this much?

He cleared his throat. 'Sweetie, I'm sorry. But I've had enough. For years I've put up with your mother and now I know that I'll be spending our next anniversary in jail because I am going to kill her very soon.'

5

Taking the Plunge

With the clan gone and everything back to normal, I worked up the courage to tell my husband exactly what I thought of his baby idea. That babies shouldn't be marriage fixers, that I was too old, we were too busy and he was never around anyway. Besides – look at the trouble big families brought. All perfectly solid reasons, right?

But when he brought me breakfast in bed (how sweet was he?) I decided that, at the end of the day, Julian was completely different from my family and that he *should* experience the joys (the pains were all for moms) of fatherhood. And that he was definitely worth nine months of gastric reflux, chronic backache and swollen feet. (He liked me even when I was cranky.)

'We should do it,' I said while I took a sip of my coffee, the kids still in bed.

'Do what?' he asked, looking up from his paper.

'You know, the kid thing,' I whispered into my mug, feeling my face go hot.

Rustling of paper. Intake of breath. His. I was already holding mine.

'Really, Erica?' he whispered.

I put my mug down and straightened my hair, flashing him my version of the famous Cantelli smile – all teeth and no confidence whatsoever. Because Renata's words kept ringing in my ears. *A baby fixes a marriage.* Did I really agree with her? My mind said I didn't. My heart told me I was crazy, but *me* was terrified of getting pregnant for all the wrong reasons. All I could think was: *What if we do need a baby to change things?*

'Yeah, absolutely. I've thought about it. I'm ready.'

Julian squeezed my hand and dropped a delicious kiss on my lips and pulled me out of my chair with a mischievous, sexy smile that promised a couple of fun hours.

Judy and Renata, zero – my marriage, one.

'Keep your legs up, sweetheart,' Julian whispered as he finally pulled out of me some time later. Did I say *finally*? I didn't mean it like that, but he was really taking his time. I mean, don't get me wrong – he has never been hasty in the bedroom; on the contrary, Julian's always been deliciously thorough – but now, it was like he wanted to make extra sure his parcel had been delivered and signed for. I sure hoped it would work. I hated to see Julian disappointed.

But then again, not being a parent would actually spare him some other major disappointments, i.e. some huge milestones in the parenting process. Like when your kids become teenagers and eat the flower of Superior Knowledge. Suddenly they know everything and all *you* are is a blooming idiot. Nothing you say holds its weight anymore. You've lost all your clout and they spend more time in their bedroom doing God knows what when we only had a telephone and magazines, a stash of junk food, plus the occasional joint. What harm could we get up to?

But this generation – if you so much as even *looked* at them in a manner they didn't like you'd get a shower of expletives that would last you a week. But a mother's gotta be a mother, no matter what. I was the opposite of my own flaky, glamorous stand-in mom in every way. And to be honest, it was important to exercise my authority over my children while I still could. It made for great learning moments to remember throughout their lives. And boy did I make sure I did it thoroughly.

'No, Maddy. You can't wear high heels,' I later told my daughter. 'They're bad for your back and Mila is against them. And I'm against them.'

'Mo-om!'

'They ruin your posture. Besides, you're already five foot eight.'

'Mila knows nothing,' she huffed. 'She says I'm no good at ballet because I'm too tall. She says it, like, slows me down or something.'

I took a long hard look at her. Her ballet instructor had a point. Maddy's long, lanky legs gave her a funny gait that her hips hadn't quite yet mastered. While Angelica had already filled out, Maddy was still on the slender side and a little jealous of her friend's confidence. As much as Maddy flaunted her prettiness at home and acted cool in front of her friends, I knew she was scared of not being accepted. She was the Terrified Leader who was waiting to be caught out for not even believing in herself. Remind you of anyone?

But there was a big difference between us. Maddy was afraid of *others* not appreciating her. She personally appreciated herself immensely, and when she referred to her thighs as ham joints, she didn't really mean it. Apparently it was the thing to talk bad about your body nowadays. Today when girls say they don't like their body, they mean they absolutely love it. In my day, when we didn't love our bodies we just shut the hell up, hid inside huge sweaters and hoped to go through life unnoticed.

So if her dreams of ballet dancing were quickly disappearing, was she really aiming toward being a model as she had lately announced? Please God, no, I fervently prayed. She had artistic talent and a flair for fashion. Why not put it to work as a fashion designer? But ultimately whatever she decided to be, I only hoped the definition included the word *happy*.

Which made me wonder if I had been an adequate mother after all my efforts. And while asking myself that, I asked myself what the hell had possessed me to agree to have another kid with Julian. Blimey, as Julian would say, did I really have any clue at all? Kids these days were more difficult to handle – they weren't the shy, docile idiots we… well, *I* was once upon a life ago. These kids today were like tsunamis. If you didn't want to get in their path you had to run to higher ground and pray for damage control. Which I did.

'Madeleine,' I finally concluded. 'I'm not discussing high-heeled shoes any further with you. Now go wash your hands and set the table.'

At that, Maddy stared at me, wide-eyed as if I'd just been assigned to her that very instant as her mother and had started giving her orders and rules out of the blue for the very first time. Then she huffed and marched out of the room.

I groaned and rubbed my aching head. Maybe I was still in time to change my mind and retract my baby promise to Julian?

Ironically enough, a few weeks later I found out Julian's precious parcel had actually *arrived* at destination.

I stared at the stick, my mouth opening and closing like a fish's. A pregnant fish. Pregnant. I was actually, *really*, pregnant. At forty-three years of age. Now really, what were the odds *the minute I went off birth control*? Had Julian speed-delivery-*ordered* the kid?

'Exactly why do you want to be a father, again?' I asked Julian as we were finishing dinner that night, my big piece of news burning a hole up my sleeve. Maddy was having another sleepover at Angelica's and I was glad for the privacy.

Julian pushed his now empty plate forward and folded the tablecloth over to rest his arms on the clean, crumb-less underside. Although I hated it when he did that, tonight I hardly noticed.

'Erica... are you having second thoughts?'

'Of course not. I'm... happy to do this. And...' I flashed him a shy grin '...that's one thing we can cross off our list now, by the way.'

'What is?'

I smiled, pushing my own crumbs before me into one little pile, Julian-style. 'Baby Mission accomplished, baby...'

His eyes widened. 'What? You're... *pregnant*?'

The look on his face told me that there was no crisis to worry about. Screw (or, as Julian would say, *sod*) Renata and Judy and their paranoia. This man was in love with me, no doubt.

I smiled. 'Uh-huh...'

'I'm going to be a father!' Julian yelled, lifting me and twirling me around the kitchen like in a cheesy Monday afternoon movie, but the look in his eyes opened up a new world to me. A world I never knew existed. Jesus – all these years he'd wanted to be a father and never *told* me? What did that say about our marriage? Paradoxically, now I was even more worried than before.

'Oh my God, Erica, this is so amazing, isn't it!' Julian cried as he smacked one last delicious kiss onto my mouth.

'Oh, yeah, wow, it is!' I assured him, not quite sure how I felt about it. I mean, I could have been happy, but my joy was overclouded by The Big Doubt – why Julian wanted this baby in the first place. He had a career, a business, two stepchildren whom although he loved immensely, had given him much ado the past seven years. Why go through it all over again just when you are about to sit back and begin to relax for once?

'Idea!' he cried. 'We'll decorate the study and paint—'

'The study? But you *love* your study!' I argued. 'That's your sacred ground! You don't let anyone in there.'

'But a baby's a baby! Honey, we're going to be parents!'

I already was one, and so was he, but pointing that out would be party-pooping at this point. Still, I had to draw the line somewhere. 'Hold your horses, Julian. I haven't even had an official blood test yet.'

'You don't need one. I *know* you're pregnant.'

Yes, so did I. I could feel it.

Surreal, Julian had called my pregnancy. It turned out he was right. It was a surreal, *three-week* pregnancy, followed by a major, major period. And according to my gynecologist, Dottoressa Bardotti, probably one of my last.

The thought was unbearable and I swallowed and nodded in a business-like manner as she sat us down with my file and test results. When I explained our situation she blinked. I tried to convince myself it was just a reflex or a spasm, but who was I kidding?

'Hmmm…' she said, flipping through my file, and by the time she looked up I was hanging on the edge of my seat as Julian squeezed my hand under the table, paler than my grandmother's linen embroidered sheets.

'So you're looking to get pregnant,' she said matter-of-factly and I almost expected her to add, like Judy, *What the hell for?* 'Well, given your age I suggest we get a move on. Every month is precious, you understand.'

No, I didn't understand. I had always been *very* fertile. If it hadn't been for birth control I'd have stocked the entire NFL, given enough time.

And now this woman was telling me I was a monthly time bomb, waiting to go off; that is, to dry up into arid, horrid menopause? She was practically saying if we didn't crack our eggs pronto there would *be* no baby. Great. Why did Julian decide *now* that he wanted a child? Why hadn't he told me before, preferably seven years ago when I was still bursting with eggs like a bloody Mexican piñata?

I had been happy with Julian and the two kids. But now, as you can imagine, hearing the doctor say that I couldn't do it was a slap in the face to me. I had failure-phobia. Not because I had never failed before, but because I had failed only too many times. Hearing Dottoressa Bardotti say that becoming parents wouldn't exactly be a cinch because we only had a margin of virtually what – twelve, twenty-four more periods if I was lucky – triggered in me a number of contrasting, gut-wrenching feelings. She explained that the menarche occurs when a girl has stored at least seventeen percent of body fat. As you can imagine, having always been quite plump, I'd had my period very young, meaning that I would very probably face menopause earlier than most women.

So there you go – once again, fat had managed, even retroactively, to ruin my life. There was no escaping from it. My weight had kept me a social pariah throughout my school years. It kept me standing against the wall at my high school prom (Peter DeVita, the closest thing I'd ever have to a boyfriend had just moved away and Tony Esposito had dropped out, thank God). I thought I could beat the effects of fat on my life with a good job, but even then fat had left me sweating buckets on my first job interviews, making me look like a real loser. Fat did nothing good for me.

But I'll always be grateful to Mr. Farthington who didn't care about looks and just wanted the job done. He got me as far as I wanted. But life was not full of Mr. Farthingtons. Life was teeming with young, skinny-assed women having children right, left and center.

Sometimes I wished I could be a thin, non-existent paper doll, like one of Maddy's childhood, pretty-in-pink, lifeless creations. You know, all legs and no room for any organs whatsoever, much less a heart to break, or a soul to ache.

Paul and Maddy would sit for hours on end at our kitchen table back in Boston and draw all sorts of outfits for these size zero sticks. Everything looked good on them. Funny how no one's ever made a pregnant paper doll. I imagined drawing one with an eight-month bulge. That would be fun.

And to think I'd got over all this. To think I had finally reached a stage where I was OK with everything. But according to my doctor, my weight was still too much. Countless doctors had told me I was never going to be a stick figure, so seven years ago, at eighty-five kilos and thirty-six years of age I had come to terms with myself and had started to accept myself – and more desserts as well.

I'd *tried* dieting but my weight yo-yoed miserably. Even when I temporarily got back to seventy-five kilograms, I was always told that The Former Me would always have the upper hand. Because my lifestyle as a fat woman had taken charge of me, ruining me for good.

And if at first having Julian's baby wasn't exactly on my Top Five Things To Do Before I Die, now it had become a *necessity*. Not just because I'd wanted to make Julian happy, but also because I needed to succeed in this relationship. My previous marriage had left me devastated. I couldn't be a loser anymore. I had lost most of the battles in my life and was just beginning to savor an equilibrium within myself. The kids were doing great. Julian was doing great. Me, I wasn't so sure anymore. Especially if I failed at this as well.

And now when I thought about it (because now, dammit,

I could hardly think of anything else), I actually *missed* the nausea, the all-nighters, the endless, sleepless nights of dragging myself out of bed and looking at my bump in the mirror, trying to guess what sex it was, what he or she would look like and sound like. The memories of pregnancy had returned with a nostalgic sweetness, waiting to become a mother. Again. Was I nuts or what?

I must have been, if I was willing to do it all over again, even the hard parts. Pregnancy was nothing, compared to what came after that – the parenting. *That* was the hard part, the part that absorbed you completely, sucked you into the parallel universe of multiple sacrifices and absolute self-effacement.

My doctor gave us a list of tests to run, first of all – you guessed it – Julian's sperm. It turned out to be super-sperm (why was I not surprised?) – particularly lively and healthy. I could almost imagine them not swimming but *shooting* around in the Petri dish, showing off. *Look at me! Wee! I can zing and dart across the universe! Yay! I'm Super-sperm!*

And all while my little, *old* eggs watched in awe, thinking, 'Oh, he'll never want to stick around *us*!'

Well, at least we now knew it was all my fault. And so the ordeal began. By ordeal I mean a one-thousand-two-hundred-calorie-per-day diet to up my chances of conceiving.

As per Dottoressa Bardotti, there was no point in IVF or anything of the sort if I weighed what I weighed. Prior to the procedure I'd have to take fertility drugs that would have the same effect on me as on a cow (yes, she really said that), that is, none whatsoever, unless I lost weight. *Lots of it*.

But because time was running out, I took hormones against my doctor's *professional* advice, although, between you and me, she said, 'What the heck, go for it – it's now or never.' I guess female solidarity stretched beyond professional boundaries. Fine by me.

So if on one side I was supposed to be losing weight, on the other side they were fattening me up with artificial crap intended to make me more fertile but in actuality was only making me more bloated. And turning me into a raging grump. No one could say anything to me that sounded remotely related to confrontation, and even the slam of a door would ignite me and I'd burst into tears.

'Sweetheart,' Julian said. 'I don't want you in this state. Let's not do this.' To his credit, he was concerned for me. But after weeks of munching on carrots and rice cakes, I had passed the point of no return. Reverting to my previous eating habits would've been bliss, but I didn't want to blow the whole thing off and dash Julian's hopes. He'd done so much for me in the past seven years. Now I wanted to do this for him.

6

Hysterosalpingography Hysteria

To be on the safe side, and because I couldn't believe it was only my fat ass stopping us from having a baby when all around me enormous women my age were getting pregnant, I had some routine tests done to make sure all my hardware was in place.

The first, a hysterosalpingogram, was to determine whether my tubes were clogged or not via sticking a catheter way up there with a dye that spread all around and into them. If the dye reached the end of my tubes unhindered, it meant they weren't blocked and we were home free.

They wouldn't let Julian in with me because of the X-rays so I lay sprawled on a table with my feet up in the stirrups while a guy I'd never met before (I know I'm a bit old-fashioned but at least a *hello* would have sufficed) told me it wasn't going to hurt in the least and shoved this contraption way up inside me.

'*Yeowhh!*' I hollered, seeing spots, and they all stood

above me bewildered while I was doing my best not to pass out from the pain as he ripped my insides apart.

'*Impossibile*,' another guy said shoving the instrument even further up. 'It shouldn't hurt – this is not normal.'

'How come no one ever told you your uterus is *retroflesso*?' the doctor barked at me.

'Retro*what*?'

'Not in the right place…' fumbled one of the doctors, searching for the right word.

'Not in the right place?' They made it sound like it was someplace completely different.

'Tipped!' he said in triumph.

Tipped? Was he kidding me? I think I'd know if my own uterus was tipped.

Believe me, if I hadn't had that thing inside me I'd have jumped off the table and headed for the hills. Abnormal, my uterus? It had worked just fine for the last forty-three years.

'Oh, no, no. It's OK – false alarm. It's just the speculum that's broken inside her,' he said to no one in particular. 'Can I get a new one, somebody, please?'

And this was a private, expensive fertility clinic. I wondered what would've happened if I had been poor and sent to just any doctor. But then I realized that, according to Murphy's law, if I had been too poor to afford a fertility clinic, the babies would have spilled out of me like in Shrek's nightmare.

And so, as the doctors looked down on me, all smiles, we waited for the delivery of an unbroken speculum that wouldn't just snap inside me again.

'Live nearby?' one of them actually asked me. I raised my evil eyebrow at him and then turned away to fight back the tears burning at the back of my eyes as he hacked his guts out, wiping his mouth on his glove.

I don't know how or why, but a feeling of total humiliation was setting in. Ladies, to those of you who are in the uncertain process of trying to have a baby, or have managed to do so with great difficulty, I salute you to the moon and back. You have to really, really want a child with all your heart to put yourself through all that. I can't even begin to tell you how much I admire you. I don't think that I could ever have that kind of strength.

On the way back from the operating room to the doctor's office on the ground floor, the walls began to cave in on me and my vision became blurry.

'I don't feel so good,' I murmured before everything went black.

When I came to, I was overwhelmed with the urge to hurl, so I tried to sit up from a gurney they must've put me on, but the doctor kept pushing me onto my back.

Damn you, let me sit up! I wanted to scream, my face cold and clammy, my lips shaking, but when I gagged he finally understood and helped me up. So much for an understanding and empathic vocation.

Julian was holding my hand, his face pale.

'I'm OK now,' I wheezed, trying to fill my lungs and get up, but both Julian and the doctor pushed me back down again, Julian tearing off a piece of paper towel from a roll behind him and wiping my forehead.

'Your blood pressure just plummeted,' the doctor explained, his fingers tight around my wrist, checking my heartbeat.

So did my faith in you, you butcher, shot through my

mind, but luckily all that made it to my mouth was: 'I'm OK now.' I whispered to Julian, 'I want to go home. Please.'

But both men shook their heads.

'You're not going anywhere until I'm sure you're OK,' Julian said.

The doctor said nothing, his hand still on my wrist, eyes on his watch.

My heart was beating erratically, I could feel it pounding in my ears, but mostly, I don't know why, I felt humiliated. Like an animal in a slaughterhouse. I had never come this close to my physical fragility before. All my life I'd fought like a tigress to be like other people by using my mind, while my body had simply been something my mind dragged along behind it. And the fact that my body was now in the limelight what with the IVF and tests only made me feel inadequate by tenfold.

So being all bruised up on the inside, I did the only thing I could do – put on a brave face and keep it light.

'I must've given him a scare and a half in there,' I said as I forced a grin while Julian and I drove off half an hour later. 'There was enough material in there today for a lawsuit.'

'Never mind him – you scared the crap out of *me*,' Julian said. 'What am I going to do without you if you drop down dead?'

'Be free,' I quipped and he cast me a stern look that melted the moment our eyes met. Yeah, he'd take it really nastily if I croaked, of that I was sure. Good man.

'Seriously, Erica – why are we doing this? I can only imagine what happened to you in there to make you feel like that. You're no queasy girl.'

That was true.

'So… what exactly did happen?'

I told him, the speculum thing snapping included, and I went all clammy again. He went white himself and squeezed my hand.

'Forget it, sweetheart. I don't want you doing this. It's not worth it.'

'Oh, but it is,' I assured him. 'Having a baby is like no other feeling in the world, Julian. I don't want you to miss out on that.'

As he slowed down to yield to a tractor at the intersection near our home, he turned to look at me, his eyes soft. He was beginning to understand what a woman went through to have a child. And now because of me he might never know the joy of cradling his own kid – something incommensurable. There was nothing like that in the whole wide world. And I'd have done anything to give Julian that.

I caressed the back of his hand. 'I'll be fine, Julian. I'm a tough girl.'

If anything, I knew I needed to become even tougher, because my current amount of tough wasn't exactly going to cut it.

Soon we'd be ready for IVF. But that didn't stop us from researching every single fertility myth, including religious candles and prayer – anything that looked like someone had pulled them out of the pages of a medieval sorcerer's *How To Cast A Spell* book.

They were so out of this world they made you wonder whether there actually was some truth to them, like sex on a daily basis (which Julian strongly advocated) and others that only a man could have made up.

'Get this,' Julian read as I nestled into the crook of his

arm once safely ensconced on the sofa. 'The consumption of yams, grapefruit juice and even stinging nettles find a scientific justification as far as an increase in fertility may be concerned.'

I sat up. 'I have to swallow stinging nettles too?'

He chuckled. 'Silly... Would you?'

'Anything for you, Julian.'

He put his laptop down and stared at me. The silence was deafening.

'What?' I said.

'I love you, Erica.'

I climbed up his body. 'Enough to drive into town for a delicious *torta Cecina*?'

He laughed. 'You already having cravings?'

I shrugged. 'Might as well start practicing.'

So yes, I was on a diet but rewarded myself once in a while for my efforts. It wasn't like I was doing pushups and knocking down Ferrero Rocher chocolates lined up in front of me on the terracotta tiles on the down-stroke.

And speaking of exercise, the next day, I read about another pseudo-strategy to get pregnant. Handstands.

I hadn't tried a handstand in a gazillion years. Could I still do one? I used to do them against my bedroom door when I was ten, but now? Only one way to find out. Of course they were no help in getting pregnant – sperm knew its way around, obviously – but I didn't want to leave any stones unturned. After a night of horror spent in a hospital, waiting to see if Julian would pull through or die and curse me forever from his grave, can you blame me?

So I closed the bedroom door and kicked my flip-flops aside. Then I took a deep breath and bent forward against the door so my hands were adjacent to it. All I had to do was let my legs follow my body and keep them straight up against the door and it would be done. Staying in that position while Julian and I—? Just the thought made me giggle and I collapsed in a pretzel shape against the door in a fit of laughs.

Not funny, a voice inside me chided.

It was, but she was right. Baby-making was serious business, so I peeled myself off the floor and dusted myself off. A fertility miracle-worker or not, I wasn't budging from here until I managed a handstand. How could I not be able to do this anymore? Had I gained that much weight? Lost that much strength in my arms and hands, with all *my* dough-kneading? How had that happened, and more importantly, *when* had it happened? When had I become some middle-aged woman who had lost her suppleness and flexibility?

Was this how old age screwed you over, and overnight, to boot? One day you couldn't do a handstand and the next you couldn't procreate and before you knew it your hip snapped and you woke up all alone in an old folks' home?

'Enough of this bullshit,' I said out loud and tried again, this time against the opposite wall. I flexed my arms and shoulders and jumped up and down on the spot like a boxer about to face Muhammad Ali. It was now or never. If this wasn't going to help get me pregnant, it meant that I really was too old, so I might as well cross it off my list.

I leaned forward with my arms and lifted my ass in the air, clenching my teeth, waiting to land in a heap again, but then the back of my calves hit the wall and there I was, standing upside down. I'd done it! Yes! Now to see how long I could resist standing right way up again.

'Erica, honey?' Julian called from the stairs and I heard his footsteps as he opened the door to our room.

Good thing I'd moved away from the door, or I'd be flat on my back right now. Not that this position was any more regal.

He stopped on the threshold and, from what I could see from this angle, his mouth dropped open.

'Look, Julian!' I called proudly. 'I've still got it!'

Silence, during which I remembered that, beneath my very wide skirt, I was wearing a pair of nothings. Oh God, could I be any more embarrassed?

'Yes you have,' he said with a sexy grin (I didn't see it but I heard it in his voice). 'And no signs of fudge anywhere.'

So it was like that, was it? Don't mind if I do, actually. Julian always had a knack for good timing. I thought I might try and stand up gracefully, but there was no gracefully with having to bring your legs down one at a time like that. So I maintained my position, my arms straining, aching, but it was nothing compared to what shape my pride was in.

To make it worse, Julian sauntered over and leaned on the wall next to me. 'Need a hand?' he said softly.

'Haha,' I answered, trying to ignore the huskiness of his voice. Well, at least I hadn't put him off sex for good. 'I can do this by myself, thanks.'

He shrugged. 'OK.'

'What are you doing, standing there?' I asked, trying to hide the embarrassment in my voice with annoyance when he didn't go away.

'Enjoying the view. Nice toenail polish, by the way.'

Argh. I was starting to weigh a ton on my wimpy arms. I couldn't hold out any longer, only my pride keeping me in this humiliating position. 'Thanks.'

'Sure you don't need help?' he asked.

'No thanks. I'm… trying to break a record.'

He laughed. 'And there was me thinking you were trying to break a leg.'

'You're just taking advantage of the fact that I'm stuck here, aren't you?' I said.

'No,' he whispered. 'Taking advantage would be doing this…' And with that, he placed his hands around my ankles and pulled them apart.

'Ooh. Kinky,' I said flippantly as he leaned in closer and *Oh my God.*

'Can you handle it?' he murmured, his voice low and guttural.

Meaning, was I going to fall in a heap at his feet, just because he was pushing all the right buttons?

'Hhhh… that's not fair,' I complained as the kinkiest images available in my filthy mind were playing out literally above my head.

'All is fair in love and war,' he quoted.

'Now is not the right time to show off your literary expertise.'

'You're right,' he said with a low chuckle. 'Now is the time to see how long you can stand it for without buckling.'

So it was a contest of resistance, was it? The gloves were off then. But soon, so was every stitch of clothing. God, I loved this man.

It seemed that neither did Julian want to take any chances. So he continued taking his time. I waited as he got his breathing back to normal, his head hanging low between his shoulders until he sank on top of me and went still, my legs still bent back against my chest as if I was doing bench presses, and in a way, I was. You try keeping a six-foot-three, two-hundred-pound man off you with the sole strength of your thigh muscles.

Many minutes had passed. How long did he actually think I could stay pretzeled like that? Had he passed out? He sure was overworking himself in between the sheets lately. Had he had a stroke and died, or was he simply sleeping? Now *that* would have been a real boost to my ego.

While I was mulling these possibilities over, a sharp pain shot through my leg. 'Ow, ow, ow, *cramp*!' I screeched, letting my leg fall back down and knocking Julian over the head, but it seemed to reactivate him. 'Oh, I'm so sorry!' I cried.

'Don't worry,' he whispered. 'Are you OK?'

Apart from a screaming Charley horse and a sore lower body, I was fine. OK, truth: I was brutally pissed off. He *had* fallen asleep on me. But I couldn't blame the guy – I was exhausted myself while only doing the minimal amount of work.

'I'm fine.' I tried not to sound snappy. 'I'm not the one who got knocked over the head.'

'No sweat, I've got a hard head.'

Apparently not only that. 'Are you... *already*?'

'Ready for another round? Absolutely.'

'But I'm not...'

'That's OK, have a nap.'

A *nap*? I wanted to sleep for a month! We'd been doing this all week around my 'fertile window' and I was exhausted. I had forgotten Julian had all that stamina. I'd forgotten *I'd* had all that strength in the past. But, I was determined – hell-bent even, for this to work. So onward and upward toward ultimate joy.

It went without saying that when we sat the kids down in the living room for a family reunion to inform them about our decision, they looked at us blankly.

The words, 'Aren't we enough?' hung in the space between us, so palpable Julian and I could hear them, followed by, equally silent but still hanging, heavier than ever, 'Ah, of course. We're not Julian's *blood* children. He wants his own kid. Good to know,' followed by an exchange of glances between them, then a simultaneous shrug.

'Cool,' they finally said.

'Yeah…?' Julian exhaled, his smile widening.

'Yeah…' Warren said.

But I know my chickens. They were not cool. Or at least, not as cool as they wanted to seem. Julian caught the expression on my face as I studied them.

'You will always be my first babies ever,' he offered, but it came out lame. Even he could hear it. 'You know how much I love you guys, right?'

'Dad, it's fine,' Maddy groaned. 'We get it. You and Mom are having a midlife crisis thing. But wouldn't a time-share or a boat be cheaper?'

Julian's eyes swung to mine again, helpless.

'Guys, we are not having a midlife crisis,' I came to the rescue. 'We want a bigger family is all, and we were hoping you'd be mature enough to accept our decision without the passive-aggressive attitude.'

'Fine,' Maddy said, getting up off the sofa. 'If you want the truth, I'm not sure how I feel about it yet.'

'Maddy,' Julian said, taking her hand. 'You know you'll always be my princess, right?'

She looked down at him with all the love in her heart as her eyes grew moist. 'Yeah,' she said. 'Until the new one comes along.'

'Maddy…' I whispered, getting up, but she stepped back, her hand sliding out of Julian's.

'Let her go, Mom,' Warren said. 'You kind of hit us with a bomb. Give us some time.'

OK, I mouthed miserably as my two lives slinked out the door, Warren looking back at us apologetically.

'They'll come round, honey,' Julian reassured me. 'Just wait until they see the baby. They'll instantly fall in love.'

'We'll see,' I answered. 'We'll see…'

And then came the day of our first IVF cycle. I'll spare you the fear, the hope, but most of all the look on Julian's face when they handed him a plastic container for the second time in weeks. What did he think his part was, just holding my hand and cheering me on with a *'Push!'* at the very end?

I gave him the thumbs up and a 'Go for it' smile as he dismally disappeared into the next room.

Just to spare you the wait, the first cycle didn't take. Which I was prepared for, to be honest. And yet, I was gutted. And Julian even more so.

'I don't get it,' Julian said. 'We have the goods on both sides. Why doesn't it always work?'

'My love, it's a question of timing and chance. Never trust chance.'

'So what do we do? Can we try again?'

'Absolutely,' I assured him.

So over the months began the long string of attempts. Meaning that Julian was having more encounters with that plastic container than with me. Not that we didn't want to have sex anymore – far from it – but we were both exhausted from the stress of it all, and on the weekends the kids were home most of the time so instead of losing ourselves in the luxury of lust on the kitchen table and every other stick of furniture in the house as we used to, we would fall asleep in each other's arms as soon as our backs hit the bed.

But even at the end of another good day, our 'us time' over a cappuccino on the veranda while soaking up yet another spectacular sunset, there was always that big fat question, hanging between us like an enormous piñata that wanted to be flogged to death: Why couldn't I *naturally* give the love of my life what he wanted most – a child of his own blood? And, more to the point, would there be a huge shift in our relationship if I couldn't, pun intended, *deliver*?

And to make things worse, everywhere I looked, suddenly almost every woman was pregnant. From the butcher's wife to Maddy's dance teacher (the one who was so harsh on Maddy but flirted shamelessly with Julian) and nearly every woman in the supermarket. It was as if an epidemic had broken out in the entire province of Siena and I'd been completely immune.

And you should have seen some of these pregnant women.

The ones who got to me the most were the young, tall, slim fashionable girls with great jobs in the city that were as gorgeous as ever, not encumbered by the extra weight, but effortlessly sporting the cutest little bumps. One woman, whom I had dubbed Sporty Spice because of her pigtails and gym suits, had a collection of T-shirts she wore to the market with a decal of a beach ball on it.

No – I lied. What hurt me more was seeing the *historically huge* women pregnant. I mean, we're talking one hundred and over kilograms. If fat was a fertility inhibitor, how the hell did *they* manage to get knocked up? Every time I got my period it was a freaking tragedy lately. For weeks I'd be thinking, *This time it'll work, this time I'll get pregnant. We did it at the right time, I can feel it*. But it never happened. My period seemed very proud to be smack on time, thwarting our every hope.

Before all this, I hadn't even been thinking about having a baby until I was told I couldn't. And now all I could think about was a little girl with Julian's eyes or a boy with his calm disposition. I could already see them, just an egg-meets-sperm away. No biggie. It was the most natural thing in the world. People all over the world had sex and got pregnant. Any day now...

7

The Home-wrecker Calleth

A week later, while Julian was back in the States (having promised to be back for our Spider Anniversary, i.e. the very first time we met) I was at home, struggling to get the back door open with the portable phone jammed between my cheek and shoulder and the laundry basket on my hip. Rather than using the electric dryer, I couldn't resist the slow, calm pace of hanging each item on my airframe dryer that I'd set up on one of the terraces.

Overlooking the infinite, luscious valleys of unripe wheat swaying in the gentle summer breeze, I was out of earshot from all the hustle and bustle of the town. But not of the noisiest of noises as calling me was Terry Peterson, Julian's New York agent.

'Erica? I just got cut off from Julian's cell. If you hear from him before me again, just tell him that they loved the book. The Brazilian butt got lots of laughs.'

Brazilian butt?

'Uh, OK. I'll tell him. Thanks.' I hung up and abandoned

my laundry basket to go into his study. Everywhere on his desk there were file folders with fact sheets and, on his corkboard, cutouts of homes, cars, people and even pets, believe it or not. I thought only romance novelists did that, you know, to re-create a fictitious world. My Julian was so *cute*.

All I knew about his book so far was that his hero was a baseball player who couldn't get a contract and ended up drinking and gambling his life away. That, to my knowledge, was not autobiographical. Feeling a bit guilty but too curious to stop myself, I turned on his desktop and opened the document containing his novel. Then I immediately clicked on *Find* and typed in 'Brazilian'.

It was just a little, innocent peek. A peek that would suffice for the rest of my life. I caught a glimpse of the words, *'and a butt like a Brazilian carnival dancer'*. Brazilian butt? *Brazilian butt?* I leaned forward against his desk, my eyes skimming furtively for more. OK, so he liked Brazilian butts. What man didn't? But how come I'd never heard him say anything so chauvinistic before? It was obvious. Because I didn't have a Brazilian butt and never *would*.

And all these years he'd seen my butt and thought, *I wish she had a Brazilian butt*. Ouch. That really woke me up. Good thing I'd started dieting again. Only it made me really, really cranky. Maybe I could take up Pilates again with Gabriele. And maybe even get some massages at the local beautician to shed a few pounds a bit quicker? The last time I'd seen that place was to get my legs waxed the previous summer. OK, so maybe I needed to get down there more often.

Stop it, I scolded myself. *You're getting all worked up*

because of two words in a one-hundred-k (that's what the header said) *novel*. Really, how insecure can a woman be? He loved me, and what was most important, *I* loved me. Most of the time. So enough. I had to get away from this desktop. I had laundry to fold. Dinner to make. A kite to fly, or something. But as it was, I scrolled up and started to read, feeling my face go hot.

The heroine was a beautiful blonde celebrity, all boobs and legs. Her name was Chastity (no surname) and she was a game-show host's assistant and always walked onto the stage with little more than a bright smile and prizes for the contestants. She was the object of the hero's sleepless nights, and the male audience was in raptures every time she turned to leave because she had a butt like – to the point – a Brazilian carnival dancer. Fan-bloody-tastic.

As promised, Julian was back in record time for our Spider Anniversary.

I had the evening of our lives planned out for him, which had three basic ingredients: Julian, me and a ton of whip cream. (And, well, yes OK, chocolate chips too).

But he was so full of stories and anecdotes and he just wouldn't shut up, every other word being *Terry says* or *Terry thinks*. Now you know I never liked Terry, but as long as he didn't try to screw Julian over in any way, I was good. He'd been Julian's agent since his first book and had been devastated when Julian had given up writing to pursue his career in education.

Remember when once upon a time I said only a bomb on our house could shake Julian? That bomb arrived precisely after I got back from my beautician's. The number of things I'd had done was longer than a grocery list – leg wax, armpits, bikini line, face peeling, face massage, eyebrow tweezing, a manicure, a pedicure and almost a brain lobotomy. Suffice to say I'd spent at least three hours in there. Then off to the hairdresser's and finally to Siena to buy Julian a gift, even though I always ended up getting him the usual Polo shirt or riding accessories.

So, with my face still swollen from the waxing and plucking, I kept a low profile, trying to stay away from Julian's sight, but the bugger always insisted on helping me clean up after dinner. He said he didn't feel right sitting in the snug with his feet up if I wasn't relaxing myself too. Cute, huh?

Anyway, I was washing and Julian was drying when the phone went. He stretched out a damp hand and, holding the earpiece between his cheek and shoulder, said, 'A Taste of Tuscany, *buonasera*,' and listened as I turned the tap off.

'Speaking,' he said, eyes narrowing.

I stopped and watched as his eyebrows shot up. 'Genie Stacie? I can't believe it! How are you?'

The voice, which I could hear as clearly as a bell, was high-pitched and babbling. She went on and on and Julian glanced at me, guiltily (at least that's what I think now) and nodded, repetitively, trying to get a word in edge-wise.

'Yes, but how – sure, but – when would you—?'

In the end he hung up, dazed.

'Who the *hell* was that?' I chuckled.

He scratched his head. 'An old friend – well, an old girlfriend of mine, Genie Stacie. We dated for a spell ages ago. She found me through my agent. She's in the area, so…'

I stared at him. 'Genie Stacie? As in the model slash actress Genie Stacie?'

'Uh, yes...'

Julian had dated *her*? She was possibly the prettiest thing in L.A., with long, long legs, a slender frame and a mane of platinum blonde hair. She'd been on the cover of *Sports Illustrated* more times than I could count. She'd had a whirlwind romance with Scottish actor Tom Jackson a few years ago and had had a kid as a result. I knew all this because she was also, God help us all, Maddy's absolute idol. It was thanks to Genie Stacie's lack of taste and dignity that I'd had to speak to my daughter about her haste to grow up and the length of her skirts.

Maddy and I had had an agreement last year before she started to mutate. An agreement by which I decided and she had no choice but to accept a number of things, i.e. apart from ballet concerts and exams, no make-up until she was sixteen, and no dating until she was eighteen, the legal adult age in Italy for driving and voting and...marriage. I shuddered at the thought. She was in too much of a hurry for my taste. Luckily she was as smart as a whip and could smell lies a mile away. And she was very specific about what she wanted in a boy. I knew I could sleep sound. Except for when she was like this.

'Mom! That's so un*fair*!' she'd shrieked in her melodramatic voice so similar to Marcy's.

'That's my decision, Maddy, like it or not.'

'And stop calling me Maddy! I'm not ten anymore! I'm a conscientious teenager now!'

If she considered herself conscientious during her morning tantrums because her black tights or favorite top were still in the wash, or while screeching at anything fried on her dinner plate and saying *duh* at something I'd said in front of any of her friends, then we were in big trouble. And now my conscientious teenager's amoral lifestyle icon was coming to our home. Great, juuuust great.

'Genie Stacie says she needs to come and see me,' Julian informed me, his gaze lost in an imaginary maze of memories. Memories I didn't need to hear about, by the way. Luckily, he wasn't volunteering them.

'See you?' I echoed. 'What for?'

Julian shrugged, his hand stealing to the back of his neck, rubbing softly. Funny – in seven years I'd never ever seen him do that before. It was like a sign of... *embarrassment.*

'She said she's in a bit of trouble, and that only I can help her.'

'Hmm... I wonder what kind of trouble?'

'I'm not quite sure. She didn't elaborate. I said it's OK. Is it OK?' he asked dubiously.

You invite a sex bomb into our home where we have a twenty-year-old boy who's champing at the bit to be a man and a fifteen-year-old-girl who thinks she is *Genie Stacie and then ask me if it's OK?*

'Sure,' I said, sporting a smile I didn't feel. Please God, not that pre-divorce, teeth-baring grin again. I couldn't stand it. It had taken me seven years to gain a modicum of self-confidence, and now this. I got a terrible feeling. I was also getting a terrible migraine.

'She'll be here tomorrow afternoon around six,' Julian informed me.

'On our anniversary and just in time for dinner,' I said, not bothering to hide the sarcasm in my voice.

'I was going to take you to L'Archetto,' Julian said as he took my hand and kissed it.

Damn, my favorite restaurant. I sighed. 'Forget it. What should I cook? What does she like?'

Julian thought about it. 'Nothing, if I remember correctly. Genie Stacie eats practically nothing.'

It figured. I sighed again and turned the tap on, and an awkward silence fell as we finished our evening chores.

'I'll make it up to you, I promise,' he whispered, nuzzling my neck.

'Damn right you will,' I assured him. Then a terrible thought began to mushroom in my mind. 'Are you going to fall in love with her all over again and dump me?' I said and stopped, unable to believe I'd actually said that.

He looked up at me, surprised, not sure whether I was joking or not. So I put on my *'I'm just kidding'* face and rolled my eyes, but he still watched me. Damn, he knew me better than I thought.

'First of all, I was never in love with her. Not really,' he said, leaning in to kiss me on the lips. What the heck did that mean? How can you *not really* love someone? Either you do or you don't. Right?

'You promise?'

'I promise. Now let's go upstairs. Unless you want me to take you on the kitchen floor?'

I batted my lashes like they do in the movies. 'Maddy and Warren'll be gone for hours.'

'Hours it is, then,' said my tantric husband with a grin as he took the dishcloth from my shoulder and pulled me upstairs. Not that I was complaining.

By midnight we were cuddling, just about to doze off,

when Julian whispered to me, 'Happy Spider Anniversary, Mrs. Foxham.'

'Happy Spider Anniversary to you, husband,' I whispered back.

But an hour later, I was still wide awake and no closer to falling asleep. So I got up and went downstairs to make myself some warm milk.

On the kitchen table, there was a copy of *Vogue*. I had never bought *Vogue* in all my life, so it was safe to say that it belonged to Maddy. I really needed to push her more toward some quality books.

I leafed through the glossy pages, looking for anything that would hold my interest, but found nothing. Until I found her. Genie Stacie Grant. Model slash actress, typical clichéd blonde bombshell, all legs and no brain.

I looked closer at her butt in the magazine ads. As much as it was perfect, it didn't *quite* have that Brazilian edge I'd imagined. Maybe because of the lack of a tan. But when I flipped the page there she was again, only this time her skin was the color of leather and sand had been strewn down her back, almost a continuation of her long blonde hair that reached her waist, and a bikini thong was shoved between her butt cheeks. *Now* they looked very Brazilian.

All this time. All this time Julian had known her, had cherished the memories of sex with her lithe, lean form while my ripples of fat threatened to bury him like a tsunami wave. Some trade-in.

God Almighty, after all I'd been through, was I here again? Hadn't I flushed out all my self-doubting, my uneasiness? Hadn't I worked really hard to be who (I thought) I now was? Apparently this was something I still had to work on. It was like painting the Forth Bridge. Or being Sisyphus rolling that damn boulder up the mountain again, only to see it topple over the other side for the umpteenth time.

8

The Home-wrecker *Cometh*

'Genie Stacie? Here in our house? Oh my *God*!' Maddy squealed, jumping up and down. Sookie looked up at her and yapped, happy to see Maddy excited about something for a change. 'I have to get my hair done! And I need a new dress and—'

'Hold your horses there, missy,' I cautioned as I dished up lunch. Four hours to Genie Stacie's arrival and I was already a wreck. But, like almost always, *nowhere* near showing it.

'And Maddy – remember to act your age. She's not your best friend.' *Or mine*, I added mentally.

'But Mo-om! Genie Stacie is *the* sex icon! She is like, the *it* girl! She is sooo—'

Didn't I know it. Not happy enough with *Vogue*, I'd Googled her, too. And boy was I sorry. For a couple that had only dated briefly, there were way too many pictures of her and Julian as a couple. Parties, award ceremonies, luncheons, dinners, holidays abroad – the works.

And he was all over her; his arm around her non-existent waist, his face in a constant smile. The same smile that had kept me sane all these years. The smile I'd thought had had no past and was just for me. How naïve could I have been?

And then there were just as many photos of her on her own or with the other rogues she'd dated. She was always in the tabloids for her party-going and her men. Tom Jackson had been half decent but even that hadn't lasted. And now this man-eater was coming to our home, back into Julian's life.

A shiver ran up my arms and over my neck, making the little hairs on my skin stand up. Whatever it was she needed to see him for, it would not be good. Sure, very often we had writers, actors and actresses staying with us when they wanted total privacy, but this one shared a history with my husband, thus hitting much too close to home. *Our* home.

My absolute favorite romance writer, Elizabeth Jennings, had come to stay with us this week. She was one of the organizers of the Matera Brainstormers writing group.

Originally from a small town in Oregon, she moved to Florence when she was a teenager. Love had sent her to southern Italy where she literally carved out of the rocks what is known today as the Women's Fiction Festival – an event you have to see to believe.

Writers, publishers, agents and all kinds of media experts from around the world meet in Matera every September to join in the feast of writing, eating, drinking and talking shop.

But it hadn't always been like that for Elizabeth. After

years and years spent traveling and living out of her suitcase as an interpreter and making enormous sacrifices, she was now finally where she wanted to be, free to write from her heart and enjoying every word of it.

I was glad to spend time with her. The first thing she always said when she got through the door was, 'Ah, *Tuscany...*'

Drinking a delicious bottle of Pratile IGT Bianco di Toscano from my buddy Rolando Bettarini's vineyard called Fattoria di Piazzano, we gazed out over the hills to the golden, melting sun.

Being in Tuscany, even for a short trip, was always a treat for anyone. Who could resist the sense of infinity and serenity while soaking in a land so ancient that it was already well known longer ago than 1000 BC.? Who could come to this place and not be fascinated by every single aspect of life here, from the large brick and stone farmhouses to the history and artifacts? From the ancient *cucina povera*, that is, simple, vernacular food, to its refined wines? And the tiny medieval villages that were perched up on the most precipitous of hills and mountains, like precious crows' nests? The intrinsic value of Tuscany was based on the toil of its poorest people. Lorenzo il Magnifico, ruler of the Florentine republic, may have kept Italy safe from the greed of foreign powers, but it was the people who had built the city.

As the sun slipped over the horizon, we continued to chat about Tuscan art and the Italian Renaissance. And then we chatted about our families and I told her about my insecurities where Julian was concerned as she sipped her Pratile, her eyes never leaving my face. I could see the wheels turning and knew she'd deliver me the rock-solid, elementary facts.

'But, sweetie, Julian is still living here with you.'

'Well, yes, of course, but—'

'Then that says it all. He's never been the type of guy to stay in a relationship that didn't fit him.'

I thought about it and realized she was right. If he lived here with me it was because he wanted to. Why couldn't I reach the same conclusions on my own?

'The two of you need to get away from your getaway. Come to Matera for a while. Visit the Sassi. Stay at the spa.'

If anyone knew Julian or any other alpha male, it was Elizabeth Jennings. She had written the book – well, actually, *the books* on men like him. Outrageously masculine, protective, dedicated to the well-being of his woman no matter what it cost, her alpha male principle pretty much applied to Julian – in his earlier days. Years ago Julian would have fought for me like Elizabeth's men fight for their women, like when he'd knocked down my front door to save the kids and me from Ira's baseball bat.

But nowadays I wasn't so sure.

'Men like him don't come along so often in life – you know that,' she said, giving me a little nudge. 'Think of all you've been through and how he was always there for you. What else do you want from the poor guy?'

I looked up at her. Elizabeth was confident, successful, talented. And above all she always had it together. I could learn so much from her – and not just about relationships. 'You're so right!'

She grinned. 'I know!'

'Mom, do I look OK? Can I wear make-up just this once? Please?'

Just this once? Who did she think she was fooling? I saw the traces of foundation on her clothes and saw the make-up remover in her bathroom. But today I was picking my battles very carefully in view of the biblical one I had coming against Genie Stacie.

'Yeah, uh-huh, that's enough now, Madeleine. Hurry up and get your ballet stuff. When you get back you'll meet her.'

Maddy considered it. 'Can't I skip ballet lessons this afternoon, Mom, please? Just this once? So I can look good when Genie Stacie gets here?'

'Skip ballet? You're always telling me how you get massacred when you miss a single lesson or if you're even two minutes late.'

'Yeah, I know, but I'll make it up to Mila.'

'No, you won't.'

'Let her, Mom,' Warren said as he came in, kicking off his dusty shoes at the door. 'Otherwise it'll be hell around here.'

I turned to him. 'The only hell that we're going to have here is if you people start losing your heads because a peroxide paper doll walks into our home.' Didn't I sound just a teensy bit jealous? Tough shit – I was the mother and had to set the example of moral discipline.

'Mom, you have to adapt to the times,' Warren insisted.

The hell I do. 'No, I don't, especially if it means allowing my daughter to act like I've taught her absolutely nothing,' I replied, opening the fridge and taking a swig of milk directly from the bottle, just like I always forbade them to.

'Hey, what are my two favorite girls in the world doing?' Julian called as he appeared in the doorway behind Warren, toeing his own sneakers off. He stopped dead in his tracks when he saw me drinking and wiping my mouth with the back of my hand. Never a good sign. 'Bad morning?' he asked.

'Dad! Mom won't let me see Genie Stacie today!'

I sighed. 'That's not true. I just don't want her to skip her ballet class.'

'That sounds like good advice to me,' Julian agreed as Warren plunked himself down onto a chair, all sweaty and grinning, and chugged down a bottle of apple juice. I glared at him to remind him of his manners and he nodded at the bottle of milk in my hands.

'Just think when Stefania finds out!' Warren whistled.

'And that makes you happy?' I asked.

'Absolutely! It pushes my stock up!'

'Oh, get over yourself, you pig,' Maddy hissed. 'You think someone like supermodel Genie Stacie is even going to look at a slob like you?'

Julian grinned at me, then turned to Maddy. 'Language, my little lady,' he whispered and Maddy turned pink. 'Sorry, Dad. It's just that Mom drives me crazy.'

'Likewise. Now go get ready for your ballet class. And you two, go wash up. We don't want a diva to see the real us,' I said, pushing her and the boys out of the kitchen like a good old Italian mamma. Although I knew Genie Stacie had seen the real Julian – all of him.

Ten minutes later, I grabbed my bag, flew down the stairs and opened the car door as Maddy plunked herself next to me in a huff and we took off down our squiggly private road that led to Castellino, my mind still on bloody Genie Stacie.

Just when I thought I'd managed to be what I wanted to be – a mother and a housewife who had time to cook and didn't have to worry about wearing a suit to work. And just when I had started to get comfortable in my own skin in my new life, I was expected to compare with bloody Genie Stacie.

The hours dragged by. Deciding what to wear hadn't been a problem for me in the last seven years. It was pretty simple – sundresses from the market and flip-flops when it was warm, jeans when it was cold. Oh, and tracksuits around the house, for when I'm cleaning or cooking (which is practically always). So what could I wear now in the presence of my daughter's teen idol and my husband's former lover that wouldn't melt me right into the background?

When I got home I thumbed through my unutilized wardrobe, having thrown all my old American stuff away – business suits and post-diet outfits, but still considered as plus sizes made in Italy.

My beautiful green Krizia jersey dress looked like my best option, but it was too pretty, making me look like I was trying too hard. How about my black dress? For God's sake, could I do any worse? It had *I don't know what else to wear* all over it, like I had no imagination. Truth be told, all the imagination on earth wouldn't find me the right dress. Because there was *nothing* I could wear that wouldn't make me look like a complete nobody next to her. I sighed. In one afternoon I'd morphed from a happy-ish, satisfied and confident woman into an insecure teenager all over again. There went years and years of killing every single one of my demons. And now they were back, in the flesh of Genie Stacie, a model I hardly knew existed, like all those dolls inhabiting fashion magazines.

So at a quarter to six, I put on a brave smile, or at least I tried to, but I ended up baring my teeth like I used to in my pre-Julian, pre-Tuscany days. Luckily, in a few hours' time this would be over and Genie Stacie out of our lives once and for all. Or so I'd thought...

Of course she arrived in a Lamborghini sports car wearing a pink-colored mini-dress that looked like a baby doll nightie. She wore no bra and I suspect not even any panties, so seamless was her perfect butt. I noticed because she had her back to me as she threw herself at Julian, the skimpy dress riding high up her thighs, her nonexistent belly against his. Boy, she was a tall thing. Even taller than me.

'Oh, my God, Julian, I missed you *soooo muuuch*!' she cried, her shrill voice piercing my eardrums from where I was standing – I couldn't imagine what it did to Julian's. But he smiled and released himself from her grip, holding his arm out to me.

She looked just like the blonde in Julian's novel, or at

least the image I'd formed in my mind. *Bloody hell*. This was Chastity's reincarnation. The image that Julian had worked around, all this time. The taut, Brazilian butt.

'Genie Stacie, this is Erica.'

'Oh, Julian, it's so typical of you to hire local help! Does she speak English?'

Julian glanced at me and I managed, in the end, to close my mouth that had dropped open in shock. 'Uh, actually, Erica is my wife.'

She turned to look at me and then laughed. 'Very funny, Julian!'

Thirty seconds and she had already managed to piss me off royally. After I'd mentally torn her face to shreds, I mustered something next to a smile and said, 'Pleased to meet you, Genie Stacie. Welcome to our home.'

She put her hand to her mouth and said, 'Oh, I'm sorry, I thought—'

'Never mind. Come in,' I said, and turned back into the house, Julian and Genie Stacie behind me.

'Oh, what a beautiful kitchen!' she exclaimed, running her hands over the black granite counter.

Julian smiled. 'All Erica's doing. And this here is the hearth – it's really old but it works perfectly.'

'Look at it! It's *huge*,' Genie purred, batting her eyes at him to make sure he'd got her *double entendre*. I think even the hearth got it, along with every other inanimate object in there.

Julian coughed. 'Well, er – Erica likes to cook and we often have guests. You could fit an entire cow in there, actually.'

'Yes, you could fit *her* in there, too!' she pseudo-whispered to him with a giggle and pranced off. My jaw dropped again. I couldn't have heard correctly. There was no way an educated (?) woman would purposely offend her host. Right? I eyed the knife block on the counter, then her departing back and wondered if it wasn't too late to take up knife-throwing as a new hobby, using her narrow back as a target.

Julian cleared his throat and moved on into the living room, standing near the open fireplace. As I followed, I glared at him, then at her, crossing my arms in front of my bovine udders, daring her to continue with her cow comments.

And Julian – how dare he not even *try* to defend me! He continued his tour of the house so I had no choice but to follow them stonily around to the dining room where an old picture of a cow grazing in the Tuscan countryside hung above the sideboard. I could only wait to see what kind of comment she'd come up with, but Julian steered her away from it as if it bore some horrific truths he couldn't deal with.

The fact that pissed me off most was that Genie Stacie in person was just as gorgeous as in the magazines. And just as glamorous. She was indeed a knockout. As in, *I'd* gladly knock her out, teeth and all. This was going to be a very, very long dinner.

'What's the *matter* with you?' I demanded of Julian as we were getting ready for bed later that evening. The evening of our Spider Anniversary, in case you'd forgotten. And Genie had managed to squeeze an invitation for the night from us because by the time she'd finished demolishing my taste in decorating and pretty much my entire persona it was dark and Julian didn't want her on the roads at that hour. In fact, neither did I want her on the road. I preferred her at the bottom of a ditch, but no matter.

And now Julian stared at me blankly, surprised by my outburst.

'The "cheap-looking linen" comment! What the hell does Genie Stacie know about tradition and the value of anything! Those linens were hand-embroidered by my grandmother more than forty years ago! And the *roasted cow* comment? Why didn't you say anything?'

He shifted uncomfortably. 'Oh – she didn't mean anything by that.'

My eyes popped wide open. 'Du-*uh*?'

Julian shrugged. 'Genie's just like that. She's never liked to be exceeded in anything. It's just a weakness of hers.'

'Exceeded? The woman called me a cow.'

'No, she didn't.'

I gaped at him. 'She suggested putting me in the *oven*!'

'To get rid of you as a rival, not because she sees you as a cow,' he maintained.

I couldn't believe such words were coming out of his mouth. Me seen as a cow? What happened to *You're my queen*? But something else had caught my attention for the moment.

'Rival?' I whispered. 'Since when did she become my rival? Is there something I should know?'

Julian rolled his eyes. 'That's not what I meant.'

I rested my hands on my hips in my usual teapot gesture whenever I was furious. 'Oh, but that's exactly what you meant.'

He sighed. 'Stop it, Erica – you're exaggerating.'

'Oh, I'd love to see *you*, if I had an ex-lover staying with us and flaunting our past in your face while flirting with me,' I threw back as I shimmied out of my clothes and left them there on the ground, along with my underwear and socks. If I was going to be seen as the family stable animal, I might as well start acting like one.

Julian sighed, running a hand through his hair the way he did when he was frustrated, which was actually very rarely.

'Yes, Genie Stacie's not very tactful, but she was actually paying a tribute to you.'

'Tribute – ha!' I snapped, pulling my nightgown over my head, too exhausted to shower. If our evening ablutions usually led to sex, tonight Julian was going to remain high and dry. Roasted cow, my foot.

'Of course,' he tried to explain to me. 'All these years she's been the center of every man's attention, and now that she's seen that one man's attention focuses on his beloved wife, she goes all scared and tries to pull herself up by bringing others down.'

I threw back the covers and gave him my hairy eyeball before turning onto my side facing the wall. 'Save your cheap psychology and your lame sugar-coating for an idiot. I'm not interested.'

The bed creaked as he rolled over closer to me, and I could feel his face just above me although I was staring vehemently at one of my own Tuscan countryside paintings on the wall next to the window. And I wondered what *know-it-all* Genie Stacie would have to say about my painting technique. It was one of the first things I'd painted since we'd moved to Tuscany, when things were all hunky-dory and we were happy. Scratch that. When *I* was happy, because apparently everyone around me still was.

It turned out I wasn't so confident after all if I let a useless, shallow by-product of Hollywood get to me like this. Couldn't Julian see her for what she was?

'And did you see the way Maddy was staring at her?' I continued, but Julian didn't answer. 'Julian? What, are you sleeping already? I'm still talking to you!'

'I thought you'd said goodnight,' he said.

'I didn't, actually.'

'I noticed. I was just being sarcastic.'

'Like your friend?' I broke off. 'Already it's rubbed off on you?'

He groaned. 'Jesus, Erica – are we really arguing over Genie Stacie? After what you put *me* through years ago?'

Uh-oh. I knew this would come back to bite me on the ass. Years ago, Julian's busy schedule, his gorgeous agent – and my own ambitions for A Taste of Tuscany – had driven a wedge between us (do you see a pattern here?). I'd had one *feeling-sorry-for-myself* afternoon in the company of Chef Alberto Veronesi, exasperated that Julian kept postponing our wedding date, when Alberto had kissed me. And I'd confessed it to Julian. Big mistake. Since then, although he'd forgiven me after what had felt like a thousand years, neither of us had brought it up.

'This is different.' Way different. This woman was not

only a sex bomb, she was a ticking bomb waiting to go off. With my husband. 'And did you or did you not see the effect she has on Maddy?'

'Actually, I saw the effect she had on *Warren*,' Julian said and chuckled.

I glared at him. 'You find this funny? We've got the queen of sleaze in our home and you *laugh*?'

'Oh, for God's sake, Erica. Lighten up – she's harmless.'

'She's your blonde beauty, isn't she?' I asked louder than I'd intended.

He groaned again. 'Which blonde beauty are we talking about now?'

I crossed my arms over my chest. 'The one with the Brazilian butt. Or is that another friend of yours who will be dropping in on us sometime soon?'

He exhaled sharply, as if I'd punched him, and let me tell you I wasn't far from it. 'You went through my manuscript? I asked you to wait.'

'Yeah, whatever,' I muttered.

Julian turned in the bed. 'That's not like you, is it?' he said softly, as if *he*'d been the offended one. Huh. 'What's going on, Erica?' he asked, and suddenly I knew it wasn't just about the fact that I didn't have a Brazilian butt. The problem was that Genie Stacie did. Years of trying to build my self-confidence and now he comes up with this bloody penchant for Amazonian asses – what the *hell*?

'What made you do it?' he persisted, and I rolled my eyes.

'Oh, for Pete's sake. I was just curious. How the hell was I supposed to know I'd come face to face with your favorite kind of butt? And don't even think of denying it!'

Boy, was he mad now. 'First of all, Erica, Genie Stacie is not the only blonde *bombshell* I've met. Second of all, my book is purely fiction.'

'Right, so you managed to describe her, making men literally drool at the sole idea, and yet… you say you aren't attracted to her? Because I find that very hard to believe.'

'And *thirdly*,' he continued, 'I was attracted to her a long time ago. But then I got to know her and the attraction waned, because she was not the girl I thought.'

'Meaning?'

He shrugged, still angry, and I knew he would be for a long time to come, but what the hell, I was much angrier than him.

'Meaning that she was someone I couldn't trust or depend upon. Someone like you, Erica.'

I turned to face him, determined not to let him charm me, because that was the way our arguments ended. With me forgiving him. And, moreover, possibly even apologizing to him.

'That's why I'm with you and not someone like her, sweetie,' he murmured, bending over me, his forehead against mine. Uh-oh – I was falling for it.

'Get away from me,' I snapped, pushing him away. 'I don't trust you.'

He exhaled, exhausted, the poor guy. 'Fine. Whatever. I'm going to sleep. Goodnight.'

And so we slept, back to back, not talking, for the first time in seven years. It hung in the neutral space between us, heavy and humongous, my insecurity, back in all its glory.

I was jealous of Genie Stacie. I was jealous of the way

Julian smiled at her, took her by the elbow, placed his hand on the small of her back as he indicated for her to step in front of him when exiting a room.

Who cares? I said to myself. She was only a Hollywood paper doll. I was a real woman, a good wife and mother who cared about her kids. I was the one who had given up a career to be with them. I was the one who was going to give him a child. I hoped.

9

Genie Stacie's Stay

Please don't ask me how or why, but harmless Genie Stacie's sleepover turned into a mini-vacation (for her) and I had to sit opposite her while she picked at lunch (she always slept through breakfast-time) and dinner, making brainless comments about everything. And then Julian made the mistake of telling her we were going to show her around and take her to the largest and oldest church in Siena, which had been erected (at which she smiled coyly at him) between the eleventh and twelfth century.

'Eleventh century, really?' she breathed, batting her baby blues at him. 'Before or after Christ?' You get the picture.

What didn't surprise me was that Maddy and Genie Stacie were in total sync and there was no way of putting a word in edge-wise. By day two they were like Siamese twins. Maddy had insisted on even sitting next to her during meals, like little girls on lunch break.

'You remind me of myself when I was youn— a teenager,' Genie Stacie purred, reaching out to touch one of Maddy's curls. My daughter sat up in her chair and her eyes almost popped out of her head with pride.

'Really, Genie Stacie?' she breathed, incredulous at the divine grace bestowed upon her.

'Absolutely, sweetie. Only I started straightening my hair when I was fourteen.'

'What on earth for?' I cut in, seeing where this was going. Julian gave me a sidelong glance and took a bite of his bread roll.

'Because straight hair is so much more *chic*. Look how much better Nicole Kidman looks with sleek hair.'

'I *know*,' Maddy agreed, then turned to me for the first time that morning. 'Mom, can you drive me to Alessia's salon this afternoon? I want to get my hair permanently straightened.'

'Ooh, no can do, sorry. We've got guests arriving later.'

'I'll take her,' volunteered Genie Stacie, who hadn't budged from the property – or Julian's side, for that matter, since she had darkened our doorstep. Of course she either missed or ignored my eyebrows shooting up and down in a warning signal that only parents can understand, the kind they use in the presence of their offspring when they don't want a particular subject to be mentioned, or when they want the subject to be changed. Instead, Genie Stacie crossed her arms and beamed at me defiantly. So she wanted war? War it was.

I can tell you Julian saw the whole exchange, glanced at me, wiped his mouth and turned to our daughter. 'Sweetie, your hair is so beautiful, why ruin perfection?' he said. He knew how I felt about naturally curly hair and Maddy's obsessions about looking like a Barbie doll.

I beamed at him and Maddy sighed. Genie Stacie had the decency to sit this one out. Or so I thought.

'Dad, you don't understand. I'd look really good with straight hair.'

'You call Julian *Dad*…?' Genie whispered.

I put down my fork and shot her my hairy eyeball this time, but she didn't notice it because she was murmuring something and before I knew it she ran out of the kitchen.

'Uh, what the hell was that?' I asked, jerking my thumb toward the door.

Julian sighed. 'Maddy, would you mind leaving us for a minute?'

'And miss out on a scoop? Are you, like, kidding me?'

'No he's not,' I snapped, and Maddy rolled her eyes and took her glass of milk (soya milk, all of a sudden) into the living room.

Julian got to his feet and took our plates to the sink. I couldn't wait to hear it.

'Genie Stacie never met her father, but she had a picture of him. I saw it. We look very similar.'

'Oh, for Christ's sake, now she wants you to be her daddy, or better, her sugar daddy? Again?'

Julian sighed and ran his hands through his hair. If he kept this up he'd be bald by the time she left. Because she would be leaving soon, I prayed fervently. This whole Genie Stacie thing was affecting him (and me) more than I thought necessary. But then again, what did I know about their past relationship? Nothing, except for the selected excerpts he provided. Nothing at all, really. And then it hit me.

'Did she lose your *baby* or something?'

I swear his eyes popped out of his head. 'What? Of course not.'

'Then what the hell is this all about, Julian? She comes here, starts directing my daughter, bats her baby blues at my twenty-year-old son—'

'That's not true, Erica. She just likes the kids.'

'Oh, let me guess, she never had a brother or sister either, right?'

Julian frowned. 'That's right, but there's no reason for you to be snarky. Yes, Genie Stacie is—'

I groaned, cutting him off. 'Do you mind getting back on track here, please? I've got a busy day and I really don't want to spend it talking about Genie Stacie or worrying about what she's trying to do to my kids and husband.'

'She's not trying to do anything. She's just a very lonely girl and as for the daddy comment, she always saw me as a kind of father figure and now I guess she's jealous.'

'Father figure?' I giggled despite myself. Oh, the cheesiness of it all. 'Is that what she would do to her father if she saw him, flirt with him in the hope of getting him in the sack again?'

Julian sighed, ran his hand through his hair yet again and started on the dishes. I got up and put myself between him and the sink. Something I rarely did.

'OK, I'm sorry,' I apologized. 'Maybe that was uncalled for. But I hate having her here. She's… obnoxious.'

'It won't be for long. Three more days. I promise.'

Three more days, for a total of one week. Was that how long her *win-Julian-back* plan was supposed to take? If so, she definitely had loads of self-confidence. And I found I had less and less each day. It had taken me a lifetime to feel secure in this relationship, and look at me in the space of a few hours.

'She wants you back. Big time,' I huffed.

'But I'm married,' he said, leaning in to kiss me, pushing me back against the butler sink. 'And in love. *Big time*.'

'Yeah, yeah. Tell Genie Stacie that.'

'I will.'

But I was still mad at the whole situation and at bedtime I made a big show of reading a book. And ignoring him. He looked at me for a moment, then sighed and lay with his hands behind his neck, staring at the ceiling.

I slapped the page over and flattened it with my fist as if it was Genie Stacie's face. Julian turned to look at me again.

'Still mad?'

I shrugged, not trusting my voice.

'Erica, honey, please. Don't let a lost woman like Genie Stacie scare you. She may be famous for the long legs, but I much prefer *yours* around me – any day or night.'

Ha. It figured he'd revert to sex to butter me up. He always did. Slimy, sleazy bastard. Boy, it sure worked.

I huffed in exhaustion. 'I just think she's such a flake. And the influence she's having on Maddy is scaring me. I flew my daughter across the ocean so Marcy wouldn't damage her and…' I gulped back the words down my throat, my eyes feeling like two flooded warehouses full of wet baggage. I couldn't get another word out.

'She's leaving Tuesday night. Then we won't see her ever again, if I know her. Just be patient for a little while longer – please?' he whispered, tracing my thigh with his index.

Uh-oh. I was succumbing to his charm again. Damn. Not to give him any satisfaction, I huffed and turned around onto my back again, crossing my arms over my chest as if to tell him there was no way we were having sex tonight. He took his cue like a pro, pulling my arms away from my body and nuzzling my face. I sighed again, this time a little less loudly. The bastard knew *exactly* how to butter me up.

'OK,' I whispered. 'But Tuesday she's gone and out of our lives, agreed?'

'Oh, yeah,' he moaned as his mouth found mine.

10

Goodnight Vienna

Gene Stacie would do anything to cling to Julian. Now she'd just come up with a story about a phone call from a producer friend of hers in Hollywood and talks about Julian's new novel becoming a movie, and was he interested in writing the script? And also, if that wasn't enough, she needed his help about something *very delicate*.

Butt out, I wanted to say to her. *We're trying to keep our family together and you're not helping*. Especially because whenever she was around Julian and I ended up arguing.

Don't get me wrong. I was thrilled for Julian. He deserved his novels to be made into movies, and more. But Genie Stacie could not be a condition necessary for that to happen. I realized that she had managed to make us argue just hours after giving us the news.

She was talking to producers and one in particular (I can't remember his name because you could only believe half the stuff she said) was watching Julian's sales closely and interested in talks about a movie. Not that I didn't believe a producer was interested because Julian's books were beautifully written, and his sales certainly warranted such interest. You don't become a *New York Times* bestseller for nothing.

So, given all this interest in Julian, Genie Stacie had – wait for it – *booked him a flight back with her* to meet said producer. Without even checking with him if it was OK. Evidently it was.

'What do you think?' he asked me when we were alone in our bedroom.

I shrugged, still wary of her. She could be lying. It could all be a ruse to get him back to the States where I couldn't watch her like a hawk.

Support your man in all weathers, I told myself, although it was storming brutally between us at the moment. But I guess if it was all bona fide, then he had to give it a shot.

'I'd talk to Terry before I took any of it for the truth. But if it is, it sounds like a wonderful opportunity.' *Gawd*, could I have been any more lame? 'If you think it's not a waste of time, by all means, go for it.'

'I think I will. Goodnight,' he simply answered and turned out the light. And goodnight Vienna.

The next day was Julian's forty-sixth birthday. I always wished I had more time between our Spider Anniversary and his birthday. I didn't do very well in the creative department so I always ended up flogging my brain for an original birthday gift, which never happened.

And just for the occasion, Genie managed to actually surface before noon, wearing a barely there burgundy dress, the same color as my *no-sex-I'm-on-the-rag sheets*. I couldn't help but think that when Julian glanced at her, he was thinking that her burgundy meant nothing *but* sex.

She flipped her platinum blonde hair so it rested all on one shoulder and flashed me a smile. The smile of a woman who knows she's prettier, sexier, richer and more successful than you. The smile of a woman who can steal your man in a heartbeat if she decides to. In my heart, I already knew that was why she had come. In my heart I knew I had no chance, but somewhere a little atom of me hoped that Genie Stacie would be just a tiny, harmless little scratch on the surface of our life. And boy, was I wrong.

Before I could produce my surprise gift from under the table, she whipped out a present like a rabbit out of a magic hat. I stared at her as Julian's face lit up in surprise.

'What's this?' Julian asked. As if he didn't know.

'You didn't think I forgot your Burberry day, did you?'

Burberry, for those of you who didn't know, was Julian's favorite designer, being British and all that. But Burberry *day*? Please kill me now…?

'Ah, Genie, you didn't have to—' he said, and I wanted to clobber him over the head with my stupid gift.

'Nonsense! I always liked buying you presents, remember? Now let's see how it fits!'

And, as God is my witness, before my very eyes she dived for the edge of his T-shirt (the one with *I love Siena* on it, my first present to him in Tuscany) and yanked it up his body and over his head with hardly a protest from him. They so obviously had done this thousands of times before. Before he was married to me, that is.

'You're as ripped as you always were, you Fox!' she said as she patted his lower abs, too close to south for my comfort. Was that where Southern Comfort came from, I wondered? Then she helped him into a beautiful, I have to say, beige cashmere sweater.

I coughed. I didn't mean to, because part of me wanted to see how far Julian would let her go, while the rest of me wanted to punch him and pull Genie Stacie's straight blonde hair out of her dark curly roots. Then she turned to me as if she'd suddenly remembered we were in the real world and not her own personal dream and said, beaming, 'Fox was his nickname on the team.'

'Uh-huh,' I said, clutching the measly Polo shirt I'd bought him, this time a bright blue (I had already gone through the gamut of greens ranging from pale aquamarine to dark green over seven years of birthdays, Christmases and Valentine's days). OK, so I wasn't very original with gifts, but it wasn't as if I *always* bought him Polo shirts. I also bought him sweaters, trousers or swimsuits, according to the season. What the heck was he going to need a sweater for in the summer? At least my gifts were ready for use. And so was she, judging by the way she swayed from side to side. I definitely had competition here.

'Don't be silly,' Renata chided as she poured me some minty iced tea. I huffed and rested my chin on my knuckles. Whenever one of us was down, we'd run to the other like magnets to a lodestone. However silly our doubts or fears, we always needed the other to tell us precisely that. 'Besides, that woman doesn't really look like that...'

'Oh, rest assured, she does.'

Renata stopped, mid-pour, and looked up at me. 'Really?'

'Really. She's so beautiful, she looks fake.'

'But surely the make-up…'

'Oh, of course, I've never seen her without her make-up. But I can assure you that the body is all there, Brazilian butt included. If anything, in person she looks even slimmer.'

'Mamma mia…'

'I know, right?' I said as I snapped my head back and took a huge gulp of tea as if it were *Rhum*. 'And what's worse, is that Maddy is fawning over her.'

'But that's normal, Erica.'

'I know. But I resent her undoing all my hard work. It takes me months to undo Marcy's influence when she stays over, and I'm so worried that my daughter will grow up with people like me in the minority. Everywhere I look, I see more and more people being so superficial.'

'That's the way the world turns, sweetie,' Renata said, shrugging her shoulders.

'How are you planning to keep Chiara solid and good?' I asked.

'Oh, she's still much too young for that. But when the time comes…?'

'Yeah…?'

'I'll send her over to her favorite Zia Erica to put her in place!'

'You laugh…'

'I'm serious. I think your values are rock solid and I stand behind them.'

'Then why can't Julian?'

She shrugged. 'I'm sure he does. Only I don't think he takes all this as a threat.'

'Well, then, he'd better wake up! This woman is wheedling her way into my home and—'

'Will be gone before you know it,' Renata reassured me. 'And in the meantime, all you're doing is putting pressure on your relationship with Julian. And you need to stop doing that right now. Even your sister would agree with me. Call her and ask her, if you don't believe me.'

I groaned. 'I know you're right.'

She took a sip from her own drink. 'Good!'

But, just for good measure, I called Judy all the same when I got home.

'I agree with Renata, it's all a bunch of crap,' Judy said when I related my fears to her. I always listened to both Judy and Renata, and then compared notes. Usually they agreed on almost everything, luckily.

'The guy's all eyes for you, Erica! Don't you remember me making fun of you two? You're both so gooey-sweet!'

We were? Damn right we were. But then why did it hurt so much to read about his ideal (and unrealistic) woman? I mean, come on. I was his wife, his rock, his companion. She was just a little bimbo he'd had while he was a baseball star and too young, superficial and fame-hungry to know any better.

'Besides,' Judy continued, yanking me back from self-pity, 'all men dream of a Brazilian butt and a leggy blonde.'

I knew that was true, but Julian had always been so

sweet and passionate *only* with me, I'd almost forgotten that he was, at the end of the day, a hot-blooded man in his mid-forties. And then I gasped as it hit me. A midlife crisis!

'Steve confessed something to me once,' Judy said as she lit a cigarette with a squeaky lighter and exhaled loudly.

'What do you mean?'

'He said he loved me but he needed more variety.'

'Was this before or after you cheated on him?'

There was a silent pause. 'After. I guess I opened up the sluice gates for him, because before that, he had never even hinted so much as being interested in anything besides me.'

'You're not thinking of pulling a threesome, are you?' I asked. I would die if Julian even joked about something like that.

'If that's what it takes to keep my man interested…'

I guess it wasn't too difficult for her to accept. Judy always was a bit more unleashed than me.

I imagined myself and Julian, plus Genie Stacie, all in the same bed, and I wanted to laugh. And then I wanted to cry, because I pictured the two of them, both statuary in their beauty, a twirl of cinnamon and vanilla (Julian was tanned now) lost in the throes of passion, and me taking up half the bed with my un-Brazilian butt, waiting for my turn, assuming she hadn't worn him out. Because there'd be no way I could ever compete with Genie Stacie, with her perfect camera-ready body, face and hair. Plus, they had a history of lots of sex, sex, and even more sex.

'In any case, if Julian chose you, I wouldn't worry about it. He doesn't seem like the kind of guy who just dumps his wife for a paper doll like Genie Stacie.'

'Maybe, maybe not. You don't understand, Judy. Julian seems to have this soft spot for her. He forgives everything she does or says, even if it hurts me.'

'Yeah?' was all she said.

'Yeah. Is that normal?'

'Not really, no. Maybe it's for old times' sake.'

For some reason Judy had shifted from supporting me to supporting my fears and my ears pricked up.

For old times' sake? Just how important had Genie Stacie been to him? I wondered. *Good enough for a roll in the hay* important, or *I want you to be with you forever* important? Well, neither of those scenarios were an option any longer if I could help it.

Later that day, as I was making lunch – a nice dish of shepherd's pie, Julian's favorite (he was still a Brit at heart) – I had the horrible idea of glancing out the window onto the patio.

There, in our very own private pool, the one that was used solely by Julian, the kids and I and our personal friends, was Genie Stacie, floating idly.

Julian was in one of the loungers doing some paperwork, totally oblivious as he always was when working.

Genie Stacie was talking and laughing and Julian looked up a second to acknowledge her, but I could see it was a polite smile and nothing more. She said something and laughed and when her bikini top magically slipped out of place, she simply whipped it off and threw it at him. As an answer to her invitation, Julian jumped to his feet and left her there.

Needless to say I was fuming at this tramp's gall. But I was also proud of my gentleman. It wasn't every day that a guy walked away from a bare-breasted Genie Stacie.

Alone and defeated, Genie Stacie reached for her bikini top again as I watched. What I hadn't calculated was Julian coming back through the kitchen doors.

'Hey, babe,' he breathed, blocking my view of Genie Stacie through the window. 'Can I help you cook lunch?' He was probably trying to rebalance his karma. Even if he'd behaved in a gentlemanly way, he was probably still shaken by Genie Stacie's free show.

I turned to face him. 'You can move out of the way now. She put it back on.'

Julian stared at me, blanching, raising his hands in protestation, an explanation already forming on his lips.

'It's OK, honey,' I assured him. 'I saw the way she cornered you. Now will you believe me when I say that she is after you, whether you are married to me or not?'

He closed his mouth and nodded.

I handed him some potatoes. 'Good. Peel these for me, will you?'

He took them from me as if they were precious stones. 'I love you, Erica,' he growled softly.

I reached up and caressed his jaw. 'If you love me now wait until you taste this shepherd's pie.'

And, for a while, we worked in companionable silence, grinning at each other from time to time for absolutely no reason at all, like we used to in the olden days of our love, when we were sure about each other, and excited to discover 'us'.

*

At ten o'clock the next morning Maddy and Genie Stacie came down the stairs together, twin gaits and dressed almost the same, refusing breakfast and hustling out the door.

'Maddy,' I called after her. 'Just where are you going?'

My daughter rolled her eyes and sighed, throwing a 'Shopping, remember?' over her shoulder. 'In Florence. Back tonight.'

'Florence? But Maddy, we were going together…'

'Don't worry, Erica, it's on me!' Genie Stacie sing-songed as they left, arm in arm. The shopping in Florence, I remembered very well. It was supposed to have been a chic treat for my daughter and myself. I'd half-pinned my hair up like I did on special occasions and even dressed up in my turquoise dress with the daring neckline Maddy approved so much of. Today she didn't even notice.

Before I could add another word, they were out the door, laughing. Should I have chased them? Embarrassed them both by vetoing their plans? Just how much clout did I have left over my daughter, and would I risk finding out in front of a gloating Genie Stacie?

As her Lamborghini roared into life and sped down the drive, I slumped onto the bench in the hall and took off my fancy shoes, my feet already thanking me after only five minutes, and threw my car keys onto the side table, staring after them through the open door as Genie's Lamborghini could still be seen as it sped its way down the hill, the wide wheels gripping the old, winding roads. My daughter in the passenger seat of an expensive sports car driven by a raging idiot who thought fifteen-year-old girls should be on the pill just in case they met someone one night. What a sight.

Enough was enough. I was Maddy's mother, not Genie Stacie. And it was my duty to protect my daughter. I should have stopped them immediately. Refused to let her go. Nipped this madness in the bud. What grown, mature woman takes another woman's teenage child without having previously asked for permission? The truth was, I realized, that Genie Stacie was not a mature adult, but simply considered herself like something akin to Maddy's older sister, and that they could do whatever they wanted under my roof. When they got home I'd have to bring them both down a notch or two.

But when they finally did make it back through the front door that evening, I almost fainted dead away.

'What have you done to your hair?' I cried, my hands flying to my mouth as I looked upon my daughter who looked like something between Marcy (who always straightened her hair even now that it was thinning) and Genie Stacie, only a much younger version. It looked like her head had been forcefully wedged through a crack in the front door.

'I straightened it!' Maddy cried back triumphantly. 'Doesn't it look, like, awesome?'

'No, it *doesn't*!' I whispered as Julian came through the door and stopped dead in his tracks, his eyes huge.

'That's nothing compared to the gorgeous clothes I got her!' Genie Stacie cried, like she was about to burst into tears with the sheer joy of it. 'Maddy, show your mother and Julian what I bought you,' she urged as she dropped her designer bags and skipped to the bar in the corner and poured herself a martini, Marcy's favorite fuel. Anybody see a pattern here?

'Look, Julian!' Maddy casually addressed her stepfather as she pulled out a strip of black cloth smaller than my cloth duster from a bag with D&G on it. I didn't know what was worse – what I'd heard or what I was looking at. I stared, wordless.

And my man, who'd coughed at the sight of the mini-outfit, didn't miss a beat. 'Young lady, when did you stop calling me "Dad"?'

'Isn't it *gorgeous*?' Genie Stacie squealed and Maddy joined her, and soon they were stomping their dainty little feet against the terracotta tiles as if they badly needed to go to the bathroom.

'It's so sexy, isn't it?' Maddy squealed as she put it against herself. Julian stood up, his face tight. 'Uhm, Genie Stacie, can I have a word with you in the living room?'

Genie Stacie looked in my direction, satisfied, inflating her chest under Julian's blinking gaze. 'Of course, Fox,' she purred, sashaying before him.

I watched them go, then turned to my fifteen-year-old. Now, just to make sure: did my daughter just ask her father if her outfit was *sexy*? The man who used to play in the sandbox with her and teach her how to kick a ball? To the man who told her bedtime stories and tucked her in? Maddy had *always* referred to Julian as *Dad* until now. What kind of garbage was this peroxide flake piling into my daughter's head?

'Maddy, why did you call your father by his Christian name?' I asked her the second the door closed.

'Genie Stacie said Julian's not my real father.' Maddy shrugged.

'Yes, well we didn't need her to tell us that, did we now?'

'I know, Mom, but Genie Stacie says that girls today don't use the words Mom and Dad anymore. And besides, Julian is really only thirty-one years older than me, which is not a lot, if you really think about it.'

I raised my eyebrows at her. Maybe Genie Stacie could marry an old geezer like Tom Jackson, but my daughter was doing no such thing.

'*Only* thirty-one?' I aped.

'Look at Genie Stacie. Tom Jackson is thirty-five years older than her.'

'Yeah, and look how that ended.'

'I want someone older than me, too. I'm sick and tired of these young pups.'

Young *pups*? 'Maddy, you are to stop this nonsense now. And you are returning these things immediately.'

'Mom! No!'

'Maddy, *yes*.'

'But they're so beautiful!'

I sighed. 'Not on my fifteen-year-old daughter, they're not, Maddy.'

'And stop calling me Maddy!'

I stared at her. 'You let her,' I said, losing my ground.

Maddy shrugged. 'Because she's so cool. She can call me anything she likes – I don't mind.'

I had a couple of names to describe Genie Stacie, but I wasn't going to repeat them in the presence of minors.

'Now pack this stuff back up. Tomorrow we are returning them.'

'You're just jealous!' she spat in fury.

My mouth dropped open. Was it that obvious? 'Maddy—'

'*Jealous!* Because she is gorgeous and famous and men all over the world are crazy about her, including Dad!'

I know it must have taken me a few minutes to close my mouth, because nothing I could say would do my thoughts justice. So I settled on being me. 'All right, that's enough! Go to your room. I'm having these, thank you,' I said, taking the bags of designer postage-stamp-sized couture from her.

All men including Dad. Was I so blind I couldn't see what was sitting astride my nose, mocking me?

'I know, I know, please don't say anything,' Julian said, holding his hands up as he came into our bedroom later that night. 'I think I got through to Genie Stacie though.'

'Thank you!' I said. 'You see what I'm talking about?'

'Oh yeah.' He sat down on his side of the bed with his back to me and pulled off his socks.

'And?' I prompted.

'And she says she's sorry. She'll never do it again.'

'Damn right she won't, because she's finally leaving our home! She is a horrible person and she has offended me and my home!'

'Our home. And she hasn't offended anybody. Not intentionally. I told you how her mind works.'

'I don't care how her rotten cabbage-mass of a brain works! There is no excuse in this world for her to come here and act like she is better than all of us except you!'

'Erica...'

'I'm not finished! It's your fault, too! You assume that just because you slept with her years ago that we all here have to live by it? Maddy is fifteen! I don't want her impressionable mind to be influenced by all this Genie Stacie crap. And you should be on my side, not hers!'

Julian's mouth tightened and he said quietly, 'I *am* on your side. But Genie Stacie is very fragile.'

'I. Don't. Care. I didn't even know she *existed* in the flesh until a week ago and now I'm supposed to worry about her psychological *balance*? What is she even still doing here, Julian? It was supposed to be just a short visit and she's invaded our home and our privacy, not to say turned my daughter against me!'

'She hasn't turned her against you...'

'You think? Maddy won't talk to me because I won't let her wear those three stitches that Genie Stacie chose for her!'

'Calm down, Erica...'

'No, I can't and I won't calm down, Julian. I have a fifteen-year-old daughter to raise, don't you *understand*?'

'*We* have a fifteen-year-old daughter to raise,' he corrected me as he pulled off the rest of his clothes in one swing and stood up, naked.

Damn, even through my haze of fury, I could see how gorgeous he was. And he was, until it was irrefutably proven otherwise, all mine. I instantly felt like an impostor sitting at a queen's banquet, dreading the moment someone would catch me out and take him away from me. Yeah, I know I sound nuts, but you try living with him and Genie Stacie under the same roof for a week. Deep inside I couldn't blame women for admiring him, but I damn well could for them trying to steal him from me.

I watched as he strode into the bathroom, turned on the shower and brushed his teeth, ignoring me now. Which caught my attention big time. He *never* did that. OK, so he was mad. I had exaggerated. But certainly a little argument wasn't going to keep us from... atoning? Was it? The shower had always been our make-up place since our very first fight. In view of this we had had a mega-shower built with a seating ledge. Worked like a charm. And I intended to make sure it worked like a charm forever and ever.

As he stepped in and began to lather his hair, I pulled at the buttons of my shirt. But when I got under the jets next to him, he kept his eyes closed, as if he didn't want to see me, let alone make up.

'I've decided I'm going to the States with Genie Stacie tomorrow to meet this producer. Don't bother driving me. I'll hitch a lift from her.'

I froze under the jets, wide-eyed. 'Oh.'

He finished washing and left me alone in the shower without so much as even glancing my way. Hadn't he agreed earlier that she was exaggerating? Hadn't he agreed that she had overstepped her mark? So what was happening, here?

It had already started. This was only the beginning of Genie Stacie's *Get Julian Back* project. First she reconnects with the excuse of a movie for his book. Susses me out, figures out I'm no danger to her whatsoever. Moves in on my daughter to make sure she has an ally. And then gets him to leave the country with her. Her next move would be to get him to sleep with her while convincing her that he shouldn't be stuck on a remote farm somewhere, when he should be shining and dazzling the screen, and the entire world, by her side. After all, she was a celebrity. And I was an absolute nobody. No contest.

11

Secret Loves and Love Secrets

The next morning, the morning of Julian's departure, wouldn't you know it, I got my period.

No, no, no! I cried inwardly. I was so sure this time! I'd even convinced myself that my exaggerated mood swings had been due to my hormones already preparing to host a new life inside me!

So much for IVF. Forget about timing and chance. Perhaps it was fate. Maybe fate knew something I didn't?

I washed the tears from my face and trudged down to the kitchen, eyeing Julian as he threw down a glass of orange juice, kissed the top of Maddy's still-sleek head, patted Warren on the back and headed toward the front drive where Genie Stacie was already tooting her horn, probably because she was dying to get past the first bend in the road and out of view to jump into his lap and—

At the door Julian turned to look at me, waiting for me to kiss him. All I wanted was to throw my arms around him and tell him that IVF had been a failure. But I couldn't bring myself to give him yet another reason to be disappointed by me. Besides, I was still mad at him. Even more now, as if the IVF disaster was his fault.

'Aren't you going to wish me luck?' he said.

'Good luck,' I said through clenched teeth. I wanted things to go well for him, for these Hollywood talks to lead to a movie. He deserved success. But I also wanted him to have a horrible time with Genie Stacie. I wanted her to get air sick and puke on his trousers. And he'd be stuck with Smellie Stacie all the way over the Atlantic. Talk about turning a man off.

Maddy and Warren stared back and forth between us. They were used to kisses and hugs and all sorts of mushy stuff between us. But thanks to Genie Stacie, in the space of a week, all that had changed. She had worked her Hollywood magic on him, while I had turned from loving to resentful, and Julian from sweet to impatient and distant.

But now he cocked his head at me, halfway between being with an expression that was half hurt and half wanting to say, *Come on, sweetie – it's still me, your loving husband Julian*. Only he didn't actually say it, but the look on his face was enough for me. And so I flew into his arms, burying my face into his shoulder as he squeezed me tight.

'That's more like it,' Warren murmured and Maddy snorted. She never liked our public displays of affection. While good old Warren had always been faithful, I realized I had to win my daughter back from the Shallow World of the Paper Dolls. And after this sudden turning on me by my former little, precious princess, I still *wanted* kids? I had to be absolutely insane. But for Julian, and our family, I was ready to do it all over again.

'Have a safe trip and call me the minute you know something, OK?' I whispered as we walked through the front door, still a tangle of arms and hands, toward Genie Stacie champing at the bit in her Lamborghini.

'I will, honey. And please be happy in the meantime, OK?' he whispered, and I swallowed hard and nodded.

'Don't worry, I'll take super-extra care of him,' my nemesis chimed as she drove my husband off our property and away from me.

I drifted upstairs and put my burgundy sheets on the bed. Even if Julian wasn't there, I needed a reminder that I wasn't going to have any sex this week, and as per the mathematical transitive property, wherever he was, neither was he.

'Hi, sweetie,' came Julian's deep warm voice over the phone and immediately that Julian-shaped place inside my heart tingled with warmth. He'd been gone only one day and I already *missed* him beyond normal.

'Julian...' I breathed, half-expecting he'd forget to call. 'How was the flight?'

Julian groaned. 'Gruesome. Genie Stacie was sick all over me.'

Was I a witch or what? I hoped something and it had happened! What had started on my behalf as a dainty, controlled giggle turned out into a big healthy belly laugh. 'Oh, Julian, that's horrible!'

He chuckled. 'I've had a shower but I still can't get the smell out of my nose.'

As much as that was ungentlemanly, I loved him for it.

'How are the kids?' he asked.

'Warren's in his room studying.'

'Without Stefania?'

'Without Stefania.'

'Wow.'

'And Maddy's out with Angelica.'

'Again?' School was out and the two were relatively free to rampage around town. I was confident, everyone's eyes would be on them in the village, from Nando, owner of the bakery-café in the piazza to our butcher, baker and even the candlestick maker (I'm not being funny; there actually is one in town). There was nowhere they could go (they weren't allowed outside of Castellino without our permission; Angelica's mom agreed with us on that long ago) without being seen. We had them practically tagged like two little bunnies.

'Uh-huh. And oh, she still hates me.' Which was the usual lately.

'Nonsense. Hug them for me, will you?'

'Oh, I don't think I can get that close to Maddy. She's at the hissing stage.'

Julian laughed and more than ever, I really, really wanted him home next to me. 'Look, sweetie, Terry's due in a minute and I have to finish getting dressed. Talk tomorrow, OK?'

'Is Genie Stacie with you?'

'What?'

Me and my big mouth. 'I mean, in the same hotel.'

'Of course not. She went home.'

'Did you find out in the end what it was that she needed you for? The problem that *only you could solve*?'

'Uh, kind of. I'll tell you about it when I get back.'

'Tell me now.'

I heard Julian call, 'It's open,' and then Terry Peterson's loud booming voice, 'Hey, Fox, you ready to hit the town?'

'Ah,' I said, resenting the man from even this far. 'OK, Julian, have a good time.'

'I'm meeting that producer for dinner,' he said softly. Apologetically, almost.

'Great!' I said. 'Good luck, then.'

'Love you, sweetheart.'

'Me, too! Bye!' I chimed and hung up before he could answer. Not that I cared about Terry Peterson constantly being on the prowl – that was his business. I trusted Julian. But how the hell was I going to get to sleep wondering why Genie Stacie had elected Julian as her only savior? And why was he the only one who could help her?

I pretty much trudged through the next few days without him, preparing meals, directing Caterina and Rosina, my precious housekeepers, with our changeover days and guests and meeting up with Renata for lunch.

'Where's that husband of yours gone, to the States again?' she asked over our *pasta alla carbonara*.

'Uh-huh.'

'With that flaky blonde?'

'Renata, please don't rub it in. I'm pissed off enough as it is.'

'Shut up. Tell me all!'

So I did. Marco was away on business too, only without the blonde. My kids played with Renata's younger ones as we enjoyed a bottle of *vino rosso* and each other's company. Warren was fake-wrestling with Graziano, Renata's boy, while Maddy had momentarily shed her princess aura and was braiding little Chiara's long black hair.

'What else is wrong?' she asked.

'You should see the way even Maddy was on my case,' I whispered. 'I think she likes Genie Stacie more than she likes me.'

Renata took a huge swig of her wine and I followed, enjoying the taste of our hard work in the vineyards. It had taken years to get it right. Just like my relationship with men. And myself. And Maddy.

'Silly. You are the most likeable mom there is. And besides, Maddy doesn't count – she's a teenager, an unreliable species.'

I grinned at her and nodded. 'See, Renata? That's why I love you so much. You always take the drama out of everything.'

She took my hand and smiled. 'You will be fine. Your family is safe. Don't let a paper doll scare you.'

We drank to that and turned our heads over a loud rumble, then a roar followed by a loud honking as a red Ferrari materialized as the dust settled. Renata paled and said, 'Wait here.'

Warren and Maddy looked up and followed me following Renata to the gate. There, in flesh and blood, stood Leonardo Cortini, otherwise known as *Leonardo il Bastardo*.

What the *hell* was he doing here?

Leonardo closed the car door and strode up to Renata, his face so close to hers, the chicken-wire gate being the only thing between them. He stepped back when we all appeared in his line of vision.

What was all this about? And why was Renata suddenly

so pale? My memory went back to the afternoon I'd crossed paths with Leonardo on the road between Renata's property and our own. Come to think of it, I'd seen his car several times, but had thought nothing of it as Renata's farmhouse was on a crossways, so he w

asn't necessarily going to hers rather than just past hers. But Marco had told me that Renata had almost married the bastard. Was Leonardo trying to get his own back? Was he trying to get her back? Could it possibly be…? No. Renata would never do anything like that. She was a fantastic woman. Yet… she *had* loved him once. If my theory of Flames Rekindled was something to go by, maybe Renata still felt something for him? How many times had he driven up that road in the hope of seeing her?

'What do you want?' I demanded, pushing my big body before Renata's scrawny little form. I could take the impact better than her any day. Besides, I'd always wanted to sock him good. For all he'd done to those poor women, many of them too young to know any better.

'Nothing,' he said with a shrug. 'I… need to talk to Marco.'

'He's not here now,' Renata said softly, her eyes lowered as he eyed her hungrily. 'Please go,' she whispered.

He made to move toward her, but I took a step forward, pretending to be brave, and Warren, good soul that he was, stood next to me, his jaw determined, his eyes unwavering. Warren was not new to confronting men, least of all his own biological father Ira, years ago in Boston on that night of unleashed madness.

Leonardo gave him a once-over, registering my son's tall, strong body and figuring he would have the crap kicked out of him. His mouth clamped shut in frustration and he spun on his heel, leaving us all standing there in shock.

'What the hell did he want?' Warren growled.

A question I couldn't bring myself to ask Renata. It was so obvious he was back on her case. After all these years. Or… had this been going on ever since?

'Nothing. He's been pressuring some local businesses to close by not allowing bank loans…'

'Can he even do that?' I asked.

She shrugged. 'Officially, no, but he's in cahoots with the bank manager. They're bosom buddies, so…'

'Do you guys need a loan?' I asked. 'You know—'

'Erica, please, not here…'

I shut my mouth. 'Right. Sorry.'

'He's supposed to be like some real lady-killer or something?' Maddy asked, but no one answered her.

'Well, he's gone now, kids. You can relax.'

'Thank you,' Renata whispered, her eyes not meeting mine.

'What is it you're not telling me, Renata? Is he bothering you?'

'Me? Of course not. Stop worrying about me all the time. I'm fine.'

'Are you sure you don't want me to stay until Marco gets here?' I asked.

Renata shook her head and attempted a patient smile. 'I'm all right.'

'No, Renata, you're not all right. Look at you. Marco told me… about you and Leonardo,' I whispered as the kids gathered their things, Chiara showing her long braid off to Warren who patted her on the head, a big smile now splitting his face. He loved kids.

Renata stared at me, then shrugged. 'That was a long time ago.'

'Yes, but you were the one that got away, in a sense. Did it take you a long time to get over it?'

She pursed her lips and looked at me. 'Sometimes it's very difficult to get rid of some people, no matter how hard you try.'

'You're telling me. Renata, what does he want? You can tell me – I'm your friend.'

But she stood in silence, her jaw working. I could see that she needed a real good cry, and if she was anything like me I knew she needed to be left on her own. 'Remember that.'

'I will, Erica. Thank you.'

'And you're sure there's nothing you want to tell me?'

'Like what?'

'Like…' I faltered. 'You wouldn't be the first person to have… an affair.'

At that, her head snapped up and our eyes met. Hers were angry. 'I think you should go,' she said.

'I—I'm so *sorry*…' I whispered, realizing what I'd said.

Renata turned away from me, busying herself with her earring. 'You need to go, Erica.'

'OK, Renata. But I really am sorry. Please forgive me.'

So I drove my family home, sad at how such a happy afternoon had been ruined by a dirty bully and my own big mouth. So I decided to keep a closer eye on her from now on.

'That's so awesome, a man wanting another man's

woman so much he'll even come to your front door in broad daylight,' Maddy swooned as our gates swung open.

'As opposed to what, sending you impersonal text messages or emails?' I countered. These kids today. 'And besides, he's not in love with Renata.'

'Oh, no?' Maddy snorted. She was still mad at me. 'And what do you think he wanted from her, candies?'

'No,' I said. 'I think he's a very bad man who likes to push people around.'

'Why?'

'Because he thinks he can.'

Which got me thinking. Had he bullied Renata into seeing him again? Or had it just happened, for old times' sake, and she couldn't get out of it because the pull of a past flame was just too strong to get away from? Or because there was something missing in her marriage? Or was I imagining everything? And if so, then what business did he have hovering around Renata's house? Did he want to take her down memory lane? Did he want her back? And how did she feel about that? As much as she and Marco were solid, would she entertain a little foray into the pleasures of adultery? I just didn't know.

But it was common knowledge that Leonardo *was* good in bed, and we all know what married life is like after you've had the kids and the years have dragged by. Or so they say. Me, I've never thought about anyone else. And it had better be the same for Julian.

And then the thought – was Julian going through the same thing with Genie Stacie? OK, he wouldn't cheat on me (right?) but maybe all these memories from his carefree, jet-setty past were coming to the fore?

I guess it's normal for everyone to compare their past to their present, to see how they've done for themselves in life. Personally, anything after Ira would have been a huge improvement, but I'd be lying through my teeth if I didn't admit that with Julian I actually lucked out a million times over.

But when he looked back at his life and where he was now, did he think the same thing about me? Now I know what you're thinking. That he did, and that he was happy with me, because I'm your average underdog who got a long-deserved break, and for that I thank you. It's nice to see our kind finally getting a piece of the pie.

But say, for argument's sake, that when Julian looked back and analyzed his own choices... that I didn't come up among his best? And say that he wished he hadn't made the decision to come to Italy (not so absurd, seeing as he is constantly leaving it) and that he actually felt trapped in this Tuscan life with me, and that he longed for the days when he was free and didn't have to report back – or even come back?

And say that the only reason he did come back was that he felt duty-bound to do so because in a moment of mad love, he had adopted my two kids?

And say that he didn't have the heart to tell me any of this, but was waiting for me to figure it out by myself so he wouldn't have to be the heart-breaker?

Well, one thing was sure. If he could have his cake and eat it too, so could I. Who said he was to be the only one enjoying the simple pleasures of life outside the family sphere? And who said I was to wait patiently, like Penelope forever weaving on her loom, for her man to come home?

*

The next afternoon as I was down in the front garden giving my brand-new (and hunky) gardener Piero instructions, my cell phone rang inside my pocket. I squinted at the sunlit screen and Julian's face beamed up at me. Despite myself, my heart skipped a beat. Damn, would I never be indifferent to his charm?

'Hello?' I said.

'Hi, honey, how are things?' he asked from the other side of the Atlantic Ocean as if he could do anything about it otherwise.

Exactly the way you left them, would have been my first response but I bit my tongue. After all, I was supposed to be working on us, at the end of the day. I didn't want to make things any worse, did I?

'Good, everything's good,' I said as coolly as possible, when all I really wanted to do was say, *I miss you. When are you coming home?*

'And the kids?'

'The kids included.'

'Good, good. Sorry, honey, but I've got bad news. I'm going to have to cancel my flight home,' Julian said.

Bingo. What did I tell you? I know my chickens, they say here in Italy. Only I think the real chicken here was me. No, actually, it was him as well, because he didn't have the guts to come right out and say how things really were. But there was no use starting yet another one of our arguments across the ether, was there?

'What? Why?'

'I'm so sorry, but this producer wants me to meet some financers.'

'Erica, how do you like it – is it big enough for you?' Piero asked from the back door, referring to a new rosebush I wanted planting.

'Who's that?' Julian asked.

Shit. I covered the mouthpiece but it was too late. I hadn't told Julian about Piero yet. Years ago we'd agreed to make joint decisions on everything, but he wasn't around when I needed to hire another gardener. So much for breaking it to him gently.

'Uh, that was our new gardener, Piero.'

Silence.

And then, to make things worse while trying to make them better, I explained, or tried to. 'I needed him to plant my bushes.'

Silence again on the other end as I could hear him trying to make sense of it and it wasn't looking good. 'You mean you're meeting more money people?' I asked, trying to get the conversation back to safer ground. 'That's great!'

'You hired a gardener without even telling me? I thought I was in charge of your bushes,' he added.

Yeah, so did I. 'You *were* in charge. And you did a great job. But you're never around anymore, and they need tending to.' OK, this was getting farcical. So I tried to explain. 'I'm not good with plants – you know that. Remember my succulents, the ones on my windowsill in Boston? Remember how you used to water them just in the nick of time?'

'Erica, what the hell?' Boy, he wasn't letting this one go, was he?

'Are you jealous?' I asked hopefully.

'Bloody right I am,' he swore, his Liverpudlian accent at its most obvious when he was angry, which was very rare.

'Good. I'm sorry, but you were away. I needed the job done. Be thankful I didn't need anything else instead.'

Dead silence.

'OK, that was a joke.'

He sighed loudly. 'You could have at least let me know what was going on.'

Piero looked at me expectantly. 'I'll be with you in a minute, Piero. Honey, I have to go.'

'Piero *Honey*?' Julian echoed me.

'What?'

'You just called him honey!'

'What are you talking about? I called *you* honey, not him.' I shot a glance at Piero who was waiting patiently. Luckily his English was non-existent. 'Julian – *honey*, I have to go. Piero needs me.'

'Indeed,' Julian said, rather teed off.

'I have to go now, Julian,' I repeated.

'Fine,' he snapped. 'Goodbye.'

'Goodbye,' I replied and pressed the red button.

So he was angry. Good. It served him right. If he could have Genie Stacie, I could have Piero. I wondered how we had managed to start this silly *I'll-show-you* game. Although it was childish, it made me feel better. For about two minutes.

Had Julian jacked me up so much with how great I was all these years that the minute he was away I needed male attention? *Shouldn't* it have been the opposite – that Julian had jacked me up so much I actually didn't *need* any more attention? Was I at the point where I needed a man to keep me uplifted? Whatever happened to *me*, the old Erica Cantelli who ran her life and raised a family single-handedly while bringing home the bacon? Well, she got depressed and lost her confidence while trying to have a baby, that's what happened.

Ah, but not for long! Because things would eventually change. Maybe even on a dime. Yes, why not? I could do this! Keep my man *and* give him a baby, no matter what Dottoressa Bardotti said – for all we knew, I could get pregnant in a few weeks' time. And where did your smarty-pants theories go now, Doc? Huh? Too old and too fat my foot.

The next day I went out and got some more stinging nettles, famous for enhancing fertility. I wished I could call Renata up, just to tell her, just for a laugh. But she had been clear. She wanted to be alone.

12

Games People Play

One week later Julian came home.

At my mea-culpa-esque questions about his trip, he quietly answered that yes, he'd met the right people, established new contacts, and was now waiting to hear. But he didn't want to elaborate, and did I mind if he had a nap because he was tired?

Too tired to just sit and talk with me? Oh boy. He *was* still cross with me. This was starting to look like when we last fell out. I prayed *that* would never happen again. I couldn't take losing him.

Because I didn't want to make him any more miserable than he already was lately, I still didn't dare tell him about the IVF failure. Because he seemed less sympathetic every time, less worried and probably more concerned with other matters. I only wish I knew what they were. It seemed that lately my nearest and dearest had maxed out on me and needed their space.

'OK,' I said. 'Uhm, good nap, then. And sleep well...'

'Yeah,' he answered distractedly and as he scooped up his cell phone off the counter, he leaned in, surprising me, and kissed me hard, almost angrily, as if he wanted to get back at me for the gardener and my bush joke. And make sure I knew *he* was still head rooster in this yard. That was a good sign at the end of the day then, right?

'Does this mean you forgive me?' I ventured.

He growled, 'Don't push your luck.' And then he happened to look out the window to where said gardener, dressed only in a pair of teeny-tiny shorts, was washing his heavenly bod under the outdoor shower like in an old Coca-Cola ad. Or was it Levi's? I can't remember.

We both watched as the Adonis shook his wet mane of the excess water and rubbed his face and time seemed to slow down as the droplets seemed to reluctantly fan out around him, not wanting to leave. He was indeed something to look at. He also looked like I'd planted him right there and then with a script: *barely clad hunk stretches his fab bod under the water jets in slow motion.* Well, let's be honest, I could've hired Mr. Alessi, Renata's elderly gardener. But he didn't look anything like Piero. Even a straight man like Julian had to admit it. I figured it was payback time for bringing Genie Stacie into the house.

'Bloomin' *heck* – is that him – the new gardener? Where'd you find him, in an issue of… never mind.'

I said nothing. He hated when I argued, because, according to him, I could turn a saint into a psychopath.

Julian's mouth clamped shut too as he turned away from the window. Not good.

'So,' I said breezily. 'Tell me more about your movie talks?'

'Not now.' And with that he plunked his bottle onto the counter and picked up his suitcase from where he'd left it, throwing his laundry into the washer just off the kitchen. Shirts, trousers, socks, briefs.

Shit. I had some major damage control to do here. 'Tell you what,' I ventured. 'Why don't we go upstairs and have a nice shower?' Which was code for, *Let's have sex and forget about the whole thing, yes?*

To which he readily responded, 'I'm too angry right now,' while snapping the washer door shut and brushing past me. 'I'm going for a ride.'

'But I thought you said you were tired…?'

'Not just physically, Erica.'

'Julian…?'

'I need to clear my mind.'

And with that, he stalked out of the kitchen and out of the house as a slow, licking flame of panic began to burn inside me.

A minute later, Maddy arrived and opened the fridge door.

'You're late. Where were you?' I demand.

'At Angelica's,' she replied, opening a carton of juice.

'That's funny. I called Angelica's mom who said you were out. Do you want to tell me what you're up to?'

'Me? Nothing?'

'Then why all the cloak and dagger?'

She shrugged, and I could see in her eyes that something was troubling her. But she wouldn't talk to me.

'Honey, please listen to me. I *made* you. No one in the world loves you as much as I do. I am here to help you with whatever problem you have. You can trust me. I am here to protect you and guide you and make sure you are happy and well. Just remember that, sweetheart.'

For a moment, just a fleeting moment, her eyes searched mine and I could see a relenting of tension. Then she rolled her eyes. 'I know that, Mom. But I'm fine.'

'Are you sure?'

'Yes!'

'You'd tell me, right!'

'Mom – you need to back off. You're suffocating us. Even Dad is sick of you, you see?'

I stopped and looked at her. Was it that obvious that I was losing everyone? My entire family was falling apart, and there was nothing I could do, because whatever I tried, it only managed to pull us further apart.

So I called my second partner in crime, my dad.

'Erica, honey, they're just kids. They need some time. Not every kid is like you.'

'What does that mean?'

'That when Judy and Vince were born you always wanted to feed them and hold them and sing them lullabies. You were adorable.'

'So you're saying that they'll come round?'

'Of course they will. You guys are a family. I'll bet once Maddy sees the baby she'll hardly let you anywhere near it.'

'I guess…'

'You'll see.'

'Thanks, Dad. And you? How are things?'

'Good, good. Business is doing well. I'm actually thinking of retiring, letting Vince take over completely.'

'Finally! You don't have to worry about Vince, Dad. He's good.'

'He is,' Dad agreed.

'And what about Marcy?' I asked.

He snorted. 'Marcy is always Marcy. She's planning a shopping trip to Paris with Judy. Why don't you join them?'

'Me? No thanks, Dad.'

'I know she made a mess of it last time, but I think she'd be happy if you did.' He chuckled. 'God knows Judy would be happy to share her with you.'

'Dad...? How do you... get over these huge arguments, when she goes overboard like that? How do you manage to forgive her at all?'

He sighed. A long, drawn sigh. 'I don't know, honey. I guess I just get on with it. What else is there for me to do?'

Of course he had options. But he seemed oblivious to them. God knew we'd all support him if he chose to leave Marcy. But he didn't seem capable. I think he felt very sorry for her. But can pity hold a marriage together? Little did I know, I was soon to find out myself.

Later, much later that evening, Julian made his return to our bedroom. Which was a big thing, considering I thought he would sleep in the guest room. It certainly wouldn't have been the first time and once again because of an Italian man. Instead, he crawled into bed and lay next to me in silence, as if waiting for me to say something. Well, he'd have a long wait. Even if I was wrong, I rarely admitted it these days. If he wanted to suspend the hostilities, then he would have to be the greater man and talk to me.

But after several minutes had passed and still not a

word, I turned my head toward him. He was sweating and breathing shallowly. He didn't look good at all. I whipped to my knees.

'Julian? What's wrong?'

Silence.

'Julian, are you OK?'

He finally groaned, ever so softly.

'Talk to me? What happened?'

'I went for a ride on the new stallion…'

'Oh my God, did you fall?'

'No… didn't use a saddle…' he rasped. 'I'm bruised… down there…'

'You went *horse* riding without a saddle? What are you trying to do, play Tarzan?' I ran into the bathroom, giggling hysterically now, happy he hadn't fallen off and broken his neck, and also relieved that we had breached the wall of silence. I returned with a cold washcloth.

'Here, let me have a look,' I whispered, and he winced.

'It's not a pretty sight,' he warned me.

I looked up at his face. 'Trust me, it never was.'

Despite the pain, he chuckled, then coughed and winced, all in one breath.

'It serves you right,' I whispered as I laid the cloth on him and ran downstairs to get some ice, an ice bucket and a bottle of champagne, which I hid under the bed. With a relationship like ours, you never knew how the evening might develop.

'How could you be so stupid to ride off without a saddle?' I asked as I wrapped the ice in a washcloth and placed it on his disaster area.

'I was – ow, ow, ow… angry.'

'Yes, you made that quite clear, thank you.'

I wiped his sweaty forehead and dried his damp hair, and when he turned his head, our eyes met. 'I'm sorry to have been such a jealous wanker,' he moaned. 'I should've known better.'

'I'm sorry, too.'

And we lay there for a long, long while as out in the night the crickets creaked and chirped their evening song, Julian's arms around me. I snuggled up to his chest, my favorite place in the world. Here I was safe. Here anything would be OK. Here there would always be understanding and forgiveness.

'Julian?'

'Hmm?'

'I have to tell you something.'

'What's that, sweetheart?'

OK, deep breath now. 'IVF? It tanked again.'

He twisted to look at me, his hand rising to caress my cheek. 'Jesus... why didn't you tell me?'

I shrugged, blinking back the tears. 'I didn't want to disappoint you. You want a baby.'

'Erica, it's not that important...'

'But, but... you said so.'

'Erica – I want you. And our family. Anything else is a bonus.'

I studied his face. I knew he meant what he was saying. But I also knew that he really did want a child of his own and if his eyes and posture were anything to go by, he was more than simply disappointed. This whole IVF thing was taking its toll on him as well as me. I hadn't forgotten how he'd done the Happy Dance when I'd got pregnant for a whole three weeks. And now that I wasn't, he was only pretending to take it on the chin.

'Erica,' he said, sitting up in bed, wincing slightly.

'You OK?' I wanted to know.

'Much, much better. The ice helped. Thank you. Let's just concentrate on the good things we've got. Which are so, so many.'

'I know…'

'There's our family, our home, our friends, our work. This beautiful, beautiful life we have together. Remember when you and Ira were divorcing and even a minute with each other seemed like a godsend?'

When you put it that way… 'Yeah.'

'There's my Erica smiling,' he coaxed.

But I sincerely hoped that he believed what he was saying. Because sometimes he didn't convince me all that much, and after each IVF failure it was getting more and more difficult to get back in the saddle, if you'll pardon the pun.

'I love you, Julian. I really do, you know? Even when I'm being a bitch.'

He grinned and pulled me close again. 'And I love you, my little nutter. Through thick and thin.'

'Then you won't mind if we keep trying? To have a baby? Because I'm ready for my next treatment.'

He stared at me. 'You are?'

I stared back. God, not two minutes of even keel and we were doing this again?

When I didn't answer, he shrugged. 'OK.'

'You sure?'

He wrapped his arms around me. 'If you're ready to start again, I'll postpone my book tour. No biggie.'

Postpone his book tour? His career? How was I going to be sure he wouldn't regret it soon enough?

'No, after you make your, uhm, deposit, you can go. I can handle the rest on my own.'

'You must be out of your mind if you think I'm going to leave you at a time like this,' he said, kissing my forehead, and I wished he'd kissed me on the mouth.

'No, really,' I choked. 'It won't work anyway, and you'll have lost an opportunity for nothing. Really.'

'Don't talk like that,' he whispered, rubbing the back of my neck. I closed my eyes, relishing the feel of his hands on me. It was a shame that any future child will have been conceived without the two of us actually making love. But it was what it was.

'You need to be positive, my girl.'

I nodded, trying to keep the tears back. I admired his strength and encouragement and loved him all the more for it, but we both knew it wasn't working. It was just a waste of money, hopes and time. I hated to see Julian become so hopeful and then deflated. But he sure as hell did a great job hiding it. Especially now that his book was out and he was whizzing around the world faster than his Super-sperm ever could.

'Tell you what,' he said. 'When I get back, why don't we go for a little vacation, just you and me? We'll leave Maddy with Caterina, and Renata can look in on her from time to time.'

'Sounds good to me,' I said, kissing him on the lips.

Long gone were the early days when he was convinced it was going to work. When we'd built our hopes up together, snuggling up in front of the TV, reading the papers, breakfasting endlessly. ('More coffee, sweetie?' 'Oh, yes, thank you, and can I have another muffin, please?' 'Of course, sweetie.') Happy. Hopeful. Renewed enthusiasm. At the end of the day we knew that family was the most important thing and if we didn't succeed it was no tragedy.

But now he looked at me. 'So you're sure?'

'I'm sure I want to at least try.'

'OK. But only if it doesn't stress you out.'

'Oh, I'm sure I can find the silver lining in having to have sex with you,' I teased.

'You little devil.'

'By the way, is this injury going to put the project on hold? I don't want to rush you or boss you around.'

He grinned. A painful half-grin. 'You mean like you usually do?'

'Me? What are you talking about?'

'Oh, well, let's see. The thermal vests I have to wear in the winter or you have a sulk? Or the vegetables you pile into me?'

'But I'm just trying to take care of you...'

'Honey, I've got this far without you mothering me to death. I think I have a chance of surviving without your cauliflower.'

I was about to say that the minute he'd made his own decisions he'd gone and jumped onto a horse bareback, but I decided against it. Why wake the dog that was falling asleep? So I clamped my mouth shut. 'Right. Got it.'

'You're not offended?' he asked.

'I will be if you turn around and tell me you don't love me anymore.'

He stared at me, trying to sit up. 'Erica, please. You have to stop this madness. You're behaving like a teenager.'

'No, I'm being practical. Say you wanted a divorce. Would you tell me?'

He groaned. 'I'd have to, wouldn't I?'

'Just answer my question, will you?'

He sighed. 'Listen to me, and listen good. I don't want a divorce. Yes, recently you're being a real pain in the arse, but this is just a bad spell and it will all go away once you understand Genie Stacie has no hold whatsoever over me. So how's that for an answer?'

'Bloody good.'

'I just wish that you would talk to me instead of inventing twisted scenarios in that maniac mind of yours,' he breathed as I flipped the cold cloth over. 'Ouch, easy, babe.'

I smiled down at him. He hadn't called me that in a long time. I was glad *I* was still his babe instead of a dumb blonde with long legs.

'How do you put up with me?' I asked as I nuzzled his neck.

'Just tell me what's really bothering you, Erica.'

Ouch. Ack. 'I just… hate not being in control of my life – of this… *baby* thing,' I whispered, surprising even me. My shrink in Boston would have applauded me for my candor.

At that, he groaned. 'Honey – you are in control of practically everything else.'

'I am.' I nodded, then looked up. 'I'm sorry. I'm bossy – you're right.'

'That's OK. I like you that way.'

'You do?' Of course I knew he did, but I just liked hearing it.

'Hell, yes. You're an absolute control freak but that's fine because I like the way you like things too.'

'Yeah?'

'Of course.'

Wow. 'Wait – what do you mean? Am I really, really that much of a control freak?'

Julian unfolded his arms (good sign) and sighed, taking me by the shoulders and speaking softly the way you do to a mental case.

'Sweetie – yes. You are a complete war chief.' He grinned, and I knew everything was OK once again.

The next morning, after a night with his rocks on the rocks, Julian was much better and we had a good session of (careful) lovemaking and came down the stairs hand in hand like two teenagers who couldn't keep their hands off each other. It was amazing, the power of love. And of *make-up sex*.

'How about an espresso?' I offered as he kissed me. 'Not that you need any waking up.'

'*Sì, grazie*,' he said with a grin and I reached for the espresso pot on the top shelf as the house phone rang.

'Hello!' Julian answered, all chipper.

'What the hell, man, your cell is off,' thundered Terry's voice over the phone, loud and clear. Jesus, I'd get a new phone system just so I didn't have to hear the jerk's voice. 'I get you Marty Liebermann, the best producer in Hollywood and you won't even *meet* the man because your *dog* is having surgery?'

Julian glanced at me, his ears turning pink, then stepped away as his hand stole to the back of his neck like whenever he was embarrassed. 'It's true,' Julian lied, now scrubbing his nape.

'It has to be! I've never heard of anything so ridiculous!'

'Terry, I've got to go. I'll call you later, OK?'

And before Terry could bark back an answer, Julian hung up with a sigh of relief.

I put my hands on my hips in my usual teapot style and looked at him. 'Sookie is not a spring chicken anymore, but she's hardly at that stage that she needs surgery, is she? What's going on, Julian? Why did you skip out on a producer?'

Julian shrugged. 'I just needed to stay home for a bit, that's all.'

'And you turned down a meeting with a Hollywood producer? *Why?*'

'It doesn't matter anymore, Erica. Really. Where's that espresso you promised me?'

I stared down at the mocha that was still in my hands and tried to twist it open.

'Here, let me do that,' Julian said as he took it from me, unscrewed the top and filled the bottom with cold water and kissed me on the lips so tenderly that I wanted to cry. He'd ditched a producer to be home with me at such a tough time for me. I mean for *us*. And then I understood I had to stop playing goddess, or my version of it.

'Call Terry back to tell him you're going to meet Marty Lieberstein.'

'Liebermann.'

'Liebermann. Now go call Terry and book your flight. I'll bring your espresso into your study.' He looked at me longingly, torn. 'I don't want you making more sacrifices than necessary for me, Julian. Go.'

He kissed me again as I packed the coffee down tight so it would come out nice and strong, just the way he liked it, while a million questions roiled around in my mind. I had to stop being a control freak and let things be as they were. I decided right there and then that if anything was going to change, it was me – effective immediately. My heart felt like it was coming out of my ears but hey – this was a new, better me. A stronger me.

I breathed a sigh of relief at the sight of Renata's slight figure at her gate as she called her dog Argo back. I hadn't seen her in ages. She had needed some space, and I was too ashamed to show my face for what I'd implied. How could I have been so stupid to think that she would actually have an affair with Leonardo Cortini?

'Hi from your neighbor, who's missed you,' I scarcely managed as I got off my bike and pushed it through the gate.

'Come in, come in! You must be crazy riding around in this heat.'

'Only mad dogs and the Foxhams.'

She snickered, and I knew we were OK again, just like that.

I followed her up the stone steps leading to the main floor above the storage areas. Her house was a typical Tuscan stone farmhouse, very similar to mine in structure, with the living quarters on the second floor.

'How's it going, the IVF?' she asked, pouring two tall glasses of iced tea as I sank into a chair.

'Ooff, not well. Failure after failure. I think Maddy's jinxing it.'

Renata laughed. 'She's not happy about a new addition to the family, then?'

'She's not happy about anything since Genie Stacie left. She's hated me since the woman arrived. I guess there was no contest with a Hollywood celebrity.'

Renata chuckled. 'Silly. She just think she does. Mothers were born to be hated. Where is she now?'

'She's at Angelica's.' Angelica's house was much more feasible when they wanted to see people. All Angelica had to do was open her front door, step into the piazza and be right where it was all happening. Maddy loved Angelica's house.

'She's spending a lot of time there, don't you think?'

I raised my eyebrow. 'Are you trying to tell me something?'

She shrugged and took a sip of her drink. 'Just that now that school's out they have more time to get themselves into trouble. Especially since Angelica's mother works in the afternoon.'

I swallowed the last of my iced tea and smacked my lips. 'Angelica's a good girl. She's a great student – I only wish her habits would rub off on Maddy.'

'Maddy is a sensible girl. And she's smarter than you think. Sorry. I don't mean to sound patronizing.'

'Silly. Just keep looking out for us like you always have.'

Renata squeezed my fingers. 'I've never stopped, Erica.

I was coming over to bring you this,' she said, hefting a grocery bag. 'I'm sorry about the IVF.'

'Why do you think it's not working, Renata? What am I doing wrong?'

Renata reached out to the pitcher on the table and poured me some more iced tea, then one for herself, slipping slowly. '*Oyoy*, it's because you're strung as tight as a bow – look at you, shoulders almost to your ears. Here,' she said, plunking the bag before me.

I sat up a bit higher. 'What's that?'

Renata smiled. 'This is my especially designed for you baby-making kit.'

'Oh-kay.' I laughed.

But she was serious. 'Just listen to me, Erica. You have to look at the problem objectively. You and Julian want a baby but no luck so far, yes?'

I crossed my arms in front of my chest. I didn't have the time for the, as Julian always says, *Bleeding Obvious*, nor for a recap of my failures. 'Ye-es…'

But she was on a mission, and with that glint in her eye that only promised mischief. 'Let's see, where is it? Ah, *sì* – here, look!'

A candle? 'What am I going to do with this?' I said. 'Stick it in Genie Stacie's mouth? Or make my eggs more attractive?' But she was already pulling out other objects: lavender oil, a CD, feathers, a silk scarf and a green bottle.

'Forget Genie Stacie. This is not about your eggs. This is about… *communion*.'

Not that New Age and ancient Chinese medicine stuff, please? We'd tried just about everything *but*.

And yet, the more I thought of it…

'Communion,' I repeated bluntly.

'Here's what you do,' she said. 'When he gets back, you send the kids to my place—'

'Renata…'

But she only raised her voice above mine. '*And* you cook his favorite dinner. No restaurant – it's too distracting. You need to be completely alone.'

I opened my mouth but shut it again at the look on her face. Boy, she was good. She had me enthralled in two seconds flat. 'And then…?'

'After dinner, you leave the leftovers and dishes on the table – you'll need them later – and then you entice him upstairs with The Look.'

'What look?'

She smiled. 'The female, *come hither* look that every man recognizes – it's universal, yet everyone has their own. You have yours; I have mine.'

'Right.'

'Light the candle while you are both undressing—'

'Who says we undress?' I quipped.

'Erica – do you want this baby or not?' she scolded me and I sobered instantly.

'Sorry. Go on. Please.'

'Use anything and everything in this kit to stimulate each other's senses. It's not about sex. It's about *connecting* – feeling the other. It's a joining of two souls, not just two bodies, you know.'

I groaned inwardly. Time to dig out my mini-*Kama Sutra*? I might have even thrown it away. Julian and I didn't need it. We were completely happy with each other. And yet… you never knew. Was there a baby-making section I'd missed?

'Just take your time, Erica. Don't think of how many times you're doing it – just think of how much you enjoy each other's company, in and out of the bed.'

'Gotcha…'

'And… start taking this every morning on an empty stomach.' She shoved the glass bottle full of some green cloudy liquid. Not stinging nettles again?

'What the hell is that?'

'Aloe vera,' she pronounced it *Alloway Vayra*. 'This will clean your system completely of all toxins and—' she shrugged '—who knows? You might have a *bambino* on the way this time next month.'

Fat chance. I unscrewed the cap and sniffed suspiciously. 'Whoa, what are you trying to do, kill me?' I sniffed again. 'Is there booze in here? The morning's looking up.'

'Well, it's a part of a natural fermentation process, yes.'

'I've never heard of such—'

'You won't even try it?'

'Damn right I will.'

She grinned. 'Good. Drink a half-espresso-cupful every morning. It should last you about a month. I've got some more where that came from.'

'Thank you, Renata.'

'You're welcome. And one more thing.'

'Yeah?'

'Have *fun – it's not a chore!*'

She was right. After our last bout of make-up sex, getting back to the baby-making business almost felt like a chore. Not that we didn't enjoy it, but Julian seemed to think that reading the same script over and over again made us learn our lines better. Well, it didn't because the whole time lately I'd be thinking about the baby, imagining my teeny-tiny egg venturing out of an ovary, hoping to meet a pack of his big bad wolves, hoping the best would sink his teeth into it.

I also started to imagine I could feel my egg nestling into my uterus and Julian's swimmers roaring, *Mission accomplished!* Just how much did we women hurt ourselves, hoping and imagining too much when we should just relax and sing *Que sera, sera*, whatever will be, will be? But of course you know me, the supreme control freak. I could never relax and sing to *that* tune.

If anything, with Genie Stacie gone, I wasn't so insecure when Julian announced he was off to the States again in a few days.

The doctor called at three in the afternoon. I grabbed the phone as if my life depended on it. Because, who were we actually trying to kid here, it *did*.

'Dottoressa Bardotti…?'

'Erica, hello. I'm so sorry. This cycle wasn't successful.'

My eyes darted to Julian's face. There was acute hope in it even if he tried to conceal it. He would be gutted now. Me, I was past hoping anymore.

'OK, I understand. Thank you for calling.'

I rang off and turned to face him. He took one look at me and folded me in his arms.

'I'm so sorry,' I wept, hanging on to his shoulder blades. 'It's not working.'

'Shh… it's OK, sweetie.'

'But it's not OK,' I argued. 'I know you really want a baby.'

The reality finally hit him, and to his credit, he shook his head. 'I want you. Now dry your eyes and let's go for a nice drive. How about a hot air balloon ride?'

'Really?' I said, swiping my eyes. 'You're not disappointed?'

'Naw. It'll be fine. Now go and put on your sneakers.'

I caressed his cheeks and kissed him, pulling him to me. 'Don't tell anyone, but you're the best husband a gal could have.'

'I know,' he said with a grin.

He held me close for a long time and kissed the top of my head. 'Shall we give it another try?'

My eyes swung to his gratefully and I nodded.

He smiled. 'Get an appointment for before I go.'

And so on Monday morning after a quick 'deposit' at the fertility clinic I drove him to the airport.

'I hate to leave you now of all moments,' Julian whispered, his fingers playing with the strings on my hoodie (I was hitting the gym more and more lately and Gabriele was very proud of me).

'It's important to pursue your dreams, Julian.' *If the outcome depends on you*, I mentally added. Getting pregnant was out of my control. This part, the waiting, was the worst and, deep down, I really needed him there with me. But I had to put on a brave face.

'Go. I'll keep you posted.'

'I'll call you the minute I land,' Julian promised as he

planted a tender kiss on my lips, but his right leg was already out of the car. He couldn't wait to go. That was the truth. Couldn't wait to get back to his other life.

I pulled him back and he turned in surprise as I kissed him hard, almost hurting my own mouth. 'Come back home to your woman soon, Fox.' *Validation. Letting him know how much you love him.*

Julian's lips turned into a smile, which he planted against my lips again, returning my kiss like he hadn't in a long time. He may have been leaving for now, but judging by that kiss, I'd say he was back for good.

'Hey, I'll be back before you know it,' he said, drying my tears with his lips and nudging my nose as he used to. 'I'll miss you, sweetie…'

I looked up and smiled. I must have been a mess. I'd started wearing make-up again (which Maddy didn't even notice because she pretty much avoided me like the plague) and I could feel my mascara running down my face. So much for glamour.

'Just go, OK? I don't want you to miss your plane.'

He held me in silence for a long moment, until his embrace became stronger, tighter and he bent to kiss my mouth.

With Julian gone during the few days of my next blue window, I decided to not concentrate on what I didn't have, but what I could lose if we didn't reconnect pronto – our relationship. And so I began preparing Renata's Improve Your Relationship strategy.

I'd surprise him when he returned with an improvised trip to the Apuan Alps. And with a lacy little number I'd found in an Intimeria in Siena, far from indiscreet eyes. A pair of knickers, to be exact. *So what?* you might think. Ah, but these were special. In fact, they were completely made of, *wait* for it… *chocolate*. Yes, edible underwear, which I had to keep in the fridge for obvious reasons. There was no limit to my imagination. Or to my desperation.

Julian tooted his car as he pulled up the drive and I breathed deeply to calm my nerves. It wasn't fair to keep the IVF failure from him. He was expecting good news, the poor fella.

I delayed it by kissing him at length, and he responded with the usual fervor, his hand cupping the back of my head while he took my mouth in an ah-mazing kiss, which told me he'd missed me. So far, so good.

'You never told me what it was Genie Stacie needed your help with,' I said, cursing my big fat mouth. You'd think I'd avoid mentioning her just before I began my seduction scheme, right?

Julian sighed and flung his arm around me as we climbed up the steps. 'Oh. *That*.' He gave me a sidelong glance before speaking, as if trying to gauge the degree of openness of my mind. 'Genie Stacie did this amateur porn flick years ago and now this guy's threatening to go public with it.'

Somehow it didn't seem like the right moment to tell him about IVF tanking again, so I kept quiet. If I hadn't been so despondent about my period I would've appreciated the trivia, reveled in it, even. I am a terrible person.

But what did a porn flick have to do with Julian? *Ohmygod!* I caught my breath. 'Did you star in it, too?'

Julian cocked his head and looked at me. 'Do I look like the kind of guy who'd star in a porn flick?'

'Well, then? How is it your problem?'

Julian shrugged. 'Her agent says she should let it go public. It would give her notoriety a boost.'

'I'll say. That would let people get to know her for who she really is.'

'Erica…'

'What? She stars in a porn movie, for Christ's sake, and you're still defending her?'

'Erica, she was very young, she didn't know what she was doing. And in any case she's a producer now.'

I stopped. 'What? When? I thought she only *knew* some producers. I didn't know she was one.'

'Well, in fairness, this would be her first project. She's reading my book as we speak.'

'She can read? Some people never cease to surprise me.'

'Come here, you,' he said softly as he always did at the end of the day, and I buried myself in the nook between his arm and his side. Only it wasn't the end of the day, and I felt that this one was going to be an all-nighter.

'You know, Genie and I had one thing in common. We were both abandoned by our parents.'

I suffocated the snort and the retort that had flared up naturally. Seven years in idyllic Tuscany, seven years of soaking up the warmth of its sun, the sweetness of its wines and the most delicious recipes and I still hadn't managed to mellow. I was a lost cause. 'Right,' I said to fill the expectant silence before he told me her sad story of abandonment and probably teenage prostitution, judging by the look of her, but I kept that to myself. For now.

'We only dated for a short while, that's true, but she opened up immediately (I suppressed the urge to snort again) and I saw her softer side (was he doing it on purpose now, or are men just born dumb?) because she was very lonely in her environment.'

Oh, come *on*! 'She doesn't look lonely to me.'

'Oh, she is, trust me. All the women were jealous of her career and all the men just wanted to get her in the sack.'

'You included,' I said, relieved he couldn't see my left eyebrow that had lost itself in my hairline somewhere, like a natural facelift. No wonder I didn't have many wrinkles. I was too sarcastic to let my face stagnate.

'Including me, yes. I was attracted to her—'

'Long legs?'

He chuckled, and drew me closer. 'I was going to say fragility, but yes, her looks weren't exactly an obstacle.'

'How gentlemanly you are,' I said, more sweetly, thus more sarcastically, than I'd intended.

One thing for sure, this was going nowhere good. Genie Stacie had found her way back into our lives again and didn't look like she was going to forget our address anytime soon. I wondered how much longer I could put up with this situation. Just knowing she existed was bad enough, but then she started calling his *cell phone*. And that's when I recognized her telephone manners from before, when she'd called me in the middle of the night. I should've remembered her squealing voice. She had already had his cell phone number. She must have called him after she hung up with me. And Julian had never mentioned it. Why, if he wasn't hiding anything?

Why had he feigned surprise when she called to say she was dropping by for a visit? For my benefit? Was something going on and I was totally in the dark? You might think

I'm a paranoid woman who can't forget the past. *You* try discovering that your first husband, whom you thought was working late almost every night, actually *got off*, and you'll pardon me the pun, precisely at four thirty every afternoon to drive his secretary, who was expecting his baby, to a beautiful condominium *you* had actually paid for because he'd asked you for a loan to save his company from bankruptcy.

Thank you. I knew you'd see where I was coming from, insecure or not.

So now my main questions were:

Number One: Will my husband still love me, as he promised, through thick and thin?

Number Two: Does Genie Stacie represent a threat or not?

Number Three: If so, am I going to murder her?

Number Four: After I've murdered her (see Question Number One)?

In record time I'd managed to twist myself into such a knot I was a live wire threatening to electrocute anyone who had enough guts to come anywhere near me. And on top of everything else, no, *more* than anything else, I hated the way Julian treated her. Like he *cherished* her. *Genie Stacie was abandoned. Genie Stacie never had any friends. Genie Stacie is fragile. Genie Stacie needs me.*

And *I* needed Genie Stacie to disappear.

Did Julian feel validated by Genie Stacie's attention? Was I neglecting him? Was that what all this was about, and now it was too late to get my husband back? Had I let him fall out of love with me?

'Are you happy, Julian?' I blurted out.

'As long as you and I are like this, I'm happy,' he whispered against my mouth, and I wondered whether the toothpaste still held its freshness before I decided it didn't really matter and kissed him deep and hard.

'Come here, you,' he murmured as he pulled my legs around his waist and peeled off my top. I pulled his shirt off in turn and leaned back and admired his ripped body, running my hands up his arms as he kissed the side of my throat, which he knew was my Immediate Ignition Button.

And then the house phone rang.

I sighed and peeled myself away from him and went over to the phone, already knowing who it was.

'Hi, Erica, is Julian there? I tried his cell phone but it's off.'

Damn right it was.

'Yep, just a second,' I said and stonily passed the house phone to him. He tossed his bunched-up shirt to the side and sighed, possibly for my benefit. I turned and left him to it. It was a good thing we were leaving for our little trip alone. Now I'd have to sex the hell out of him to erase The Genie Stacie Effect.

As Julian drove our Jeep high up into the hills, he hummed along happily to an old John Legend song, 'All of Me'. Well, I was definitely going to give him *my all* this weekend. Anything to bring us back to where we used to be. I was going all out. Two nights, just for us, in one of the most beautiful hotels in the region. Operation seduction was under way.

I lifted my legs onto the dashboard with the oldest trick in the world of my stockings having a run in them.

'To what do I owe this lovely surprise getaway?' he murmured as his eyes darted to my legs which, I have to say, didn't look that bad from this angle. Had the rice cakes and carrot sticks finally started to work their magic?

I rubbed my calves gently, up and down. 'Nothing, just to you and me.'

'Well, then, Hello, you...' he drawled.

Yes!

'Hello, yourself,' I whispered huskily. 'I'm wearing a new bra I bought while you were away. Too bad I won't be needing it this weekend...'

In the penumbra, I saw him swallow, steal me the sexiest look I'd ever seen, and drag his eyes back to the road, which was twisting and turning up the mountain now. Perhaps this was not a great idea. Maybe I should wait until—

'Aren't you going to show me?' he whispered.

Ooh good, he was hanging off the edge of his seat now. Just as long as we didn't end up hanging off the edge of the cliff as a result.

'I might. But can you handle it, with these curves?' I quipped.

His eyes twinkled at my *double entendre*, the sap.

'Babe, I know your curves better than anything,' he drawled. He was such a ham lately. Was it the Genie Stacie effect? *No, no, no – don't think about her. Think about the sweltering hot sex awaiting us.*

'There's always something new to discover,' I whispered, moving in closer to lick the side of his neck.

He shivered and murmured, 'I swear I'm going to crash if you keep this up...'

I giggled – as throatily as I could, mind you – as my hand touched his thigh. I didn't need to go there or turn on the overhead light to see he was... intrigued.

What guy could resist any kind of foreplay?

When we finally arrived, he came to a stop, his breath ragged, his eyes glistening and hooded. At the end of the drive we were rewarded with an amazing hilltop view and a tiny, lodge-like romantic hotel and restaurant.

First, a romantic dinner, to which Julian responded with a flush of pleasure. He knew where this was going and was already, shall we say, *visibly* in the mood and eating quickly, but I slowed him down. Tonight it wouldn't be about making a baby. It would be about making love. Our love.

I'll spare you the smoldering looks we cast each other during our meal. Suffice to say that when we got to our room I quickly slipped into the chocolate knickers and oy – you should have seen the look on his face when I stepped out of the bathroom dressed only in my edible underwear. A look I hadn't seen, let's face it, in a long, long time.

'Is this wonderful sight for me?' he murmured.

'Dessert's ready,' I teased him and as he pushed me back onto the bed, nibbling on my earlobe and kissing me and... I swear to you in two seconds flat I was a goner. And then... he began to consume his dessert.

I lay back, taking in the magic moment, the way it used to be. Yes, this was Julian, and this was me. And together, we made a wonderful *We*. Forget about everything else. He loved me. We were a family. And we were on our way back to being like we used to be. Full steam ahead.

As I was enjoying his attention, Julian coughed. Then again, making a wheezing sound. I lifted myself up onto my elbows. 'You OK?'

He shook his head, gasping and clutching at his throat. He was turning red and desperately trying to breathe, but nothing was happening. Was he choking on the chocolate? I shot to my feet, beating his back right between the shoulder blades, but it wasn't getting any better. His face was turning purple now as he staggered to his feet, me trying to help him.

Wearing absolutely jack squat, save what was left of my edible underwear, I reached for the phone and dialed for an ambulance, threw a tiny towel around myself and flung the door open, shouting for help down the stairs into the darkness of the night.

When he opened his eyes, Julian found himself all tubed up and an IV needle stuck into his arm. His hair all sweaty and matted and his face extremely pale now, he was a real mess (said by the woman now wearing a hospital nightie and with traces of chocolate where chocolate can be fun but only for so long).

He looked at me over his mask and I took his free hand, trying not to sag with relief that the ambulance crew had arrived in time.

'You're OK,' I said quickly. 'Nothing to worry about.' Ha. Talk about underwear understatements.

He closed his eyes and blinked once. That must have meant *yes*.

'Mm-hm-hm?' he asked, meaning, *What happened?*

I blushed. 'It was an allergic reaction.'

His eyebrows shot up in question. *To what?*

Now this was going to be embarrassing. 'Uhm, remember my chocolate underwear?'

He blinked once. He remembered. Not that anyone could forget that. 'I'm so sorry – I *thought* it was chocolate. But it was actually *Gianduia* hazelnut fudge…'

Made with the best hazelnuts in the whole of the region. And Julian (how could I forget?) was highly allergic to hazelnuts. He'd had an allergic reaction once when he was a kid that had almost cost him his life.

His head fell back with a mutter muffled by the mask and he closed his eyes in the notion that he had once again narrowly escaped death from a hazelnut. And I was the uber-nut who gave it to him.

'We'll look back on this one day and laugh?' I said helpfully to Julian.

He blinked twice for *no*, coughed and exhaled so heavily through his mask he sounded like Darth Vader. Leave it to me to see the funny-ish side of things.

Luckily the hotel had been near the Guardia Medica. Memories of the night before zapped through my mind, leaving me cold with horror.

'Is he allergic to cortisone?' the doctor had asked me dutifully, his needle poised, ready to inject into Julian's vein something that would either save him or give him the *coup de grace*.

As Julian's thrashing continued I had tried to remember, my mind mush.

'*Signora! Sì o no?*' the doctor had prompted, his voice belying the rising panic that a doctor should never show as my mind raced and searched for any memories of other allergies.

OhGodohGod. What was he allergic to? Oranges, peanuts, cabbages. Hazelnuts, of course. But cortisone? I couldn't remember. He was allergic to some kind of drug – I always remembered it, but last night, with Julian suffering and the doctor screaming at me I couldn't think clearly. It was like my mind was in a thick, stagnant fog and there was nothing I could do to shift it.

Was it cortisone... or something that sounded similar?

'*Signora!*'

And then, like the sun bursting through the clouds, I had it. 'Cardizem! He's allergic to Cardizem!' I cried and the doctor's needle immediately sank into Julian's vein.

In a few seconds he was whisked away and I was left behind the swinging doors, propped up against a wall where I took deep, calming breaths. He'd be OK. He had to be. I couldn't lose him. And my edible underwear just could *not* be the cause of his demise.

With a sinking sensation of stickiness, I turned to look at the wall I was leaning against and gasped at the big brown hazelnut stain my butt had left on the pristine surface. I frantically tried to rub it off with the palm of my hand, looking around to make sure there were no witnesses to my abstract art piece.

When that didn't work, I brought my bare knee up against it for more pressure. Still nothing. A nurse stopped short, stared at the nutter (me) who looked like she was trying to crawl into the wall, sniffed the air and nodded for me to follow her down the corridor to a door, which she opened and gestured for me to follow her.

Inside what looked like a linen closet, she gave me a few towels and a new nightie and led me to the bathroom where she nodded knowingly.

'I heard your husband is allergic to chocolate?' she asked.

'*Gianduia* fudge,' I answered and she nodded again.

'Mine, too. I almost killed the poor man. Next time try caramel,' she suggested and left me with a grin.

13

By Hook or by Crook

About a week later, Julian had fully recovered from his anaphylactic shock and was back to being his old self. Or almost. I had noticed a slight shift in his demeanor. Was it because he had been traumatized about almost being killed by my underwear? I could understand that. And yet, something was off.

'You OK?' I asked him as we got ready for bed.

'Yep,' he murmured, folding his T-shirt and putting it on his chair. A task that was taking him a mighty long time, when you consider he usually threw his clothes over the back of said chair. By now one hand would usually be tugging at mine while plucking at my buttons with the other. But tonight? Nothing. It had been seven days and seven nights, which, after all these years, would have seemed even normal, but Julian and I had never had a problem in that department. Until now, apparently. Perhaps he really was traumatized, and perhaps more than I'd thought.

I stood to my feet and rounded the bed, holding out my hand to him. 'Fancy a shower?'

I swear, I think I startled him, he looked up at me with those huge eyes. 'Uhm, no, I'm good, thanks. I'm tired, anyway. Goodnight...'

Oh. *Oh.*

'Good... night, then...'

I knew something was going on. He was still mad at me. But it wasn't like I had done it on purpose, was it? I mean, really? How many times did I have to apologize?

With our romantic buzz dissolved like ice-cream cones on a windy day, at this point getting pregnant was going to be very tricky as Julian no longer seemed to have the inclination to make love to me, almost as if he was afraid I'd manage to kill him after all in between the sheets with, I don't know, poisonous pillowcases or something.

Funny, because while I was married to Ira, I'd had all sorts of fantasies about all the different ways I could kill him. In the past few weeks after our last failure, it had become obvious that Julian was having issues, which I hoped were temporary, because we had a baby schedule to stick to and as my doctor said, it was now or never. I needed to secure a pregnancy now. The rest, we could hash out together later. Right?

So like every other woman rapidly running out of ideas while nearing the end of her fertility tether, I surfed the net (alone, this time) in case I'd missed any of the gazillion tricks listed, keeping his allergies in mind. Medieval, magical or mystical, I was going to try them all.

Daily sex – and feeling sexy in general – seemed to be the top one, or rather, didn't seem to be it, because sex was instead recommended every other day during your fertile windows. Oh thank God! Now I could stop dreading bedtime. Dread? Ouch, that was harsh even for me. I didn't dread bedtime. No, the baby project had to be rushed full steam ahead.

Scrolling down the long list of miracle-workers were, in case you wanted to get pregnant and didn't know, grapefruit juice, leafy greens, raspberry leaves. Raspberry leaves, really? Never seen that one before. Stinging nettles (been there, done that – it doesn't work, BTW). Neither do grapefruit and yams.

'I have to go to the States again the day after tomorrow,' Julian said out of the blue a few weeks later.

What the hell, you just got back, I wanted to say. And I was just getting back into the swing of things. Why couldn't he just stay put for a bit and be a husband? And work with me on the baby thing? No. I would not go down that road. 'New York again?' I asked, trying to sound neutral.

'No, Los Angeles.'

Right into Genie Stacie's den. 'Oh.'

And so after what seemed like only a few hours had gone by, Julian hefted his bag (the one permanently packed in the corner of his office) containing his passport, his American driver's license and his British driver's license, a toothbrush, toothpaste, shaving kit, a few changes of boxers and undershirts and socks, legal copyright documents and a copy of his latest novel, but absolutely no condoms. I know because I had a (shhh) snoop in there one morning while he was out in the barn with his horses.

I dropped him off at the airport from where he'd fly to Milan, double parking outside and turning to him bravely. Things were still not going well. With new hopes for a baby rapidly dissolving and Genie Stacie calling at all hours, gnawing at my last shreds of security, and Maddy's constant ignoring me, I felt like life's biggest loser. How much longer could I hold out?

'I'll be in touch,' he said distractedly, not even turning my way to kiss me. Before I could stop myself, I pulled him in for a sudden kiss. Pathetic of me, I realized immediately.

Because he seemed resigned. Of course he wasn't going to meet up with Genie Stacie. Just because it was her city didn't mean—

'Come on, Julian, we're going to miss our flight!' came an unpleasant squeal and my blood froze. Wide-eyed, Julian turned and saw her as she stuck her head in through the car window. 'Erica, let go of him already, he has to get a move on.' She giggled as she opened the door and literally dragged him out and his lean figure sauntered toward the entrance doors that slid open, Genie Stacie linking an arm through his and turning back to wave at me.

But I could only stare after them, helpless, like a child being relieved of her candy. What could I possibly do, go after them and beg him not to go?

So I selected first gear and took the highway home, my

stomach in shreds, and wondering how long she had been in Tuscany, how was it that she hadn't dropped in on us and, most important, how she knew he was taking that precise flight on that precise day. I also conjured up all sorts of scenarios of them having dinner, then a few drinks up in his room. She'd use all her charm to get him back, or at least to get him in the sack. Because Genie Stacie thought that sex was the be-all and end-all of it. I pictured Julian as he resisted, once, twice, three times, even. Then he'd finally shrug his shoulders and think what I didn't know wouldn't hurt me.

He would shed his clothes, all the clothes I'd washed and ironed for him, to stand naked, in all his splendor, in front of her. He'd take her in his arms and lift her onto the bed and… I closed my eyes tight and shoved the idea out of my head. My cheeks were wet.

I had loads of ironing to do when I got back, but no will to do it. So to cheer me up, I propped my cell phone on the counter of the laundry room and dialed Paul via speaker phone.

Paul was closer to me than my own brother. Vince and I barely spoke except for at Thanksgiving and during the summer holidays when he brought his family out to stay with us. And even then it was only: 'So how's things?/ Good thanks, and you?/ Good, good. The kids have grown./ Yeah, yours, too./ You hungry?/ Yeah./ Let's go eat.' That was the extent of my relationship with my younger brother.

But Paul? He was my life coach, my image coach, my stylist, my make-up artist and even my beautician, having waxed the hell out of me several times, including that stubborn hair on my chin, which not even Julian knows about, thank God. I couldn't even begin to tell you the trouble we used to get into together as if we were primary school students. And to think that we'd met as adults. Well, he was an adult, while I was acting like a baby, crying in a changing room at Macy's. He'd heard me, picked me up and promised me that life could only get better from there on. So who better than my old Paulie to have a restoring chat with now?

It rang five times before he picked up. 'Hiya, Sunshine,' he chirped.

'Hello, handsome. Still using the old trick of not answering immediately so you'll look busy?'

'I am busy. Crazy busy, but I was just about to call you because I'm bursting with some fab news! You are never gonna believe this.'

'You and Gabriele are getting married?' I quipped.

'No, but you're close. I just got a contract for the celebrity engagement party of the decade! If I can pull it off, the wedding's mine, too!'

'Paulie! That's great! Who is it?'

'Promise me you won't tell. Because, as per contract, I am not allowed to say a single thing. But you, I trust. And if you can't keep your mouth shut, you'll owe me a gazillion dollars.'

'Promise. Who am I going to tell?'

'Not even Julian, OK?'

'I said I promise. Now who's your filthy rich bride?'

'Genie Stacie Grant.'

I almost dropped my iron. 'Genie Stacie?'

'I know! And I have you and Julian to thank. Remember she doesn't want anyone to know – you least of all.'

This made no sense. 'But… but… who is she marrying?'

'That's the thing! I'm not allowed to know until she gives the go-ahead.'

A horrible, terrible sensation burned its way up through my insides. Of course not. Julian was already married to me. Unless…

'When is it scheduled for?'

'As soon as the groom can get his divorce. I have a little over eighteen months to plan everything. Can you imagine creating a masterpiece in such a short time?'

'And you have absolutely no idea who it is?'

'Apparently a retired sports star. But her assistant says she's been going to Italy very often. So you tell me.'

'But why would she not want you to know who he is? That's ridiculous!' Please ignore the squeak in my voice, it's only sheer panic.

'What can I tell you? He hasn't actually told his wife yet and doesn't want the world to know before she does.'

Is he *serious*? How in a million years could he do this to me? 'How… noble of him.'

'It's a mad world, Sunshine.'

'So you're planning everything without actually knowing anything? Where is it going to be, the wedding?'

'In Boston, where his family lives. Isn't this crazy?'

I could have told Paul my suspicions, but of course I'd be totally wrong. Julian would never do that to me. Preposterous. Unheard of.

So then who was the guy, and why didn't Genie Stacie want me in particular to know?

'Erica? You still there?'

Barely. I had actually sunk onto a chair next to the window (I have a laundry room with a view) and was absently staring out at the fields and the cypress-lined drive up to the house. It looked perfect. From the outside, it was all perfect. Inside, things never really were as they seemed.

I thought and thought and thought, trying to understand. 'Paul, any idea why she chose you, no offense?'

'Gee, thanks, none taken. Julian sent her my number. Remind me to thank him when this is all over.'

And you remind me to kill him when it is. OK, this was getting too close for comfort.

'Will do,' I said. 'Keep me posted?'

'Uh, OK, just as long as you remember your promise.'

It was really looking like someone else had forgotten theirs.

'I will.'

'OK. Take care, Sunshine. Oh, I almost forgot. Have Julian's measurements changed? He's looking a little slimmer, lately.'

'Julian's m-measurements…? What do you need those for?'

'Oh, didn't I tell you? He's invited.'

And there you have it. 'Just… him?'

'What can I tell you?'

'Everything you know.'

'But that's just it. I don't know anything. Gotta go, Sunshine.'

'Bye…' I croaked before I hung up.

Of course I knew it was silly. But for all things high society in Boston, who better to ask that the in-law for some intel?

*

'Erica, what a lovely surprise!' came Maggie's clear, intelligent voice. 'How is my Italian family?'

'We're good, thanks, and how's Dad doing?'

'Oh, bless him, he's taken to painting now. I've got canvases all over the house, but I'm thinking of banishing him to the cellar. Not that he's any good, mind. At least nothing like your lovely landscapes.'

'Awh, that's nice, thanks, Maggie.'

'Is everything all right, Erica?' she asked. 'You sound preoccupied.'

'No, everything's fine. I was just wondering if you'd heard someone in High Society Boston is getting married next year?'

'And you called me. Bless you, pet, but I try to keep away from those insipid people. But I will keep an ear open for you if you like?'

'No, that's OK, Maggie. Thanks anyway.'

'You should ask Julian. He keeps in touch with Marcus Mallory.'

The name sounded familiar. 'Who's that?'

'Just a local journalist. He's usually got his finger on the pulse.'

'OK. And Maggie? Not a word to anyone. It's supposed to be a secret. There's a privacy clause so if they think you know something—'

'I will keep my lips sealed,' she promised, and after asking me about the kids, she asked me what her son was up to these days. As if I'd be the first to know.

*

Days melted into weeks as life continued as usual, with me not being able to tell anyone about Genie Stacie's secret wedding. Or to get back into the nook with my husband. So I called someone I knew would die for me.

'Hey, Dad...'

'Honey! What a nice surprise! How are things?'

'Good, good,' I lied. He had enough on his plate, what with Marcy and all. 'You?'

'I'm all right. It's your sister that's worrying me.'

'What do you mean?' As if I couldn't guess.

'Every day she disappears for a few hours, leaving Steve to go out if his mind. At first I thought she had a health or a gambling problem, you know?'

'And then?'

He sighed. 'I finally managed to get it out of her. She's seeing someone else.'

'Poor Steve...' was all I could say.

'Yeah, poor Steve. I mean, if she doesn't love him anymore, why not just leave him? The boys are old enough; it's not like they wouldn't get over it. How sad am I to say that?' he asked.

'Awh, Dad, it's just the way it is. Judy and Steve have never really been that close.'

'That's true. And Steve is such a great guy, you know?'

'I know.'

'I wish she had what you and Julian have. Now that's something you rarely see nowadays.'

Ha. If I wasn't so miserable, I'd probably laugh my head off. But I was, so no laughing.

'Why do people have to have all these secrets?' he asked me. I seriously hoped he wasn't waiting for an answer.

Especially from me. For a moment I was tempted to tell him about Genie Stacie's secret engagement, but that would have been betraying Paul, which I have never done and never will do.

Secrets. Everyone around me seemed to have them, not just Judy. Marcy. My grandmother, my mother. Renata. Maddy and Angelica were always giggling about their secrets and I wondered just how innocent these secrets were.

'How are you guys doing? The kids? Julian?'

'The kids are fine, so is Julian.' I quickly glossed over the subject. I had to get off the phone because if I stayed on I knew I'd confide in my ever-understanding father. 'Sorry, Dad, gotta run. Will call you soon, OK? Give my love to all.'

'All right, honey. You too!'

And that was that. If I could keep something from my dad, I could keep it from anyone.

'When will Paul be back?' Gabriele wanted to know as I wiped the sweat off my face with my towel after one of his major workout sessions.

'Good question,' I said. 'Who knows? He comes and goes, and all you can do is be there when he returns.'

'Is it like that for you too, Erica?'

If he only knew. 'Oh yeah. A bit of advice? If you get him to commit, make sure it's his decision and not you convincing him.'

He paled. 'Why, what has he told you?'

'Absolutely nothing. It's just my personal opinion, that's all.'

'But do you think I stand a chance?' he wanted to know.

'With Paul? I couldn't say. He is pretty much focused on his work right now, and I don't think he'll be back soon.' Not for another eighteen months minimum.

14

Stefania and Melania

Although Julian came and went, I was sure glad he was home on this particular day. Whenever I was nervous, I cooked batches of food or did laundry. Going against my house rules of 'If it isn't in the laundry basket it doesn't get washed', I knocked on Maddy's door to fetch some laundry.

Now usually she had music on full blast, dancing her little heart away with her BFF Angelica. But this time I found her sitting with Warren on the bed, both sets of eyes downcast.

My own instinctively dropped to the small object in her hands. A pregnancy test. I clung to my laundry basket as if it could keep me from swooning.

'What are you doing with that?' I finally croaked, my voice barely audible, my lungs barely working. Maddy? Impossible. I always knew her every move. She was a little crazy but she wasn't stupid. She would never do anything like that. 'Are you...?' I couldn't even pronounce the word anywhere near my daughter's face.

Maddy stared at me as if I'd grown another eye in the middle of my forehead. 'Me? Are you crazy?'

My eyes swung back to the packet of the pregnancy test. 'Then who is? Someone I know? A friend of yours?'

Hair-raising silence. 'Maddy…?'

'Er – sort of.'

And that was when the door to her bathroom opened and she emerged, pale and drawn, her eyes huge, like a lost child's: Stefania. Friggin', bloody *Stefania*.

'Can you believe it?' I shrieked, a moment from pulling my hair out of my scalp.

Julian's hands came down around my shoulders and I burst into tears all over again.

'What the hell is wrong with these kids? They act like they know everything and they can't even manage to put on a stupid condom?'

'Calm down, Erica. We'll take care of it.'

'How?'

'You have to allow for her age. She's very young.'

I snorted.

'For Christ's sake, Erica – stop being so judgmental,' he urged.

'Judgmental?' I repeated. 'That is my – our son! Who's going to have a kid! I'm furious, and scared to death, not judgmental!'

He stuffed his hands into his pockets and huffed.

'People make mistakes, Erica. You can't jump onto their backs every time someone falls out of line.'

I swiped at my cheeks in silence. I sure as hell hoped he

wasn't talking about himself. And Warren? If this was true, his life was practically over. His plans for the future, his studies, the chance of seeing the world. And falling in love with a nice girl. All over.

Julian cleared his throat. 'I know you're scared and angry and hurt. But Warren is all that, too. Tenfold. Trust me.'

I sighed, wanting to let go and get angry, spew out a few bad words. But I forced myself not to because every time that happened, I felt that big demolition ball swinging in my chest like in the old days. To which I didn't want to go back, but right now, it was difficult for me to live and let live. This was my family we were talking about here. What was the matter with everybody?

'Is this only about Stefania getting pregnant or maybe just a bit about you not getting pregnant?' he asked.

'Oh, that is such a *crass* thing to say!' I flung at him, but couldn't help wonder how much of it was a lie.

Warren knocked on our bedroom door and poked his head in, his face ashen. The last time I had seen that look on his face was when he had been eleven and he was in trouble for punching a kid on the field.

'Come in, son. We'll work this out together,' Julian beckoned him in.

Warren stuffed his hands into his pockets and sat down at the writing desk where I paid our bills. Boy, this certainly was the biggest bill ever – my son's freedom and youth. When you had kids you never knew what was around the corner. But I knew Stefania's greedy mother Melania inside out.

She'd had four kids when she was very young, realized she couldn't cope with them and started blaming their father who was always at work trying to raise the money to feed them. The fact that he could get away from her screeching voice was just a bonus. Mealtimes in that house were a nightmare, not to mention homework time.

Melania was so inept (I can't think of a better word to describe her) that she always ferried the kids off to a friend's house in the hope they would help her take care of them. Needless to say her so-called friends would soon tire of her and ditch her, and Melania would have to move on to a new friend. She was cheerful and cute enough to attract people, but soon it would become evident that she only befriended people who could give her something.

That sounds cruel and judgmental (which, alas, I am. I can't help it. It's stronger than me. But over the years it's helped me keep the creeps at bay). OK, let me put it this way.

The truth was that Melania couldn't keep a job, nor a clean house, nor her own kids. She kept changing religion – and therefore her so-called friends – every change of season. She was unfocused and flaky. She would drag the kids to temple, or the tent, or the pagoda – whichever religion seemed in vogue at the moment, just so she wasn't alone with them. And whenever confronted, Melania – frustrated and incapable of an adult-level of thought or communication – would use her middle finger as a sign that the conversation was over.

Rumors had it she had become a steady drinker and always delegated someone else to pick her kids up (it had even happened to me six or seven years ago) as she was already floored by five o'clock. Now you see, *that* was the kind of wife my ex-husband *Ira* had deserved. Not conscientious, underestimated *me*.

Neither was Stefania really anything to write home about. To me she looked like a younger version of Melania. Yet Warren was smitten because she always told him what to do. Go figure. When I tried that all I'd get from him was a grunt. Then Stefania would walk in and he'd rise as if magically levitating, his eyes filled with the divine light of her beauty. Love did work in mysterious ways, but it was a good thing that Warren had parents who cared.

I saw her through the crack in the door. She sat haughtily, straightening her fake Chanel dress, her bangles clanging with the brisk movements. On her face was the look of greed. If Stefania really was pregnant, Melania would do her utmost to milk the situation as much as possible. And from the way she was smacking her lips in anticipation, this was only the beginning of it.

'How's she looking?' Julian whispered.

'Still like mutton dressed as lamb,' I whispered back, calmer now that I'd had a heart-to-heart with my son and assured him we would be behind him all the way to hell and back.

Julian nudged me forward. 'Come on, let's get this over with once and for all.' In a sense, I was grateful that this thing, whatever it was, had brought us back on the same team, or so to speak.

We opened the door and she jumped in surprise. She was probably silently counting our money.

'Hello, Erica. Hello, Julian,' she said, sitting up straighter.

'Hello, Melania,' I answered back. 'Will Diego not be joining us?'

'My husband? No, he's at work.'

The odds were that her husband didn't even know about this whole charade, poor man.

'I will be making the decisions today. Obviously Warren will marry my daughter and support her,' Melania began.

'Warren is twenty years old and a medical student,' I said pleasantly. 'He hasn't got a euro cent to his name.'

At that Melania's eyeballs popped out of her head and I thought I'd have to catch them in mid-air.

'You lie!' she shot back, spreading a hand across the room. 'You have a big house – a good business!'

'My husband and I have a big house and a good business, yes,' I agreed sweetly, unwilling to take her bait. 'And we work very hard for it. If Warren abandons his studies to support a family, he will have to go out into the world and earn his own fortune.'

But Melania's mind was way ahead of me. Actually, it had rushed all the way to my deathbed. 'But you have to leave it to someone when you die!' Melanie said in a panic, realizing she'd hit a hard spot and that her usual pushiness wasn't going to get her very far.

'Eventually, yes. But we're hoping to live a very long life, Melania.'

Julian was silent, letting me enjoy the talking, and if I'd glanced at him even fleetingly, which I didn't in order to not seem weak before this gold digger, I knew I'd have seen him struggling to keep a straight face.

'But you have to give them *something* now that she's pregnant!' she insisted.

'*If* she's pregnant,' I countered with that painful grin still plastered onto my face. 'And *if* it's my son's—' (she opened her mouth to say something but I raised my voice like Marcy would have at a saleslady in Macy's rudely walking away from her) '—then and *only* then we will discuss the matter again – and the options open to them.'

'*Mamma!*' Stefania wailed, whether in surprise at the revelation or worry that they weren't getting anything out of us, I wasn't quite sure.

'*Zitta!*' she hissed at her daughter to be quiet.

'Warren – say something!' Stefania urged, pinching him in the side. He winced.

'That, my son, is just a teensy-weensy preview of what's going to happen if you shack up with these two ladies.'

'How dare you talk to me like that!' Stefania spat at me, then turned back to Warren. 'And how dare you let her! What's the matter with you?'

Julian stood up and said, 'Warren. You are old enough to know what you want, but too young to ruin your life. Think about it and tell us what you want to do.'

'I already know what I want to do, Dad,' he said, and cleared his throat. I stared at him, feeling my face go pale. *Oh, God*, I thought. *Please make him see the light. Please don't let him become this girl's slave.*

Warren cleared his throat again and took Stefania's hand. 'Stefania and I are going to need five minutes alone, if you don't mind.'

To which I thought bitterly, *Yeah – that's what got you in this mess in the first place.*

Melania nodded and scoffed at me as if to say: *You lose, I win a big beautiful house with swimming pool* and *horses!*

*

They weren't in there for more than five minutes but it seemed like my life had come and gone. Melania checked her watch so many times and every time she glanced my way she had a smirk on her face. I wanted to smack it off and bounce her head around the terracotta tiles.

Was my son going to sign his own death warrant? Renounce university, his entire future because he'd knocked up the girl who would do everything in her power to turn him into her doormat? Years and years of my sacrifices flashed by me, from ferrying him back and forth to soccer practice, baseball, Italian lessons, summer camp – everything I'd done to make sure he would one day be a strong, intelligent man in charge of his future. Which was now going down the toilet thanks to a white-trash girl and her social-climbing mom.

When the door opened Stefania emerged but I couldn't see her face. As she headed for the door Melania scrambled after her, an expression of sheer terror in her eyes. Jesus, we weren't that rich. It wasn't like she was losing out on a millionaire's lifestyle.

Warren closed the door after them and heaved a huge sigh.

'What did you say to her?' I whispered.

Warren shrugged. 'That I had serious doubts it was even mine. There have been some rumors and frankly I believe she's capable of scamming me into marriage. When I asked her for the truth she broke down and told me she was seeing someone else but that he doesn't want to know about the baby. So her mom had told her to pin it on me because we have more money.'

Julian slapped him on the back. 'Well done, lad,' he said, beaming.

'Good for you!' I hurrahed, clapping my hands, relieved my son's brain and backbone weren't on his private parts' payroll and that Melania and I would never be related after all. But, I had to admit, I was sad that Stefania had felt the need to turn to someone who wasn't the father of her child.

It turned out that she was pregnant with Leonardo Cortini's baby. But Leonardo had brushed them off saying he'd never pay a euro cent to a bastard.

No girl – not even Stefania – deserved to be treated like that. Had Stefania been two years younger the law would have slapped Leonardo into the slammer *senza complimenti*, aka, unceremoniously and gladly. The authorities, I imagined, were looking to catch him out on anything – even littering – just to throw the book at him, like getting Al Capone (or Ira Lowenstein) for tax evasion. People like that had it coming. But so did Melania.

As for Warren, he'd acted irresponsibly despite Julian's constant warnings about staying safe (and free). But in the end he'd been mature and wise enough to see through her.

God, I missed the eleven-year-old who'd given Billy Blackmoore eight stitches.

15

Agony Aunt

A few days later, while Julian was away as usual, the home phone rang over and over and I let it go to voicemail lest Melania had already bounced back with another scheme to wriggle her way into our family.

'Awh, come on, Erica, answer me.' I'd recognize that low growl anywhere. Terry, Julian's agent. He was like a grizzly bear, thick-necked and barrel-chested. And as bossy as they come. What did he want with me, though?

I picked up. 'Terry?'

'Hey, Erica. I knew you were home. Listen, there's a couple of newspapers that want you to write for them.'

'What?' Had he misdialed the number after all? Maybe he was looking for some other Erica, a writer?

'On a regular basis, Erica.'

I didn't get it.

'Each week you get questions sent to an email account we set up for you, and you answer them.'

'You want me to be an agony aunt?'

'Only without the agony. Be flippant. Irreverent. Funny.'

'Ah. Then it's a dead duck. I don't do funny.'

'Of course you do. Julian's told me all about your dry humor.'

I wondered what else Julian had told him. Terry had been his agent for quite a while. Did Julian confide in him about our personal life as well? I'd heard somewhere that Terry was also Genie Stacie's agent. Did he know about the wedding? Or, gulp, was it all his idea in the first place? Like a PR strategy?

'Why me, Terry? I'm not a writer.'

'No, but you're Julian Foxham's wife.'

Of course. 'And I'm supposed to write about being Julian's *wife*?' That alone was a year's worth of reading.

'Julian's a big celebrity, you know – especially with his last few novels, he's bigger than big.'

'So?'

'So women will want to ask you for guidance. You know, marital problems. You two have a good marriage. Who better to answer their questions?'

Good marriage, I thought. Good-ish. But it needed a lot of my attention if we were going to stick together. 'Uh, thanks Terry, but no thanks.'

'Erica, don't turn this opportunity down.'

'Opportunity for what?'

'To tell the world about your opinions. The media gives you power.'

'I've no doubt, but what am I going to do with it?'

'Don't say no. I'll call you back at the end of the week. They pay really well.'

And with that the phone clicked and he was gone.

I imagined Terry being born with his rough looks and manners, smoking his cigar in his crib. Power. What kind of power could a housewife possibly have from writing a few thoughts down? Really, this guy was unreal. And yet… me getting paid for expressing my opinions? It was, really, a no-brainer.

So the next day, after a night of unanswered questions to myself, debating about Julian and our future and the baby and Maddy and a thousand other things, I rung Terry up and said I'd do it. Ten minutes later he emailed me the contract. And immediately Julian called me.

'Terry told me you accepted an offer for a column?' Julian asked, sounding loud and clear as if he was calling me from a payphone around the corner and not the other side of the world. The subtext was: *Why didn't you tell me?*

'Yes, I accepted.'

'Are you sure you want to do this?'

'Why not? You afraid of a bit of competition?'

'Don't be silly, Erica. It's just that Terry can be very persuasive, and I want to make sure you're not being bullied into it.'

'Bullied into speaking my mind? Have we met?'

He thought about it. 'OK, have it your way.'

'Good. You don't mind if I mention you in my articles, do you?'

'Me?'

'Well, the wife of a celebrity can hardly talk about men without mentioning her own man, can she?'

Julian said, 'Just as long as you keep our private stuff private.'

'But I can talk about your career, right?'

'Well, don't make it too obvious. I don't want to look like my wife is pimping me.'

'Of course not. You have an agent for that.'

'OK, hon, gotta go.'

'Wait, Julian – did you read the contract Terry sent me?'

'What? Yeah – it's pretty much standard. Welcome to my world, luv. Got to go now. Bye!'

And he hung up. End of conversation.

Was that it? No, I'm so proud of you or anything? *Blimey*, as he would say, we had a friggin' parade when he'd decide to start writing again and all I got was a 'Welcome to my world'? Did my accomplishment mean absolutely nothing to him? Maybe he was a talented writer, but I was a housewife with a new career. Well, maybe not a career, but a fun thing to do in the mornings rather than do the ironing. Or think about ominous, secret weddings.

Don't misunderstand me here. I left a fantastic career in Boston because it was killing me. I wanted to be a housewife and have my own business. And now I do. So answering a few letters every morning is not a career move – it's not denying who I wanted to be. I'm still a housewife. Only I'll have a little more fun.

So out of the blue and with absolutely no merit whatsoever, I was answering the questions of poor, unwitting women writing for help for my new blog called 'Erica Can Tell U'. Boy, at least that part was true – the stories I could tell you. Terry recommended I should be honest and not afraid of speaking my mind. Ha. Some of the questions were light and breezy. Like what was it like to be the wife of a celebrity, *et cetera*. But others brought me straight back to my past, like this one:

Q: *Dear Erica,*
   My husband is not a physically violent man but he is verbally abusive. He'll mutter nasty words under his breath – so only I can hear him – about how fat I've become. This really hurts and I swear I don't recognize the man I married fifteen years ago. Everybody else, including my family, thinks he's a saint. I feel so lonely and hopeless. What should I do?
   Signed,
   Desperada

What had happened to flippant and funny? I shook my head and typed.

A: *Dear Desperada,*
   I deeply sympathize with your plight. Marriages are never as easy as they show on holiday, jewelry or real estate commercials. Marriages take a lot of working out the kinks and most probably, in time—

I stopped typing. In *time*? The poor woman had been putting up with this shit for fifteen years. (Remind you of anyone from a long, long time ago?) How long was she expected to go on, smiling and pretending to be an idiot while she was slowly dying inside?

If even for a moment I'd doubted I had anything to say to other women, I was wrong. I now realized I had bucketfuls to say, and that I had no doubts or qualms whatsoever.

Besides, it was renowned the page had a humorous take, so there was plenty of room for poetic license. I hit 'Delete' and started all over again.

A: 'Dear Desperada,

Get rid of the little shit. Bury him in someone else's garden (but leave an anonymous apology note for digging up their flower bed) and get on with your own life. No one will miss him anyway.'

There. That ought to do it. It served the bastard right!

My phone rang the day Julian returned and as I was getting dinner ready. I can tell you over the last few months I'd developed ESP. I *knew* when it was my doctor calling with my results. My sixth sense has never failed me.

'*Pronto?*'

'Erica?'

'Dottoressa Bardotti—' (gulp) '—hi. What's the news?'

'I'm sorry, Erica…'

There was no need to add anything. I closed my eyes, envisaging yet another little guy going down the drain. And Julian trying to hide his expression of… was it relief I was seeing? Relief? Seriously?

He had asked me to have a baby, and this was the umpteenth time IVF had failed – how many times would we have to go through this torture to have a baby? Did we want to book another IVF cycle, the doctor asked? Yes, unless Julian came out in the open and clearly discussed what had changed between us in the past few weeks. No one gets that angry for an allergic reaction.

'Of course, Doctor,' I said sweetly, looking Julian straight in the eye. 'Next Monday at nine? We'll be there, thank you.'

I hung up and watched Julian's face change as if I'd slowly poured acid all over his lap. 'What?' I prompted. Let him finally take a stand and be clear for once and for all. Tell me he didn't love me anymore and that he was getting engaged to Genie Stacie as soon as he dumped me.

'You still want to go through with it?' he asked.

'Why not? I'm keeping my promise to you. You said you wanted a baby and I'm gonna give you a baby.'

'But… this would be our fifth attempt, Erica.'

'So? Usually it never works before the fourth.'

'So how long do you want to keep trying for?' he asked.

'Until it works.'

Julian stood to his feet and pushed his hand through his hair, looking like Superman staring at a big pile of Kryptonite. And yet he couldn't bring himself to tell me the truth.

'Listen, Julian. I'm doing this because *you* asked me. And now it depends on if *I* want it?'

'I didn't say that.'

'You didn't have to,' I said, my throat getting dry. 'Having another baby was light years away from my mind, remember? It was your idea.'

'Meaning you're OK if we stop trying?'

So that was what he was up to? He'd changed plans mid-way, obviously after I'd almost killed him with my hazelnut underwear. That night had been like a watershed in our relationship, along with Genie Stacie's presence. After that, things had started to go awry. We hadn't had sex since. Which had never happened before, if you don't count our Alberto row years ago. So he didn't want a baby anymore, was that it? Or he didn't want me anymore, and didn't know how to tell me? He probably figured that if I was the first to want to stop trying, it wouldn't be his fault if we never had a baby. Smart guy. But I was no less smart. I decided to call his bluff.

'No. Monday morning we'll give it another go.' Which sounded like *'Let's see if you're man enough.'*

Silence. He must have thought the same thing.

Q: Dear Erica,

My husband is cruel to me. Whilst I appreciated your heartfelt answer to a previous reader to whom you suggested stabbing, I prefer a more bloodless approach. What do you suggest?

So she wanted bloodless?

A: *The next time he has a bath, throw your hairdryer in the water and close the door behind you. You don't want to be bothered by the look on his face once you've done it, believe me.*

Among my Ira-killing fantasies, that one had been my absolute favorite.

As I continued to scroll through my emails, Terry called. 'You've become a celebrity,' he said. He'd got into the habit of calling me often. I wondered why he wasted his time. The Q&A got lots of laughs. So what else did Terry want from me, I wondered. I knew him well. He didn't do nothin' for nothin'.

I instinctively snorted. 'Who, me?'

'Are you kidding? You are huge in the States. Everybody loves your politically incorrect approach. You're the best thing since Howard Stern.'

'Who?'

Silence.

'He's...'

'I'm only kidding, Terry.'

'Ha. You're like a breath of fresh air. And there's already a book option for you.'

So that was what he wanted. Was he absolutely nuts? 'A book? But I'm not a writer,' I assured him.

'Not yet, you're not.'

'No, and I never will be,' I protested. I'd had a hard time completing reports on my staff when I worked at the Farthington, let alone parking my ass on a chair to write a book. I mean, anybody can start one – but to actually finish? Yes, I did have stuff to say about husbands, especially my first one. If I said yes to this offer, I'd be trapped. I'd have to finish it. But what if I just went blank and couldn't?

Plus, Julian was the family writer, not me.

'Don't you worry, you will be a writer,' he assured me. 'People like you always have something to say.'

'I'll take that as a compliment.'

Terry chuckled. 'Get back to work. And don't lose track of the most important thing – your page. Gazillions of women out there are literally waiting for your piece of mind with their morning coffee.'

'They are not.' Were they?

'Of course they are.'

'Well, Terry, to be honest, I wouldn't know. I live in the old world. Maybe I should come out there for a bit, get the feel of things. I've been away for eight years now.'

Silence. 'Absolutely not, Erica. Your take is original because you *are* out there.'

Huh?

'If you were here, you would ruin the magic.'

I wondered whether it was the same for Julian and me?

'How's your column going?' Renata asked me the next day as we were having a drink on her terrace.

'Umph…'

'I read it – it's funny.'

'Really? It's crazy. People are crazy. And now Terry wants a book.'

'A book? Wow, that's amazing, Erica!'

'I don't know if I have one in me, but I said I'd try. At least it'll keep my mind off—'

I swallowed as I imagined a 'fill in the blanks'. Writing kept my mind off Genie Stacie's wedding plans, the widening gap between me and Julian, the baby that just wasn't happening, my narrowly escaped grandmother-hood and Maddy who was constantly changing before my very eyes. And that was only on this side of the ocean. My calls with Dad told me that things weren't any better on his side of the pond. God knew when Marcy would stop aggravating him after that three-day disaster of a trip. I wondered if Judy and Steve were OK after Marcy's revelations, and how my sister-in-law Sandra was taking the fact that everyone in the family knew about Vince's infidelity. My family was so screwed up and even if Julian had told me that I couldn't take the weight of the world on my shoulders, most of the times it felt like I should.

Renata filled my glass with some more white wine. 'Keep your mind off what?'

I took a sip and looked at my flip-flops. 'Oh, lots of stuff...'

'Julian?'

'Among other things. He and I... have grown distant lately...'

'How is that even possible? You two are like... is it the stress of IVF, then?'

I shrugged. 'We said we'd try again, but it sort of sounded like a dare rather than a promise. I just don't know what's happening to us. After his allergic reaction, it's like he's completely changed. He's not the same old Julian. And—' I bit my lip. I had to tell someone. It wasn't right for me to keep this burden in my heart all to myself.

'What is it, Erica? Your *face*...'

I look up from my chalice. 'Paul asked me not to tell anyone, so please keep this to yourself...'

'Of course...'

'Genie Stacie has hired him to plan her wedding.'

'But that's great! You see, you were all worried about her. Who's the guy?'

'That's the thing. It's a huge secret because the groom hasn't actually left his own wife yet. Not even Paul knows who he is.'

'What?'

'And… Paul asked me for Julian's measurements…'

'Oh, come on, Erica, really? Is that what you're thinking? It's absurd!'

'Is it? The groom is a celebrity sports star who lives between Boston and Italy. Does that sound so absurd to you?'

'Of course it does! It's just a coincidence. Julian would never in a million years do that to you!'

'Yeah, that's what I keep telling myself, but things have changed, and not in a good way.'

Renata looked at me as it finally sank in. 'So what are you going to do? Surely you're not going to give him up that easily, are you?'

I shrug. 'I can't give up what's not mine. If he wants to go, there's nothing I can do to make him stay. He and Genie Stacie were a hot item way before he met me. They have history.'

'So do you, besides two kids,' she reminds me.

'The kids are growing up. I hardly think that would stop him. Him and his bloody midlife crisis. I wish he'd just get himself a sports car or something.'

'He's not the type,' Renata says.

'Well, he used to be. Maybe he changed because of me, and now wants to be who he used to be before he met me.'

Renata studied me, twisting her lip in thought, probably thinking that I was right.

As it turned out, after all the toing and froing with Julian's agent Terry, I did have a book in me. Well, an idea of a book, really – a story that had been inside me all my life. My working title? *Youth and Other Albatrosses*, that is, the fictionalized story of my teenage years and how they helped me – not – to navigate and understand my own teenagers' lives.

And now that I had a subject, whenever I sat down to write, my fingers glided across the keyboard as if I was playing some mad symphony I'd invented in my sleep. I wrote and wrote about a teenager so dangerously full of herself but also so naïve and thin-skinned, teetering over the edge of sexual maturity, and a boy who had barely escaped teenage fatherhood.

But not a word on Julian. I couldn't bring myself to analyze what was going on with us. I was afraid that if I didn't let sleeping dogs lie, they would wake up and attack me, finishing me off once and for all.

Because this mystery engagement was killing me. Come on, what are the odds? He's from Boston, a former celebrity sports star, still married, but now lives in Italy? And he's the only one of us invited (as if any of us would want to go; I trusted that my kids would have my back in an eventual kick in the teeth like that). Factor in Julian's distancing himself from me completely, his avoiding talking about the baby, or even the future. Even when I asked him where he wanted to go for Christmas, he'd shrugged and said, *Let's not get ahead of ourselves, shall we*? Jesus, how close was I to the precipice without even knowing it?

A loud rumble made me turn to look out the living room window where a cloud of dust rose. Even Julian, who, for once, was sitting in the same room with me, sat up at the noise of what could only be a sports car. Was it Leonardo?

Could he possibly be going to Renata's again? I had seen his car zooming past our entrance at the bottom of the hill many, many times. But, seeing Renata's reticence and how we hadn't spoken for a few days because I'd simply mentioned him again, I'd decided to mind my own business. And yet, the thought of that creep anywhere near my friend…

But it wasn't a Ferrari. It was a *Lamborghini* – the same one Genie Stacie had rented when she had dropped in on us. Actually, not only was it the same car, it carried the same person – Genie Stacie – *plus one*.

I stared after Julian as he opened the front door and climbed down the stone steps as Genie Stacie jumped out of the car and threw her arms around him. 'Julian, Erica – I'd like you to meet my beautiful daughter Josephine Jackson.'

16

Joey

'It's Joey, actually,' said the young girl barely glancing up from her phone.

Dressed in Goth garb from her spiky black hair to the spikes in her nose and eyebrows, Joey looked just like any other pissed-off teenager. The only thing that belied her angry stance was the color of her eyes beneath all that black eyeliner: a crystal clear green with a veil of sadness. I loved her immediately.

This girl was clearly crying out for help. With a mother like Genie Stacie, either you went with it and became her mini-me, or you went polar opposite, which was what Joey had done. Where her mother looked like Barbie, Joey looked like an Alice Cooper nightmare. I get it that it was a thing in L.A., but somehow this look didn't seem to sit well with her.

Genie and Joey. It somehow sounded like an unfortunate *Thelma and Louise* spin-off. She was the antithesis of Genie Stacie. If the word *derelict* had an image it would have been Josephine Jackson's persona. Somewhere between seventeen and thirty-five, she reminded me of myself at that age. Except for a few details. My eyes involuntarily slid to her bony arms. It didn't take a rocket scientist to see she was underfed, just minutes away from starved.

'Don't slouch, Josephine,' Genie Stacie ordered, her voice like the crack of a whip, and in defiance, Joey slouched further. I grinned at her and she caught my eye before looking away. It was a sign that there was hope in the world.

As Genie waffled on and on to Julian about her week, I led Joey into the kitchen where Maddy was setting the table, which she only did lately when she was hungry.

Joey looked up from her phone, glancing at her briefly, instantly dismissing her without so much as a *Hey*.

'Maddy, this is Joey, Genie Stacie's daughter. Joey, this is my daughter Maddy.'

Maddy stared at her in shock, obviously trying to hide her curiosity. 'Don't you ever take your eyes off your phone?' Maddy asked.

'Nope,' Joey answered back as she began to text away.

'Don't you know it's rude to send messages when you meet someone for the first time?'

At that, Joey shrugged. 'I'm not sending messages, I'm connected to the world. In any case, I'm reviewing a book.'

'Oh, what book?' I asked.

'*In Cold Blood*. It's like, awesome.'

'Figures,' Maddy muttered. 'What's with all the black? You a Goth, or something?'

'Maddy, don't be rude.' I softly nudged her.

'*I'm* being rude? Look at this chick. Two minutes in our home and she hasn't even said *Nice to meet you* or anything.'

'Probably because it isn't,' Joey simply answered.

At Maddy's dropping jaw, Joey rolled her eyes. 'Would you like to be dragged across the ocean to meet *your* mother's old boyfriends? This is like, the twelfth or something.'

'Not particularly, no,' Maddy admitted.

'Didn't think so. So I'm going to lie low until we can get out of here already. No offense, Mrs. Foxham.'

'Oh, none taken,' I assure her.

'You must live in a world of your own. What's it like to be Genie Stacie Grant's daughter?' Maddy asked, pulling herself up to sit on the counter despite my historical pleas not to.

Joey snorted. 'I'd rather have a normal life.'

Maddy grinned. 'You're only saying that.'

'No, I'm not. We're off to another movie set now and I've begged my mom to not drag me there, but she just won't listen.'

'Oh?' I said.

'Yeah. Caterers, hotel rooms and paparazzi in your face *all the time*. And I'm not even *in* the movie. What I wouldn't give to stay in my own house. Not that that's any more private.'

'But your mom is Genie Stacie Grant!' Maddy marveled. 'How can you not be happy with your life? And a mom like that?'

'Actually, I'm thinking of moving out. Then I can eat, drink and do whatever I want.'

'Not a bad idea. Maybe I should do it, too. My mom is a real pain in the ass,' Maddy considered as I stood right there in front of her. Well, how long exactly had I expected our atonement to last?

'She looks cool to me,' Joey answered as I donned my oven gloves and pulled out my tray of lasagna. Did I mention that I loved this girl at first sight?

By the time we all sat down Genie Stacie hadn't even stopped to draw in a breath, with Julian listening and nodding politely, but I could tell he was on stand-by, and Joey, who was practically salivating at the idea of a square meal, readily held her plate up.

'Thanks, Mrs. Foxham,' she said, surprising me. 'I love lasagna.'

'No, don't eat that – it's full of grease and calories,' Genie Stacie scolded, slapping Josephine's hand and in the process, mine as well. The ladle full of lasagna fell onto my grandmother's precious linen tablecloth.

I stifled a gasp of mortification as Julian's eyes met mine. How could a mother treat her kid like that? After years of Marcy doing exactly the same to me, I still hadn't learned to gloss over things like that.

As far as the ruined tablecloth was concerned, it served me right. *Never give pearls to pigs*, my grandmother used to say.

'There's other stuff,' Maddy offered, pushing the tray bake of vegetables and chicken her way.

Genie Stacie smiled at Maddy and proceeded to help herself, and, when Genie Stacie turned to Julian again, Joey eyed me and I gave her the plate of lasagna back.

Maddy saw the exchange but made no comment. I suppose in her eyes she was lucky that I didn't force-feed her.

'Joey and I are going to Africa next Wednesday,' Genie Stacie said as if nothing had happened. I wished she'd go a little further, like maybe the South Pole and stay there until she froze to death.

'Oh?' Julian raised an eyebrow.

'They're finally shooting it, Jules! They're finally shooting *Beyond the Dunes*!'

Julian's face lit up with genuine pleasure. Only he knew what she was talking about, because it went way past my head. What was so special about the sand dunes?

'It's this project Genie Stacie has been working on for years,' Julian explained to me. I made an 'Oh,' face and nodded as I cleaned up the mess she'd made. It seemed to me that was all I'd done since we met, while she ignored me as if were her housekeeper.

'I'm producing it!' She beamed.

'Genie Stacie, that's absolutely brilliant! Congratulations, old girl!'

'Yeah, congrats,' I added. 'How long are you staying away?'

'Oh, at least six months! Joey is dying to see Africa, aren't you, sweetie?'

Joey, who was busy surreptitiously stuffing her face, blinked at her mother, then at me. And fainted.

'Oh, my God! Joey, wake *up*!' Genie Stacie screamed as Julian bolted out of his seat and scooped the girl up in his arms. He laid her on the sofa as I made a dash for my salts.

'Here, put this under her nose,' I said and Julian waved the tiny bottle in front of Joey's face.

'Joey?' I called softly. 'Joey...'

She turned her head, opened her eyes, yawned and looked straight at me in wonder. I swear it was like watching her being born.

NANCY BARONE

'What happened?' Genie Stacie wanted to know. 'You're not pregnant, are you?'

Julian glanced at me and I rolled my eyes.

'Of course not, Mom,' she murmured. 'I'm just… hungry.'

As if you needed a degree in medicine to see that.

I had Julian put Joey in the blue guest bedroom upstairs and Maddy stay with her and Genie Stacie lest the idiot do or say something she'd be sorry for. The banging of my crockery downstairs spoke books on my opinion as I quickly nuked a beef consommé I kept for when the kids had colds. Forget chicken soup, in this house we ate heartily. Even Maddy, despite her protests.

Josephine turned my way as I tiptoed in with a tray and tried a smile. The poor kid looked at the bowl with lust as I shooed everyone out so I could put some nutrients into her. She must have been at least twenty pounds underweight. How can a mother *not see*?

'Drink this slowly,' I whispered as she tried to prop herself up and I recognized a faint whiff from my pregnant days.

'Did you throw up?' I asked as I patted the pillows down.

She looked up at me miserably and whispered, 'I tried to keep it down because I'm *hungry*, but I guess my stomach isn't used to eating real food anymore.'

I swear I had to fight to stop the tears from gushing. Tears of compassion, tears of fury. Tears of fear for this girl trapped in her irresponsible mother's lifestyle.

'I know, Joey. It's only normal. You need to get back to eating gradually.'

She nodded and sipped the consommé to the very last drop, raising her eyes at me in gratitude, and I wanted to cry all over again.

STORM IN A D CUP

'What do you normally eat at home?' I asked, although I pretty much had an idea. 'Does your mom always keep you on a strict diet?'

'I'm on a vegan non-dairy diet,' she explained with a wince.

I rolled my eyes.

'I know, right? She only lets me eat vegetable smoothies and protein shakes. And a protein bar every now and then. But when I'm out with my friends I'll eat a burger or something.'

Jesus, no wonder the kid was in terrible shape. She needed an intervention pronto. Good thing I'd come prepared.

'Here,' I said, slipping her a tiny chocolate bar. 'Small bites. Let it melt in your mouth.'

Her eyes widened momentarily in joy, then she grinned mischievously. 'My mom would kill me if she found out.'

'You let me worry about your mother, Joey. And we'll get you eating like a normal girl again.'

She looked up at me, hope brightening her face. 'Why are you doing this for me?'

'Because I like you.'

'You're actually not so bad yourself. I think you're the nicest of all the ex-boyfriends' wives.'

'Why thank you, Joey. Now get some sleep.'

She nodded and, satisfied, lay back against the pillows, a faint grin on her face.

'Fat!' I spat later in the bedroom as we were getting ready for bed. 'Can you imagine that? Your friend needs a reality check, Julian. She's a bloody psycho, and someone should lock her up before she kills her daughter.'

But Julian was too indignant to even answer, his jaw tight. 'She was always a bit of a flake, but my God, how could she have changed so much?' he said softly.

'She is a danger to that girl,' I blurted fiercely, feeling the tears coming back. 'She doesn't even deserve to be a mother! (If you detect a sense of anger/jealousy, you're absolutely right. I'd been trying for months to have a baby and this whacko had a true treasure of a daughter and didn't realize it.) 'She has no idea of what it means to take care of someone besides herself!'

'Hollywood is full of anorexic teenagers,' Julian said distractedly. 'Maybe it's not her fault after all. Girls today want to be slim – look at Maddy.'

'*Don't*… compare that ghost of a girl to my daughter.'

'*Our* daughter,' Julian corrected me.

'And FYI, Joey is not anorexic,' I informed him. 'She tries to eat normally when she can. And she downed a chocolate bar in three minutes flat.'

'Does that mean she's not anorexic, and that maybe she's bulimic?'

'Terrified of her mother, that's what she is,' I said. 'The girl is starving because her mother won't let her eat properly.'

Julian ran his hand through his hair. 'You're absolutely right.'

'Can you imagine that poor girl having to face the next six months in Africa with her mom?' It was obvious that I wasn't going to let Genie Stacie take Joey anywhere. '*And* live with someone like Genie Stacie?'

'Well, she is Joey's mother,' Julian said half-defensively, and I whirled around on my heels to face him. 'That is exactly what is wrong with this world. She can't even take care of herself, let alone a child. What the hell was she thinking? And doesn't Tom *whatshisface* even care?'

'You mean Tom Jackson? Genie Stacie has full custody,' Julian answered. 'Tom doesn't even pay her alimony, nor does he care about the kid.' Well, Julian seemed to know pretty much everything about it. I could already see Genie Stacie pouring her heart out to Julian about how hard it is to be a star and a single mother, and the schmuck listening sympathetically. Puh-lease!

'If a woman can't be a proper mother she should not be a mother at all,' I declared. 'She shouldn't be allowed to have children. It's just wrong and unfair to the kid.'

As my voice cracked again Julian glanced at me, but said nothing, when by now he would have wrapped his arms around me to comfort me. But he stayed where he was.

I dashed my knuckles across my eyes and nodded. I was *not* going to take this personally. 'In the meantime, other women – good, capable women – are dying to have kids.'

'Erica,' he whispered as he got up to stand before me. He seemed to want to reach out and hold me, but something was blocking him. When had this happened to us? We were usually melded to each other, couldn't keep our hands off each other, and now? The minute we decided to extend our family, we started to fall apart and there was nothing I could do to keep the pieces from sliding out of place.

'I don't mean only me... just... women in general, you know?' I sniffed, reaching out to hold him. He didn't move away, but, Jesus in heaven, he didn't put his arms around me either. So it was all true, then. This was the beginning of the end. This was his way of putting some distance between us before telling me about him and Genie Stacie. That he was going to marry her as soon as he got a divorce from me.

Oh my God, how had this happened to us so quickly? Were we really that fragile as a couple, despite all we'd been through together? Was this really happening to us, historical Erica and Julian who had been through hell and back just so they could be together?

'And you – you wanted to be a father…'

At that, he looked at me, suddenly guardedly. 'I… don't know what I want, right now…'

And there it was. The truth, in a whisper, as if it could somehow soften the blow of what he'd just confessed to me. It was so, so simple. Julian didn't love me anymore. Nor did he want a child with me.

I broke the embrace. 'You don't want a baby anymore?'

'I… I'm not sure. I've got a lot on my mind.'

I swallowed, keeping my cool as much as one can in these situations. 'Once upon a time you used to share it all with me.'

He shook his head slowly. 'Not this time, Erica. Not yet.'

'Well, when, then?'

'When I'm ready.'

'It's about you and me, isn't it?' I prompted, unable to stop myself. Might as well take the bull by the horns and get it over with.

'Erica, I said not now.'

'Why not now?'

'Because I told you I'm not ready!'

I backed away. Julian hardly ever yelled. At least not at me. There was never any reason to. Even when we argued, it was always without animosity. But here, I was seeing a huge dose of it. In his defensive stance, in the glint of his eyes, in the blush of his face, the heaving of his chest. Julian was angry, but he was also worried. Perhaps not so much about how *I'd* take being dumped, but possibly how the kids would react at being abandoned by both their fathers. Was he waiting for Maddy to finish school? Not according to Genie Stacie's plans, he wasn't.

Without a word, I swung around and left him standing there and clomped to my office. My own private hell was back.

'Give him some time, sweetheart,' my father said over the phone as I wiped my eyes. 'At one point, everybody needs a little time away.'

'Hard To Say I'm Sorry,' I whimpered.

'Well, it doesn't seem like you've done anything wrong,' he said. 'Do you feel you should apologize for anything?'

'No, I meant Chicago.' I half-laughed.

'He's going to Chicago?'

'The band, Dad. They sang "Hard To Say I'm Sorry", remember? *Everybody needs a little time away...*'

He chuckled. 'It'll be OK, Erica. Just be patient with him.'

'For how long? He won't share his thoughts with me, Dad. I don't know what he's thinking anymore, and I always know what he's thinking. I have literally no idea what's going on. Is he going to leave me tomorrow? Is he terminally ill? Are we going bankrupt?'

'Honey, have some faith. Julian is not that kind of man.'

'None of them ever are, until they are.'

He sighed. 'Princess, until he's ready to talk, I suggest you don't force anything out of him. You don't want to pull a Marcy on him. She badgers everyone until she gets what she wants.'

'How is she, by the way? Still driving you nuts?'

'Absolutely. Still drinking, too. And she won't even consider AA.'

'You are obviously not happy, either, Dad. How long are you going to keep living like this?'

'Are you suggesting I get a divorce?'

'I'm simply asking you whether it's fair on you to do all the putting up with.'

'Marcy would be lost without me. Not because she loves me—'

'Oh, she loves you, Dad. Maybe in her own sick, twisted way, but she has eyes only for you, rest assured.'

'I know. But if I died, she wouldn't know where to start. The bills, the insurance… hell, even the grocery list would be too much for her to tackle.'

We both sighed simultaneously, then chuckled.

'What a pickle we're both in,' I said. 'You in one way; me in another.'

'Love is always a pickle, in one way or another, sweetheart. Love is always complicated. Until it ends. But if it ends, it was never love in the first place.'

'So if Julian and I end, does that mean that it was all pretend?'

'You and Julian will never end, honey,' he reassured me.

I snorted. 'That's what Julian used to say.'

'Then have some faith in him.'

I sighed again. Have faith in Julian, when he was avoiding

me, pushing me away? Hard to do so, especially when we have never felt this distant ever before.

As the days dragged by, I worked on my novel and continued to answer the most serious Erica Can Tell U questions:

Q: *Dear Erica,*
   My husband doesn't want to have a baby because he says all my attention will go to it rather than to him. What can I do?
A: *Buy your husband a pacifier and stick him in a playpen and post pictures of him on Facebook. That ought to do it. Let us know how you get on.*

Q: *Dear Erica,*
   My husband is really good-looking and when we go out, sometimes he walks ahead of me, like he doesn't know me. I sometimes get the feeling he's ashamed of me. What can I do?
A: *Don't go out with him.*

Q: *Dear Erica,*
   My husband complains my career has supplanted my family time and that he sees our housekeeper more than he sees me. As a matter of fact he's bonking her. What should I do?
A: *Hire a cleaning boy and bonk him.*

Sometimes it was very difficult to know how to approach certain topics, but of one thing I was convinced. A good dose of humor always helped, at least for the minor issues. But other things simply couldn't be helped.

No one was ever allowed behind Julian's office door. We all knew that. Yet, there he was with Genie Stacie.

I could hear her high-pitched voice even if she was making an effort to talk furtively. 'Jules… she can be perfectly happy with another man… you've always told me I'm the love of your life.'

I swallowed and almost grabbed the door to keep myself from swooning. *What…?* I didn't know *that*!

Julian was silent, and I could feel him debating through the two-inch oak wood door. Oh God, had he really said that to her? Had she really been the love of his life? And most importantly, could it ever happen again? Certainly she wouldn't even go there if she didn't think she had a chance with him. And Julian? Was he going to leave me after all these years now that his lifetime love had reappeared like an H-bomb in our home?

That's jealousy for you – instead of taking the high road and pulling away from his door, I stayed glued to it. I couldn't help it, but I somehow seemed entranced more by the silences between their words rather than the spoken words I could barely grasp.

There came another sigh, almost a hushed moan and I buried my head in my hands. I dare anybody to stay calm and collected while listening to a woman throwing herself at your husband in your own home. Was Julian in Genie

Stacie's arms, letting her kiss his doubts away? I wanted to barge in on them and shriek a long-pent-up, 'Aha! I *knew* you were up to no good!' like in the old movies, but my stomach gave such a violent lurch I thought I'd be sick in the corridor. Which would not earn me any brownie points in case he was still debating, teetering over the brink between *Genie-Stacie, love of my life since I can remember and... what's her name again? Oh yeah – Erica, the neurotic, unstable and manic wife of seven years whom I constantly have to reassure and who, by the way, hasn't given me a child yet.*

No contest. No matter what Julian promised me.

Silence again. Then, a soft moan. My heart lurched. 'Let's go home, Jules... I'll produce your movie for you – star in it for free – anything you want. I *miss* you...'

I strained my ears as he softly murmured something back. It was practically a done deal. No man would turn down the chance to live in a Hollywood mansion while his movie was being funded by his lover. The movie was what Julian desired more than life itself. And Genie Stacie's presence would make sure it raked in the big bucks.

Another long silence ensued, followed by more soft moans. What the hell...?

And then just like that, the door opened and Genie Stacie sashayed out, sending me a satisfied smirk. I watched her go up to the next floor as Julian appeared on the threshold, a grim expression on his face.

'I need to talk to you, Erica,' was all he said.

Talk...? Oh God. This was it, the end. The *definitive* ending to us. This was how he was going to get rid of me to marry Genie Stacie once and for all. The engagement party, the secrecy. It had all been just a matter of time! And now, here it was, the *talk* I'd dreaded since he told me he loved me eight years ago. He wanted to leave me for greener (or blonder) pastures, and I was weighing him down. He wanted to pursue his career as an author because he believed in it – a career that he couldn't pursue exclusively from an old Tuscan farmhouse. We'd fared pretty well, if you considered all we'd been through.

Gulping, I nodded and followed him inside, every part of me shaking.

He sat at his desk, like a doctor about to give me a horrible diagnosis. So I braced myself, huffed and looked him straight in the eye. Maybe if he saw how much I loved him he'd change his mind?

He was rubbing his hands, the way he always did before facing a problem. Correction – before getting rid of a problem. I squared my shoulders, ignoring the pricks at the backs of my eyeballs. This was it. The end of an era.

'Erica…'

Erica. He hardly ever called me Erica. Mostly it was sweetie or honey. Babe in our best moments. And now we were back to Erica.

Look me in the eye when you kill me, I silently willed him.

Julian looked up from his hands on his desk as if he'd heard me and for a moment I thought I'd actually said it out loud. He plowed a hand through his thick hair, his eyes searching mine. 'I have to tell you something…'

I could only nod to indicate for him to go on, because my throat was too tight.

He looked at me for a moment longer before he huffed. 'I'm so sorry, Erica, but… Genie Stacie and I…'

I closed my eyes and swallowed. Here it came. The end of our marriage.

'Joey is my daughter.'

17

Family Strangers

There was a loud *woosh* in the room. My breath, rushing out of my lungs like a raging river emptying itself into the sea. I waited for my lungs to refill, but nothing was happening. My body had literally stalled, as had my mind. Joey, Genie Stacie's daughter, was also... Julian's...? No. It couldn't be. Despite the similarities that had kept creeping into my unconscious when I lay quietly in bed, I'd ignored them. Pushed them deep down into one of my darkest corners so that I would never have to consciously deal with it. Because this utter proof that he didn't need me anymore, if not even to make him a baby, just couldn't be true. But Julian's face was saying otherwise.

'Your... daughter...?' I heard myself rasp, while most of me was still clinging to endless possibilities.

His lips tightened and he nodded. 'I'll have to take a paternity test, but Joey's birthdate matches the time I was seeing Genie Stacie.'

But I didn't need a paternity test to know the truth. In the cold light of day, where there was nowhere to hide the facts, the rock-hard evidence was Joey's face minus the make-up, a lovely female version of Julian's features. Joey had his eyes, hair, even his teeth. How had I not had the courage to face this before? To see it with my eyes as well as my instinct? How had *Julian* never seen it before? And more so, how had all the showbiz rags missed it?

The thought kept roiling around and around in my brain, looking for a place to rest and settle. *Julian has a daughter of his own. From another woman. And I, his wife, couldn't give him what he'd wanted after months of trying.*

And now I wondered why my rival had stayed away all these years. If she wanted him as much as she appeared to, why was she only staking her claim on him now, after almost eighteen years?

As far as Joey was concerned, and with my maternal instincts, I knew that she was extremely vulnerable under that *Who gives a shit?* exterior. And a part of me, on some level, was relieved for her. Relieved that Julian could have a say in changing that poor girl's life and offer her his unconditional love. But the other part of me wondered, what about his family? What about Maddy, Warren and me, *our* family? What would all this mean for us? How would Warren and Maddy take it? And what about Julian and I? What about *us*?

And then it all came to me in a rush, adding up and slotting into place, piece by painful piece. The engagement, the secret groom and all the hush hush about everything. Every mysterious, wandering piece finally fit to shape the most grotesque picture for me. He was slowly, secretly replanning his new life. Which indicated only one thing.

'You *knew* about Joey...'

He stopped and looked me straight in the eye. 'Yes,' he finally whispered.

Something at the bottom of my stomach flopped, like a dying fish. Or maybe it was merely me, slowly starting to die inside. 'For how long?'

'Genie Stacie called me when I was in hospital.'

The fish flopped again. Once, twice. 'You've known for weeks...?'

'Yes. I've been tormenting myself, thinking of how to tell you, and now that you know, it's like this huge weight has been lifted off my shoulders. And now all I want to do is win my kid back and build a relationship with her.'

Forget that you're dying inside, Erica. You need to make some sense out of all this. I cleared my throat, but I only managed to croak out my question. 'W-why is she telling you now?'

'She told me that she's always loved me, even when she married Tom Jackson.'

So much for trying to understand. I didn't want to hear any of this.

But Julian was an ebullient fountain of information. 'Genie Stacie said that if I'd died in that hospital, I would have never known the truth about my daughter...'

My daughter. Up until this very moment, every time I'd heard him proudly say that, he'd always been referring to Maddy. His daughter, whom he'd lovingly adopted. Our daughter. And now, in the space of an instant, these two wonderful words, *my daughter*, meant something completely different. A kid. His own, biological kid!

We'd moved to Tuscany eight years ago as a family, with

a million visions of happiness in our heads – our dream home, our dream businesses, our dream *life* that we had truly earned. We deserved to finally be here, together as a family. We *were* a family. But if our dreams had finally come true, they hadn't lasted all that long.

Because now Genie Stacie, the seemingly dumb Hollywood bimbo, had outdone me. She had used all she had, daughter included, to try and get Julian back. They had history. Chemistry. And they even shared biology now as Joey's parents. That was one thing that Julian and I did not have. And, judging by the way our sex lives and IVF had been going, it was looking pretty clear that we had reached the end of the line. Was this what life had turned out to be, while we were busy creating dreams of our perfect future? Had this been fate's plan all along? To give us the illusion of happiness, only to whisk it away from beneath our feet, just as we were about to get there?

I turned away from him, trying to stifle the sobs that were now shaking me from head to foot. *Awh, hell.*

'Come on, Erica. Try to understand. What am I supposed to do, turn my back on my own blood?'

Funny life, wasn't it? First my mother turned out not to be my mother at all. Then she had a child from another relationship. Then my first husband Ira produced a child from another relationship. And now it was Julian's turn – the only person in the world who I thought would never ever do anything like that to me. The one man I had entrusted my whole life and family to, had in fact been the one to deal me The Blow of Blows, finally putting me out of my misery and annihilating me once and for all.

Because the one thing Julian had wanted from me I

couldn't give him, and life had found a way to award him for all his kindness to the world. And punish me for trying to be happy. The moment I'd most feared had arrived. Julian Foxham didn't need me anymore. Now he had a child of his own.

To think I had cried maybe once in seven years, so happy we were. *Happy times are up, girl – you've had your share, now make way for the Bad Times.*

No longer able to stifle my sobs, I slapped my hand over my mouth and fled his office. There was nothing I could say, and if there had been, I was unable to say it.

'Oh my God, Erica, I'm so, so sorry,' Renata offered as she hugged me.

'Yuh, thanks,' I managed as I tried to blow my nose, but I was still far from even being able to breathe. Renata's was the first place I ran to. My go-to person, who was always around for me.

'Julian and Genie Stacie, I can't believe it…' she repeated for the tenth time since I'd got there. 'Here, let me get you something stiffer to drink. How about a Bloody Mary?'

'How about a Bloody Genie Stacie instead?' I quipped and laughed at my own pathetic little joke. God, not even in times of duress could I refrain from making a joke?

'Here,' she said, shaking her head as she pulled a pitcher out of the fridge. 'I just made this. I had a feeling you would show up sooner or later and that we'd need it.'

What she didn't mention was our little unspoken diatribe about Leonardo Cortini, but that was another story. Right now, out of the two marriages, mine was in clearer and more present danger than hers.

'So what are you going to do now?' she asked.

Suddenly the fish was back in my stomach, flopping like mad again. 'Apart from sleeping in the guest room, what can I do? I'm still reeling here – I have no idea what to do. All these years I thought Julian and I were solid, and instead…' I broke down into such violent sobs that my chair began to creak.

Renata let me sob for a while, just to get it all out. After a long, long moment, she groaned: 'I still can't believe it… Is there any way at all you might be wrong?'

I stopped sobbing and sat up to look at her inquisitively as I rolodexed through the possibilities. There were none whatsoever, and I began to bawl all over again.

'Come, here, lie down on the sofa for a bit,' Renata suggested, guiding me off her chair. She was probably worried I'd shake it apart. 'Where are the kids?'

'Warren's in Siena as usual and Maddy's with Angelica…'

'Again? Those two are inseparable lately, don't you think?'

'Yuh,' I agreed miserably. 'I'm supposed to go pick her up in ten minutes.'

'I'll go,' Renata volunteered. 'You stay put, OK?'

'Will you bring her back to my house and tell her I've gone grocery shopping or something?' I whimpered. 'I don't want her to see me like this.'

'Of course. You just try to calm down and get some rest. I'll be back in twenty minutes. OK?'

''kay,' I obeyed, hunkering down deep into her amazingly miso-friendly sofa. 'Thanks, Renata.'

Her gentle hand ruffled the top of my head and I closed my eyes, comforted by the knowledge that I was loved, if not by Julian anymore. Renata would stick by my side. Which was what I was going to do for her if and when she decided to tell me what was going on with Leonardo. If there was indeed nothing between them, was he making their business difficult as he'd done to others? And if so, she should tell Marco. Marriages. They took forever to build and a second to tear them down.

When I got home later and all cried out, the house was absolutely still.

I tiptoed up to Maddy's room. She was lying in bed, bopping her head to inaudible music in her earphones, a half-eaten focaccia on her bedside table. I pitied her instantly, so happy in her own carefree little world. It would not last long. Sooner or later we would have to tell her and Warren about Genie Stacie and Joey and us being no longer.

I checked the other rooms. No sign of Julian and/or Genie Stacie or Joey. Had Julian moved out? I checked his closet and found a half-filled suitcase.

I gulped to suppress another sob. No. I couldn't let Maddy see me like this. I was her tower of strength, whether she knew it or not. How I behaved in consequence would imprint on her forever. I actually wanted to punch a hole in the stone wall, but what did I do instead?

I went back downstairs to the kitchen and began to peel onions. Lots of them, and soon my face was bathed in tears due to the fumes. That was what I told myself. But my onions and I knew far too well how this went. We all knew the drill, even if it had been a while. *Hello, my old friends. My, there are so many of you! And you are particularly strong tonight! Let your fumes fly into my eyes like they did yesteryear, and hide my real tears like you always have!*

Needless to say my French onion soup was delicious, and I ate dinner all by myself in the kitchen, because if there was anything lately that Maddy hated more than onion soup, it was me.

As the key in the lock ground and the front door opened, I steeled myself to stay strong. I had fled our previous meeting with Julian, leaving him in no doubt as to how I felt about the entire Joey thing. But that was the thing. I *loved* Joey. I wanted her to have a better mother than Genie Stacie. Given the chance, I would have taken care of her. The operative word being *given the chance*.

Julian tiptoed into the kitchen, eyeing me, his face asking: *Is it safe?*

Was it? Was it safe to walk all over crystalized shards of my heart?

'Hey,' he finally said, as if absolutely nothing had happened. 'Can we talk?'

I almost choked on a gob of melted cheese as I wondered, *There's more?*

Julian came to sit opposite me at the table. 'I know all this is unfair on you.'

I said nothing, just scooping up soup into my spoon and emptying it repeatedly as if on autopilot.

'But I will keep you informed. Tomorrow I should be getting the results of the DNA test.'

'How nice for you,' I quipped, completely absorbed by my spoon.

'Erica. I understand that you are upset.'

Upset? Ha. I was past that. I felt betrayed. Like he'd slit my throat while I was sleeping because he didn't have the guts to look me in the face while he drove the knife across my neck.

There were decisions to be made, of course. Like who was moving out, for instance. How we'd tell the kids about their father's new lease of life with a new wife and a new kid. All in due time. It was certainly a conversation that was not up to me to instigate.

'So is this why you are getting engaged? Or do you really love her?' I blurted out instead.

His eyes widened. 'Sorry, er, what?'

'I *know*, Julian,' I whimpered, unable to help myself as tears flooded my face, 'about the engagement party…'

'Sorry, you've completely lost me,' Julian asked, a blank look on his face. 'Whose engagement party?'

I looked up at him. Either he wasn't ready to tell me yet, or I had made the biggest mistake of my life. Better to stick to the facts. To hell with Paul's secret, this was our family we were talking about here. So I took a deep breath.

'Paul told me that Genie Stacie secretly hired him to organize an engagement party for her and her mysterious sports celebrity who lives between Boston and Italy…'

His face reddened. 'And you think it's me? You think I would actually do something like that to you? What the hell is *wrong* with you, Erica! What does that even say about our relationship?' he shouted. Really shouted.

'What was I supposed to think?' I shouted back. At least we were communicating again. 'She's always all over you and you haven't been really speaking to me since we got back from the castle—'

'Where I almost *died*,' he underlined.

'But I didn't do it on purpose,' I assured him. 'I just wanted to put some *oomph* back into our relationship, but you completely blocked me out!'

'It wasn't about you, Erica! Just because I don't want to have sex doesn't mean I don't love you anymore. I just had a lot on my mind.'

'What? So you're not in love with her?'

'How could you even think something like that of me? For Christ's sake, Erica!'

I didn't know what to think anymore. Half of me was relieved that he had nothing to do with the engagement party, and half of me was sick to the back of my teeth about this whole situation.

'And Joey! How can you possibly think that this isn't going to change our family?' I blurted out as I sank into a chair.

'I know this is tough on you,' Julian said, squatting before me. Tough didn't even begin to describe it. 'But it happened many years ago. It's not like I cheated on you.'

He hadn't cheated on me because it had happened way before me. I knew that, of course. But inside me there would always be that niggling doubt. If she hadn't left him for Tom Jackson, would they still be together today? And how can you blame someone for a fling they had way before they even met you? Julian was not at fault if Genie Stacie had passed her child off as Tom Jackson's all these years.

But he would forgive her because, one, Julian was a

forgiver by nature, and two, Genie Stacie had made him a happy man by giving him exactly what I'd been desperately trying to do for months now without any success. At this point it wouldn't matter to Julian anymore if I got pregnant or not. Now he had Joey. I felt used, like my body had disappointed him, but it didn't matter because now he had a daughter of his own blood. Tears stabbed at the back of my eyes, threatening to spill, and my mouth was filled with the all too familiar saline flavor of unhappiness.

'Honey… this doesn't change anything between us,' Julian whispered. 'You and I are rock solid – you know that…'

Did I? How could I be so sure, especially now that Genie Stacie was here to stay? If it wasn't today, it could very well be tomorrow. She knew no limits or boundaries.

'But that's just it, Julian. This changes everything.'

'No, don't say that. We will continue to be happy together, no matter what fate throws our way.'

Happy? Happy? I couldn't remember the last time I'd laughed since Genie Stacie had landed on our home like a bomb. Like the plague.

'Erica? Will you stand by me?' Julian raked his hand through his hair. 'If Joey really is my daughter, I don't want to screw this up. I need you, Erica.'

I wiped my eyes. 'I needed you, too. But look what you've done to us.'

His jaw dropped as he stared at me, utterly surprised.

Of course he was surprised. What did he know about the endless nights of worrying that she would, in the end, take him away from me? It was taking its toll on my health. I had had countless sleepless nights because of this, and I was beginning to feel queasy and sick to my stomach whenever I just thought about her, let alone saw her in my home.

I sighed an exhausted sigh. 'I know it's not your fault, Julian, but I don't know if things can ever be the same again between us. I know I should be happy that you're not running off and getting engaged to Genie Stacie and all, but believe me... this whole thing...' I lifted my hands, helpless '...her mere presence... it's truly soured me to the point that I'm sick to the back of my teeth.'

'So what are you saying?'

'I'm saying that I can't just continue like nothing happened. I'm sorry, maybe a greater woman would, but I'm finding it extremely difficult to cope.'

He ran a hand through his dark hair. 'Jesus, Erica, after all these years together, you're doing this to me? I need you by my side. You're my *wife*...'

'I'm sorry I feel this way,' I finally sobbed, dashing a hand across my eyes. 'I can't just lie and pretend it's all OK. *It hurts too much*...'

'But Erica, I did absolutely nothing wrong...'

'I'll help you with Joey, of course. It's not her fault. I can get her back into shape in no time. And I'll do everything I can to make things like they were in this family. But I honestly don't think it's enough to put you and me back to where we were. I'm sorry.' And then I began to really, really sob as the monumentality of what I was saying began to sink in.

'Jesus Christ, Erica, I'm doing my damnedest here – what more do you want from me?' he said hotly, his face red, his eyes flashing daggers at me.

'Nothing,' I whispered. 'There's absolutely nothing you

can do to fix this. You can't fix my broken heart. Only I can. And I'll try. But I offer you no guarantees that I'll be able to.'

He lowered his head into his hands.

'Julian,' I whispered again. 'Maybe, with some time—'

But Julian didn't listen to me. Instead, he shot to his feet and bolted out the door.

Talk about making things easy for your rival.

18

Strange Families

'It was just sex, Erica. And it happened years ago,' Paul said to me over the phone as I crouched in the darkness of the study during a one a.m. sob session. He was in New York doing another rich wedding. 'Although of course the bitch could've told him about the kid a little sooner.'

I snorted despite myself. 'So you'd think. I *know* he didn't cheat on me, and I swear to you I already love Joey. I loved her the minute she walked through the door with that fake confidence.'

'I know. And besides, it all happened years ago.'

'Yeah, that's what I keep telling myself, but I'm just not listening,' I whispered as a thought hit me. Why was she telling him now? Should I be thankful she'd waited all these years? Because if Genie Stacie had told Julian she was pregnant at the time, he would have done 'the right thing' by marrying her and moving back to Los Angeles. And I would have never run into him. Would they have lived happily ever after? One thing was for sure – he never would've saved me from my Spider Attack in that restaurant nine years ago. The thought scared me. What would my life have been like without him?

Would I have found the courage to come out here and live in Tuscany? Or would I have hunkered down and tried to plow through my unhappy marriage with Ira? Or perhaps I'd have settled down with a colleague at the Farthington in Boston?

'But what if it wasn't just sex? What if Genie Stacie really had meant more to him? Don't forget she was the one who dumped *him*.'

'Yeah, for an older man,' Paul said.

'All the same, the damage has been done.'

Would I never get rid of her? She was detrimental to my family in every way – to Maddy, to Warren and to me. Even her own daughter suffered because of her. In any case, I would keep my promise to Julian and support him and Joey through all of this, no matter what my personal feelings were for Genie Stacie.

Q: Dear Erica Can Tell U,
 My husband looks so much younger than me and I'm worried people will talk behind my back, calling him my toy boy or something. What can I do?
A: Buy yourself a pacifier and wear pigtails when you go out with him. Really, haven't you got any real problems?

Like maybe trying to have a kid? Especially when your husband already has one by a supermodel he once loved?

What was happening to us? What was happening to me?

Where did I stand, besides my affection for a vulnerable young woman whose mother was a flake and whose father had just been hit over the head with the newsflash of her existence?

It was official. The DNA tests returned with a ninety-nine percent probability that Julian was Joey's father. It was more than enough. So now they would have no choice but to tell Joey. And I knew exactly how strong the blow was going to be for her. Being told that one of your parents is actually not your parent, and, by the way, here's your real parent. I did not envy Joey in the least.

I steered clear of Julian's office and waited with bated breath as he steeled himself to go and speak to Joey alongside Genie Stacie. They were both still staying with us because in the light of the news that was to be delivered to Joey, I didn't want to send her to a hotel. I wanted her to feel at home when her world crumbled beneath her feet. Which meant I had to put up with Genie Stacie as well. My dad always says to respect the rabid dog for its owner. But for me it was the other way around.

A couple of hours later, Julian came downstairs to the kitchen where I was torturing a coffee cup.

'How did it go?' I asked, having bitten my nails down to the quick.

Julian signed. 'Not quite like I imagined. She already knew, or had imagined it.'

'So it was easier than you thought.'

He dipped his head. 'Yes. And she wants me to officially recognize her as my daughter before she turns eighteen.'

What else did I expect? Of course he had to adopt her. She was his kid. 'OK,' I said. As if he'd asked for my opinion. Which, I believe, he should have, even if in the end he was going to do what he wanted.

'Not OK,' Julian corrected me. 'Genie Stacie is making it very difficult. She says that unless I move back to Los Angeles, I won't be a present father figure to Joey, so I might as well forget about seeing her, which would only upset Joey.'

The right royal cow. 'So now what happens?'

'I've no choice. On Monday I'm going to follow Genie Stacie and Joey back to the States – and get myself that lawyer. I can't not see my daughter, Erica.'

'Of course. I'm behind you all the way. You have my full support. I promise you that, Julian.'

'Thank you, Erica,' he whispered, but neither of us could bring ourselves to hug the other. It was much too awkward, now.

Even if Julian hadn't confirmed it officially to the world, Terry's advice was a terse 'No comment'. No comment? I wished it had been that easy for me. Or that it would be for the kids. Because if Warren had accepted the news serenely enough, Maddy was completely shocked.

'What?' she'd shrieked as the tears immediately formed in her eyes. 'Dad, she's lying. Genie Stacie's lying! She must have slept with hundreds of men. Joey's dad could be anybody!'

'Honey, there's no mistake. I took a DNA test,' Julian whispered, taking Maddy's hands as I wiped my eyes in silence. This was something he had to do on his own, for once.

'Don't touch me!' she screamed flinging his hands off, and flew out of the room.

'I'll sort her out,' Warren offered when I made to go after her. 'For what it's worth, Dad, finding out you got your girlfriend pregnant, I understand how you feel.'

'Thanks, son. I appreciate it.'

'Us guys have got to stick together. There's no telling what the opposite sex will pull on us, right?'

Ha. That was rich. But as promised, I kept out of it all.

As Warren went to check on Maddy, Julian glanced at me miserably. 'I fucked up,' he whispered.

Oh yes you did, was my first reaction. But I clamped down on it. He didn't deserve it, really, did he?

'It'll be OK,' assured him. 'She's just a bit shell-shocked. But she likes Joey. She'll come round.'

'You think?'

'Just give her some time. Give us all time.' *Like, maybe, a million years or so.*

Because I thought it would be OK. I said it would, to Julian. I'd told him I'd support him. It had taken a huge chunk out of me to make myself OK with it, when really, I was full of doubts. Was it Genie Stacie's existence that made it all impossible? Because if I could have Joey under our roof, I'd do my best to help her. And despite my kids' sense of loss right now, I knew that they would rally and form a protective shield around Joey. She would no doubt become one of them. But Genie Stacie? Genie Stacie was a different proposition. I could never accept her. Not in a million years.

But for Julian's sake, and for my kids' sake, I would make it easier on all of us.

A few days later, Maddy seemed to have calmed down. She no longer burst into unexpected tears out of the blue as she had until now, and instead was subdued, responding softly to Julian's approaches, as if she was afraid to lose him completely despite his assuring her that she would not. Which would be interesting to see how he was going to do that all the way from L.A. while tending to his new-found daughter.

But when a few days later Maddy missed her curfew, Julian went into a panic.

'I should have found a different way to tell her,' he fretted. 'I should have assured her more. God knows where she is, if she's OK…'

'She's fine. She's just doing this to piss you off.'

'You think?' he asked hopefully. 'Because it's getting late. It's not enough to know where she is; she needs to come home when she's told. Maybe we should retract this lenient parenting style…?'

Oh, so all of a sudden he was an expert in this field? I bit my tongue. No, I would take the high road.

'Julian, you have to give her some slack. Up until yesterday she was your only, beloved daughter and now she sees her position being threatened.' How good was I at analyzing everyone else around me? 'I mean, even… IVF. Do you think they were happy about that? And that was just an idea, a germ of a kid, as opposed to Joey, a fully fledged person that you can't ignore or deny.'

Julian stopped and his eyes narrowed in an uncustomary

expression of... almost animosity. 'Well, I can't throw my only blood daughter out the window, can I now?'

My head snapped back at his stance. I understood he was still in shock too, but really? Was this the way he wanted to go? Because it wasn't leading anywhere good.

'No one asked you to do anything of the sort, Julian. And I'll ask you to chill. No one is touching your precious Joey.'

'Precious Joey? So what, you're jealous too, now? Because she's not your blood but mine and Genie Stacie's?'

I stared at him, dazed. Of all the things he could have said to make this easier on us all, he'd chosen none of them. Instead, he'd switched into attack mode. Who was this man standing before me? Because I certainly didn't recognize him. This was not my beloved husband, procrastinator extraordinaire.

'I don't recognize you anymore,' I huffed as I brushed past him, grabbing my car keys on my way out. I knew exactly where Maddy was. Sulking at Angelica's.

'Where are you going?' Julian demanded. 'I'm talking to you.'

I huffed and stopped. 'I'm going to get *our* daughter.' Did you hear that nastiness in my voice? So did he. But I couldn't help it. As much as I wanted everything to go smoothly with Joey, part of me (the biggest) was having trouble accepting this monumental change in our lives. And the fact that Maddy was too made it all the more difficult. How was I supposed to talk some sense into my teenage daughter when I, a grown woman and mother of two who was not your average shrinking violet, was having a hard time accepting all this?

NANCY BARONE

'Not on your life,' he snapped, taking the keys out of my hand. 'If anyone's going to fetch her, it'll be me.'

And with that, he marched out the door, slamming it behind him. Ouch. It looked like calm and collected Julian was losing it. With this weight on his shoulders, I didn't wonder at it. How was he expected to take this news? And how were we, as a couple, expected to survive this?

About half an hour later, I heard the roaring of Julian's Jeep as it rammed up the hill, lifting a cloud of dust in its wake. At seeing how he was driving, I was alarmed that something had happened, contrary to what I'd assured him of. But Maddy was sitting next to him, looking straight ahead, the pair of them stony-faced.

Like in a mirror, they both got out at the same moment, both slammed their doors and marched up the stone steps, Julian bringing up the rear. Their faces were bright red, but neither of them said anything as they brushed past me, avoiding, this time, slamming the front door. But I decided that if Julian was going to take Maddy on, he should be able to do it on his own until the bitter end.

It was only when they were both in the hall that Maddy spun around. 'You can't tell me what to do!' she spat. 'You're not my father!'

'And *that's* where you're wrong!' he pointed his car keys at her and yelled back. Literally yelled. At *Maddy*. He never yelled at anyone, let alone his own family. 'I am your father, and not that bloody low-life your mother married!'

Ah. Here we go. I knew it wouldn't be long before he

snapped and started taking out his problems on me. 'Hey,' I complained. 'What's going on?'

'What's going on?' Julian echoed. 'What's going on is that I found our daughter and that other princess Angelica in a car with some blokes!'

'I wasn't doing anything!' Maddy insisted. 'We were just driving around!'

'You are not allowed to get in people's cars, especially if we don't know them,' I tried to remind her calmly lest she turned on me and then all communications would be severed for the unforeseeable future. 'That was our first rule.'

'Rules, rules, rules!' Maddy shouted. 'What about you following some of your own advice, yeah? What about the two of you actually talking to each other like you aren't sworn enemies?'

Julian eyed me briefly, his face still red with anger, before he replied, 'What goes on between your mother and I does not concern you, Maddy.'

'Oh, is that what you think?' she suddenly shrieked as if he'd slapped her across the face. 'You follow my mom – and us – halfway across the world and open a business with her. You adopt us, marry her and then when this celebrity skank shows up on or doorstep, all of a sudden it's *Yes Genie Stacie and No Genie Stacie*. And then you tell us that, oh, by the way, you actually had a kid with that flake! And you expect Warren and me to just be chill about it? What the hell's gonna happen when another ex-girlfriend crawls out of the woodwork, huh? Are we supposed to embrace every woman you slept with? I don't know what's going on in my mom's head, but if I were her, I'd have already dumped your ass!'

I couldn't have said it better myself. Those were the deep, private Erica's thoughts. But how could my apparently shallow and self-centered teenage daughter have read me so easily? How did she know the real, politically incorrect me that I'd been suffocating for years? And how shocked was I, more to the point, that she was actually defending me against her idol, Genie Stacie, the *It* Girl?

'Maddy, honey, leave your father and me to speak in private, will you?' was all I could say.

She turned around and looked at me, and I could swear I saw pity in her eyes. But also anger. Sure, it was easy for her, at fifteen years of age, to talk about dumping asses.

I sighed, resigned, exhausted, disgusted. 'I can't make all this go away, Julian. I fear it's going to only get worse, for all of us.'

And that's when, atop all my other feelings, a thick veil of sadness descended. 'To be honest, I still don't... know how I feel right now about us,' I confessed. 'I'm not exactly thrilled that Genie Stacie has given you the only thing you ever wanted, but don't get me wrong. I'm happy that this all worked out for you.' In a sense.

His eyes went moist as he took my hands. 'I'm so sorry to do this to you, Erica...'

If he'd only known exactly what he was doing to me. I caressed his cheek, realizing that things would never be the same. Not because of Joey. I loved that sweet girl. But because... because...

'It's OK,' I promised. 'I'm here for you.'

'Oh thank God... thank you, Erica. 'I knew I could rely

on you after all.' He drew me into his arms and kissed me. And yet, there was still so much sadness in my heart. Disappointment at what I'd been through since I was a child, and what was still to come. No one should ever have to fight so hard just to obtain what most people have from the day they're born, that is, loving parents.

'And Joey? We'll take care of Joey, offer her a normal life,' I assured him. Because I knew that even if I was broken-hearted now, and that it would probably take me years to get over it all, that I wasn't going anywhere. I didn't want to lose Julian, and I wanted to help Joey. Genie Stacie's existence was just something I'd have to get over for the greater good.

'That's tremendously generous of you, sweetheart,' he croaked, his eyes welling up again as he kissed me again and again. 'I know that Joey is a little... difficult...'

'She's not difficult,' I defended. 'She's alone and without any support. She needs a family beyond Genie Stacie. She needs her father and her siblings.'

His face lit up. 'Really...?'

'Of course. As a matter of fact, why don't you in the meantime ask Genie Stacie if we can have Joey for the summer?' I suggested.

'Great idea. Maybe she'll mellow toward you a bit. She's a bit insecure around you, you know...'

'Ha! That's so rich! Her, insecure around me!'

'She is,' he assured me.

Probably because I was married to the one man she wanted.

But Julian was my husband and we'd been through thick and thin together. I wasn't going to dump him for all the money in the world. Well, if I have any say at all in this, she can't bloody have him.

But getting back to being able to so gleefully, unwarily trusting him like I had in the past, was another issue. To be able to trust him to not hurt me ever again was going to take time.

And so came the moment for Genie Stacie and me to address the pink elephant in the room, and by that I did not mean me, as she might have suggested. No, sorry, I was a *cow*, not an elephant.

'Genie Stacie, can I talk to you for a minute?' I asked her as politely as I could as I approached her while she sunned herself on the terrace.

She bristled and planted her sky-blue eyes on me. 'About what?'

About your starving daughter? About the way you spread yourself like strawberry jam all over my husband? About the way you totally blank out the fact that he's married to me now?

I coughed. 'Julian told me about Joey…'

She glared at me, but when she saw no animosity (boy, *I* should have been the actress, not her) she cooled down. 'Oh.'

'Julian and I would like Joey to spend the summer with us. To get to know her a little. Plus, we think she'd be much happier with kids her own age.' And not on the umpteenth movie set, I almost added.

Genie Stacie shrugged. 'OK. I'll leave her here then. Just as long as you don't overfeed her while I'm gone.' Then she threw me a disdainful look. 'I want her to still have a neck when I get back.'

I told myself not to take her bait. Tomorrow morning she'd be out of my house and hopefully out of our lives as well. At least for a while. But it still bothered me tremendously.

It was lucky for Julian (and for the entire family) that I had never stopped loving him. Not even for a minute. And now that I knew he still loved me, for better or for worse, there was still hope for us. If you didn't count the blonde fly in my champagne.

'She's so insensitive to other people's needs!' I vented to Julian, ripping off my clothes as he sat on the edge of the bed (welcome back!) watching me with a new-found lust in his eyes.

'I know. She always was. That's one of the reasons we broke up.'

'Gee, I can't imagine what the other ones could be,' I continued, dragging my hair into a ponytail. 'Just how the hell do you put up with her? I personally would like to drag my fingernails across her face. But you already know that, don't you? And oh – by the way – the next time she touches you? I will.'

Julian snorted. I stopped and pinned him with my hairy eyeball. 'You think this is *funny*? I'm on the verge of a nervous breakdown here! I really will kill her if she doesn't stop!'

'She's leaving tomorrow. Then we won't see her for at least six months.'

'Amen. I wish it was six years.'

'And now how about we think about ourselves for a while?' he ventured.

I stopped, unsure. I wanted to, of course. But somehow I'd morphed into a Mama Bear and couldn't think of anything else besides helping Joey. 'Uhm, now?'

'Hell, yes…' he moaned as he tugged at my clothes and his, leading me to our shower at the same time.

Julian slipped out of his trousers and turned on the hot water. I was watching him without really seeing him.

'I know they'll have five-star catering on set in Africa, but I'll get her back into shape here,' I said.

He pulled my dress over my head and expertly unhooked my bra.

'Panties off, luv.'

'I mean, look how skinny the poor kid has become.'

'She'll be all right once you start taking care of her,' he said, tugging at the last item on his list and pulling me under the jets. 'Now let's get you nice and soapy…'

'I'm so glad that she's staying with us,' I breathed.

'Good old you with the heart of gold,' was all he said as he lathered my hair, then my shoulders, bringing his lips down to mine, but I knew I had his approval. In my mind's eye she was already putting some flesh on those bones, ditching the indifferent façade and actually smiling. Just one summer, please. That was all I needed. I let out a contented sigh as Julian pushed me back against the tiled walls slippery with steam. We were back. The rest, we'd figure out along the way. Together.

In the space of two weeks Joey gained some weight and

some color into her cheeks. The dark smudges under her eyes were gone and even her skin and hair improved. She had blossomed under our roof. That's what a little love and healthy food will do to you. I should know.

Genie Stacie had never made time for Joey, giving nothing up – not her modeling, nor her acting. Genie Stacie had it all – and was treated like a princess, no matter what she did or didn't do.

'Honey?' Julian said as I was brushing my hair the next morning.

'Yeah?'

'I wouldn't normally do this, but since we're back on track, you and I, out of honesty and since you've opened our home to Joey, I have to tell you something.'

Uh-oh. I pulled my hair into a ponytail, frantically rolodexing through the possibilities, and my finger always landed on the negative cards. Whenever it was about Genie Stacie, it was never good. Bracing myself, I turned around in my chair and said, 'OK. I'm listening.'

'Genie has a drink problem,' Julian said with a sigh. 'She always has.'

I stared at him blankly. So Genie was a junkie. What star wasn't? 'Is that why you left her?'

'To be exact, she left me, remember me telling you this? For Tom Jackson.'

Meaning she had broken his heart and not vice versa. If he couldn't hate her for dumping him, then what exactly were his feelings for her?

Tom Jackson was still a movie star the caliber of Ewan McGregor, only older, with the charm of Sean Connery. Scotland one, England zero.

'And she needs help. Please don't feel threatened by her.'

'Whatever.'

'And… you can't ever tell her that you know,' Julian was saying. 'She's extremely susceptible and vulnerable and her self-confidence is on the razor's edge.'

Here we go again with the crystal-delicate doll attitude, I thought, then giggled despite myself. 'You sound like Dr. Denholm,' I said. (Yes, in the end I had told him about my shrink.)

'Erica, it's not funny. Not everyone's like you.'

I felt my smile fall. 'Not like me? What does that mean exactly? Sane? Because that's just a façade, you know, my all-business kind of manner, Julian. In truth, I have absolutely no idea what I'm doing half the time. So you see, my dear husband, Genie Stacie and I are more similar than you think after all. Minus the Brazilian butt, of course.'

I absently scratched at a scab on my knee and blood gushed out as if to symbolize the way I was feeling. I wanted to see blood, but not mine.

'Shit,' I swore, and Julian caught a Kleenex and bent down in front of me to wipe up the mess. I watched the top of his beautiful head, wondering how such a gorgeous guy had got lumbered with a nut like me. He reached into the drawer and placed a Band-Aid on my skin. 'There you are, sweetie. Better?'

I nodded, a strange knot forming in my throat. If only he could fix my heart. But I was doing my best to get there. 'Better, thanks.'

'What? Why are you looking at me like that?' he asked.

'I'd have married you even if you had been the hunchback

of Notre Dame,' I gushed, out of control. Which was true. After eight years, I was still under Julian's spell.

Alongside my page that was going rather well, I steadily worked at my novel about an ugly duckling. Hell knew if I had enough material for it. I had been the ugly duckling all my life, battling year after year to get rid of my albatross of youth and experience my sexual awakening. But to think that my own daughter would in a few years be doing the same made me very uncomfortable. So, in an effort to establish a stronger tie between us, I had given it to her to read.

'So what do you think about it so far, Maddy?' I ventured, mostly to get an insight of her mind because lately she wasn't talking much to me again. God knew what I had done to break the temporary spell.

She shrugged from her bed, eyeing the dresser where my manuscript lay, dog-eared and stained with the make-up she swore she never wore. 'It's OK, I guess.'

I struggled to keep my eyebrow down. 'Oh, good, I'm glad. What do you think about Lisa?'

'How the hell should I know? I can't relate to her.'

Arrgh. Brutal. 'Don't you, uhm, think other girls might?'

'Only losers,' was her verdict.

'So you can't see any of your friends reading my book?'

Maddy sighed. 'I'm not pimping your work for you, Mom.'

The blow was like a gunshot. 'I never asked you to. Thank you.'

Wow. When had my only daughter become similar to Ira?

I had done so much to keep my kids away from him and his horrible influence, but I hadn't considered that, no matter what I did or where I took them, half of him was in them. How was I supposed to control that? My guess was, I couldn't. All I could do was continue to be patient and constant with my motherly love, and maybe, perhaps one day, Maddy would 'see' me.

I took the manuscript off her dresser and went downstairs to the kitchen where Joey was making herself a sandwich. It was a joy to see she felt at home and even more of a joy to see her eat without me having to force-feed her.

'Want one?' she asked.

'No, thanks, but I like what I see. You look so much better, Joey.'

She cut the sandwich into two and wiped her hands on a paper towel. 'And I have you to thank. You took me into your home and made me better. I am really grateful to you, Erica…'

'Stop,' I said, welling up. 'Anything you need – a chat, a hug – I'm here for you. We all are.'

She stopped, her eyes huge. 'I wouldn't actually mind a hug, if that's OK?'

I grinned and opened my arms for her, and like a fragile fledgling, she flew into them. She was still so small, even with the weight gain. I'd have to have a doctor give her a check-up, just to make sure.

While my own kids were killing me, with each passing day, I literally fell more in love with Joey. Everything she did, everything she said, was cause of the deepest joy to me. Who knew I'd ever appreciate something Genie Stacie had created?

'What's that?' she asked, eyeing the pile of sheets that used to be my masterpiece in progress.

'Just a book I'm trying to write.'

'Wow, really? Can I see it or is it off-limits?' Joey asked, wiping her hands carefully.

I sat back and stretched. 'Don't worry about it. It's been through worse.'

Joey didn't answer, already reading the first page.

I grinned. 'It's a YA. Nothing like Julian's rubbish.'

She chuckled and continued to read. 'Do you mind if I take it and finish it?'

'Sure, absolutely.'

'Thank you. I'll give it back tomorrow morning.'

'No you won't. I want you to sleep tonight.'

'Mom never lets me read in bed.'

Of course not. For Genie Stacie beds were made for other activities.

19

Final Attempt

In the space of a few weeks, Joey was a newborn girl. Although Maddy was two years younger, she and Joey eventually began to hang out. She even took her to dance classes and out with Angelica and the rest of their friends for ice-cream in the afternoon and to the piazza in Castellino to check out the shops – and the boys.

I wished I could be as big-hearted toward Julian. He needed me, probably more than he'd ever needed me, and here I was, caught and weighed down by my own insecurities. But I'd do my best, because here was my moment to demonstrate to him that I was a bigger woman (no pun intended) than he'd thought, and yet, I kept screwing up his every attempt to get back on track with me. Each smile, each caress seemed like a betrayal to me, because I couldn't help but imagine what he was like with Genie Stacie. But I knew I had to shake myself out of it. There was a young girl, two entire families, if you will, at stake. And I was the lynchpin. So because Julian and I still needed to work on us in order to get back where we used to be, I gave myself completely to everyone, making sure that Maddy in particular would accept her half-sister.

One of the family pictures we'd taken during a trip to the beach was sitting on Joey's bedside table. A small knot formed in my throat. Poor thing. There were no other pictures. Not of her dad, not of her mother, not even of herself. So I went out and got her a large frame.

'You can put more in here,' I said as she unwrapped it, eyeing me, still unsure.

'Can I go get my camera then, and take some around the house with you guys?'

The knot in my throat had blocked my air passage, so I just nodded as she skipped off happily, her lanky legs like a colt's, so similar to Maddy. I swiped at my eyes and straightened her coverlet.

Denial was a vicious beast. I didn't need Dr. Denholm – or even a two-year-old for that matter – to tell me what I was going through. In my desperation to become a mother again, I was willing Joey to need me, willing her to recognize in me a dependable source of affection and stability, love and comfort. In my mind, I'd already moved her in under our roof indefinitely, enrolled her at our local school, helped her decorate her own pretty room and so much more. In my heart, I'd already built a space for her where she could stretch out and begin to live her life among us.

Sunday was Joey's birthday. I had made all her favorite dishes and Maddy and Warren had secretly collected a series of presents in my closet.

'Happy birthday, sweetheart,' I chimed as we all sang out of key, and she slapped her forehead and giggled. She seemed so different from the belligerent teenager who had darkened our door only a few weeks ago. We all hugged her and sat on her bed. 'What would you like to do today, Joey?'

'I don't mind,' she whispered.

'Oh come on, birthday girl! It's your day. Choose anything.'

She hesitated, her eyes wide as she looked at me in wonder, kind of like a mixture between love and gratitude. God, what a feeling! 'Anything?'

I beamed down at her. 'Absolutely.'

'Well, Warren and Julian have been teaching me a bit about baseball...'

'Baseball it is!' Warren called, and soon the mob was calling teams. I glanced at Julian who squeezed my hand. We had so much love inside us to give. It was such a heart-warming feeling.

Genie Stacie's movie, *Beyond the Dunes*, flopped before taking off. The producers had all pulled out, leaving an unpaid crew who fled Africa like bats out of hell. At least that's what the media reported.

'But what does this mean?' I asked Julian.

'It means that with no movie, she'll be on her way back. Possibly within the next couple of days.'

Which turned out to be spot on. She drove up our drive, slamming her Lamborghini rental as if it were an old Dodge pick-up truck. Julian was out, which could've given me ample time to try and have a civilized conversation with her. I wasn't all that optimistic, given the mood she was in. But I'd promised Julian I'd be on my best behavior.

She clopped up the stone steps leading to the front door and swung it open, dropping her bags in the hall. 'Julian!' she called, her voice echoing through the entrance.

I poked my head around the kitchen door. 'Hi, Genie Stacie. Welcome back. Have a seat.'

At that, she eyed me, wondering just how much I knew about the movie and figuring that a country hick like me would know nothing about her world. 'Would you like some coffee? Julian won't be back for another hour,' I explained as she barged in as if the joint was hers, sporting an Hermès (I know because it said so in big silver letters) bag the size of a boom box.

'Another hour? I was banking on finding him here. I have to talk with him about some very important things.'

'Yes, I know.'

At that, her eyes popped open. 'You know? I told him not to tell you.'

I bit my tongue. 'Well, Julian and I have no secrets.'

She sat back and squared her shoulders. 'Is that what you think? You know absolutely nothing about my past with Julian.'

'I might not know everything about it, Genie Stacie, but it's OK, because, as you said, it's in the past. What counts is the future.'

She snorted. 'And do you think you're going to be in it?'

I didn't take her bait. 'I can assure you that Julian and I are more than ready to do our part for Joey.'

'I don't want you anywhere near my daughter. In fact,

that's my one condition: he can't see her if you're in the picture.'

'I beg your pardon?'

'Why can't you just read the writing on the wall?' she bit off.

I stared at her. This wasn't how I'd envisaged our encounter. What writing on the wall was she talking about?

'Listen to me, Erica. Julian is not interested in you anymore. And frankly, I'm surprised he ever was.'

I stared at her. She hadn't really said that, had she? I knew that this meeting wasn't going to be easy, but I didn't envisage her being unpleasant. I thought she'd use subterfuge. I was wrong. Genie Stacie still wanted Julian back and was making no bones about it.

'Look at yourself – you're huge. You dress like you have no clue and all you do is cook and eat, cook and eat.'

I couldn't believe my ears. Why was there never anyone around to witness these moments? No one would believe me if I tried to tell them.

'Julian and I are getting back together again,' she said. 'He doesn't want to have your child. He wants mine. As he did years ago.'

No. That wasn't true. Julian loved me.

'And you even *ask* yourself why Julian doesn't find you attractive,' Genie Stacie continued smugly, tsk-tsking and shaking her head. 'Look at yourself, Erica. You're hopeless. You wear track bottoms, for Christ's sake!'

'Just around the house…'

'Yeah, and I've seen how often *you* leave this mausoleum.'

I put the coffee pot down as gently as I could, my own blood beginning to boil. 'OK, Genie, I think I've had enough. You have absolutely no right to come and offend me in my own home where my children and my husband – the operative word being *my* – live in total happiness.'

'Total happiness?' she echoed, snarling, her face so not pretty now. 'He's *done* with you, Erica. How can you not understand that? Everyone can see it but yourself. So stop writing those pathetic columns about smart women because you don't have a clue about how to keep your *own* man.'

'Stop this, Genie,' I said softly, trying to master my anger and frustration, which was so un-typical of me. Only recently I'd have pummeled her into the wall behind her, but I'd made a promise to Julian and I intended to keep it. 'I understand you want him back. He's a great guy. But he's married to me now.'

'He was mine!' she suddenly cried, huge fat tears splashing out of those vacant turquoise eyes and all I could see was a little girl crying over the loss of her favorite toy. 'Mine! And we were great together! Iconic! Pictures of us go for thousands on eBay!'

I sat back and studied her. Iconic? eBay? She was talking about him as if he was an item for sale. Was she serious?

'The whole world talked about us! I was part of something special!'

Something special. Now that she'd come right out and admitted it, I almost sympathized with her. I could understand the bond they may have had, and a woman's efforts to keep him, because life without Julian was not the same. His love had totally turned my life around. I understood what it must have been like losing him. I wouldn't even want to contemplate that. But she'd have to deal with it, like we all deal with our problems.

'Why don't you just let him go?' Genie Stacie insisted. 'You're a nobody – no one will ever notice the difference. Why don't you just crawl back into the woodwork where you came from?'

My eyebrows shot into my hair as my ears began to ring. From someone who'd made her money by appearing in magazines with half her butt hanging out, it was a mouthful. The only reason she was famous was because of the men she'd dated. On her own, she had nothing going for her except for her looks. Without Tom Jackson, or Julian, for that matter, she would be absolutely anonymous. Who did she think she was?

'And you?' I countered. 'Why don't you go back to your bottle and leave us alone?' I said before I could stop myself. And that's when, of course, Julian appeared on the kitchen threshold, looking at me in shock. And then I realized what I'd actually said.

Shit. I'd meant it as a Genie-in-the-bottle pun. I hadn't meant her *drinking* problem. I felt horrible. Julian closed his eyes and raked a hand through his hair.

Genie Stacie's eyes popped out of her head and she looked at Julian in anguish. 'You told her!' she squealed at Julian who was slowly coming up the stairs, his eyes darting to mine, hurt. I'd unwillingly betrayed his confidence in me. I'd never done anything like that before.

Shit, shit, shit. How the hell was I getting out of this one?

'Told me what?' I asked, desperately thinking of something to undo what I'd done. 'Look, I'm sorry about the Genie-in-the-bottle comment, but really, what the hell was your mother thinking when she named you?'

She looked at me, still unsure, then at Julian as she finally squared her shoulders and sniffed. 'Never mind.'

Not knowing what to do or say, I turned and went upstairs to our bedroom, seething but also feeling like the world's biggest shit at the same time. And Julian, instead of following me, stayed with her. Instead of his own wife. It would be a long way uphill indeed.

'Mom?' Maddy called from the front door later that day.

'Yes?' I called back.

'I'm going out with Genie Stacie, Angelica and Joey, OK?'

Talk about an inclusive family. 'OK!' I chimed. 'Go right ahead!' I figured she was better off not seeing me so miserable. Genie Stacie's *own* daughter wasn't enough. Now she wanted mine too. I was losing my only daughter to my rival. Might as well throw in Warren too, as a bonus.

I ditched my coffee and poured myself a glass of wine instead, sinking down into the sofa. As much as I hated to admit it, Genie Stacie was right – I always wore track bottoms or jeans. Or even my PJs when we didn't have guests. I *was* a mess. I wasn't trying hard enough to keep my man. I didn't know I had to. I thought love was forever, and although I appreciated the need to look good for your man, that had not been the first thing on my mind lately. I didn't exactly subscribe to the 'Never let him see you without make-up school', either.

It was funny, because whatever Julian wore – mainly jeans – he looked terrific, whether they were his designer jeans or his covered in horse-muck jeans. He had that innate, natural class and good looks, whereas I had to make an unbelievable effort to make sure my hair was half-decent, that my concealer hadn't rubbed off and that my clothes were something I'd actually be OK being caught dead in.

I poured myself another glass of wine, thinking I shouldn't be drinking on an empty stomach, so I made myself some popcorn. There was a Queen special on TV so I sat and watched as Freddie Mercury pranced around the stage, his melodic voice coming out of the speakers, filling the room with a tangible warmth and sense of sadness. 'Love Of My Life', he was singing, and I grabbed another handful of popcorn and jabbed it down my throat to stop the tears from surfacing. Julian *was* the love of my life – the only man in the world I could ever see myself with.

Before I knew it, I was reaching for my fourth glass, swaying now to the notes of 'Bohemian Rhapsody' – the part where it becomes pure, angry rock.

Man, I loved this song!

'Erica?'

I whirled around with my glass, spilling red wine – *shit* – all over the white rug. Julian. He took a closer look at me. 'Are you… *drunk?*'

'Of *courshe* not,' I answered. 'I'm just shinging wit' Freddie. Why do you ashk?'

But Julian took the remote and Freddie disappeared from the screen. When I groaned, he sighed and sat down, patting the sofa next to me. 'We need to talk, sweetheart.'

'I don't want to talk. I want to shing!'

'You're stoned drunk. How long has this been going on?'

'You'd know if you were around,' I snapped. Boy, could I smell a fight coming. One that would've sobered anybody.

Julian gently took my hands and I let myself fall on the sofa next to him.

'Listen to me, Erica,' he said, softly but so firmly I focused my attention on him as if he was shouting. 'I know how freaked you are because it's the same for me.'

I snorted and he put his finger under my chin so I had no choice but to really focus. Boy, was it hard, with the wine and the rhythm of the music still swaying and swirling inside me. But I tried all the same.

'Has this ever happened before?' he asked. 'Have you ever drunk this much?'

With images of Marcy's drunken and embarrassing moments of truth, I sobered instantly. 'No,' I said. 'I swear. This is the first time.'

Luckily Julian believed me. His face cleared instantly. 'Good. Because you are my rock, Erica. And I can't see you crumble. Especially when I need you so much.'

I burped. 'You need me?'

His eyes swept over my face as he got up to go into the kitchen toward the coffeemaker. I must've looked like a mess.

'More than ever.'

'Oh, I need you too, Julian,' I groaned, getting up to follow him and wrapping my arms around his neck. He hugged me tight, so tight I thought he was going to break me. I rained little kisses on his neck and ear, running my fingers through his hair, over and over again, until he pulled away to look me in the face.

'Where is everyone?'

'They'll be back soon, Genie Stacie and the girls. She took my baby shopping. Or whatever... I don't know. It hurts to think. In any case, she was awfully convincing about you and her.'

Julian looked at me at length, and then poured me a nice hot cup of coffee and drew me into his arms. 'You know that's absolute shite, don't you?'

My eyes met him. 'Do I?'

'Of course. Why would you still doubt me?'

'Because you stayed with her!' I burst into tears. 'Why would you do that?'

He sighed. 'Because I'm worried about her.'

I snorted. I was the one having a tough time, fighting tooth and nail to keep my family in one piece.

'You see?' he said. 'You're strong. Genie had been falling apart since the day she was born. She's already tried to commit suicide twice.'

I looked up into his eyes. He would never lie about something like that. 'I didn't know,' I whispered. 'I'm sorry.'

He held me against him. 'I'm sorry, too. How shall I make it up to you?'

'You want to make it up to me?' I asked, looking up into his sexy, take-me-now eyes.

'Uh-huh,' he confirmed, a big grin on his lips. 'Now let's go upstairs and shower your booze away...'

Much much later, the front door slammed and Maddy marched in, Joey trudging along behind her.

'What's wrong?' I asked as Julian and I came down the stairs, me a little more confident than before. Funny, how love does that.

Maddy slammed her bag down. 'Genie Stacie is a sell-out!'

'Oh, I'm used to it,' Joey dismissed the whole idea with a swipe of her hand.

Now *there* was good news if I ever heard it.

'What happened?' Julian asked as Joey sat down opposite us, Maddy leaning on her armrest.

'Genie Stacie took us shopping. Then we stopped for a drink.' I raised my eyebrows at her. 'Chill out, Mom, just a Diet Coke for Joey and me.'

I looked at Joey who nodded. 'I hate booze.' Which was even greater news for me. 'I've seen what it does to my mom.'

Well, at least it wasn't hereditary. 'I believe you. And then?'

'And then these guys come up to us and ask us to take them to a club in Siena for a couple of hours. As if I had a couple of hours with *your* curfew. But that's not the point. Genie just went, leaving me, Angelica and Joey, her own daughter, there like idiots. I mean, wasn't Genie supposed to stop *us* from going, being an adult and all, and not vice versa?'

I sighed and shook my head. 'You girls did the right thing to come home,' Julian said, then turned to Joey. 'Sweetie, your mom is going through...'

But Joey sighed. 'Julian, I really appreciate your concern for me, but you don't have to protect me. I know my mom is a flake.'

Now there was the truth if I'd ever heard it. At least Maddy saw the real Genie Stacie now.

'Erica?'

'Yes, Joey?

'Like, wouldn't you have told them to take a hike?'

'Uh, absolutely. Of course.'

'Just as I thought. Erica?'

'Yes, sweetie?'

'What's for dinner tonight?'

It would've been nice to say 'your favorite, sweetie,' but all I had was a kilogram of fava beans Renata had given me the day before and they were one thing no one liked.

'Tell you what. Why don't we order a pizza? We can have it on trays in front of the TV and just hang out, all of us. What do you think?'

'Sounds good,' she chimed and skipped off behind Maddy who'd extricated herself from the conversation as it was in the neighborhood of praise for me. Which was just as well as my eyes were starting to water.

I turned to Julian. 'So I guess we won't be having that talk with Genie Stacie tonight, huh?'

Julian shook his head. 'Doesn't look like it.'

I heaved a sigh of relief. 'Tomorrow sounds just as good.'

And, truth be told, the next day was the perfect day, as I began to see the slightest chink in Maddy's armor.

As I was loading the washing machine, she phoned me.

'Mom? Can you come pick me up?'

'Sure, I'll be there in five minutes. You're done early.'

Silence.

'Maddy? Is anything wrong?'

'I'll tell you when you get here.'

'I'm on my way, sweetie.' I dropped my whites on the floor and almost tripped over the heap in my haste.

When I got there, Maddy was waiting for me on Angelica's doorstep, which was odd because usually I had to wait several minutes for her to emerge, what with them not being able to separate. But today was different. Maddy's stony expression told me they had argued.

'Do you want to tell me what happened?' I asked as she got in and slammed the car door shut.

'Not really.'

'Did you argue with Angelica?'

She shrugged, then whispered, 'Yes.'

'Is it serious?'

'Dunno...'

'If you want to talk—?'

'Can't we just go home?'

'Of course, sweetheart.'

But once we got home, she didn't stomp all the way up to her room, but lingered in the kitchen instead.

'Would you like a snack?' I offered. If I offered a chat along with it, I'd lose her. So I played it cool. I'd get there.

She shrugged. 'Yes, please.'

So I pulled out the flour, eggs, chocolate and sugar and made a thick cream to eat with biscuits. To hell with my diet, my daughter needed me.

'Here,' I said. 'You keep stirring this while I pull out the biscuits.'

'OK,' she conceded, taking the wooden spoon from me, her eyes downcast. She wanted to talk, I could see it on her face. But she'd have to do it of her own volition.

'Where did you learn to cook, Mom?' she suddenly asked.

'Nonna Silvia and our aunts taught me.'

She nodded. I had never hidden anything about my real mother and Marcy from her.

'It must have been difficult, not being able to connect

with your mother,' she whispered. 'To not be able to trust your stepmother to not hurt you.'

I put the biscuits down. 'Do you not trust me, honey?'

She looked up. 'Of course I do, Mom. I trust you with my life.'

It had to be really, really bad between her and Angelica if she was being so nice to me all of a sudden.

'And Angelica, does she not trust her mother?'

'Oh, she does. But she's very strict.'

'More than me?'

Maddy chuckled softly, and my heart lifted. So there was hope.

'You aren't that strict, Mom. You're only trying to protect us from harm.'

What I wouldn't do to scoop her up into my arms. My arms ached from the effort to not hug her and kiss all her fears away. But still, it was too soon. I needed her to come to me, to understand she needed her family, no matter how hip and cool she thought she was.

Besides experiencing an unfamiliar sense of elation the first thing the next morning, I experienced something just as surreal. My period was in its eighth day of absentia. Now *that* had never happened before. Could it be? I doubled-checked the date and performed an auto-diagnosis.

Breasts? Sore, but that had been a given lately.

Appetite? I could eat a horse. As usual.

Mood swings? Come on, you should know me by now. And yet, I knew it wasn't what I was hoping.

When I found Julian, he was sitting at his desk, his head in his hands.

'Hey, honey, how are you feeling?' I asked and he looked up, his eyes unfocused. This Joey thing and possible custody battle was taking its toll on him too, I realized. There was so much he needed to figure out still.

Julian groaned. 'I'm freaked out. Confused, scared.'

'I know...'

He shook his head. 'The fact that Joey and Maddy could've gone with some jerks out of naivety, how can I protect them from that?'

'They would never have done that,' I reassured him. 'They're smart.'

'Yes. They are. But they are both still so innocent.'

Or at least, we thought they were.

20

Mixed Messages

My cell phone beeped as I rolled over, wondering if it was from Julian who used to send me messages from around the house, telling me my coffee was ready or that he was waiting for me in the shower, et cetera. Those were the good old days.

I want to lick you from head to toe, it read, and I sat up. Today was definitely looking up! I scrolled down to read the rest of the text message: *And then inside out.*

And then I realized in a split second of pure horror that this was not my phone. We had all bought them together in one go, and they were all the same. Stupid of us, wasn't it?

I checked the next message and found an even more obscene one. Whose phone was I holding in my hand? Who was having this torrid affair? My heart began to pound erratically. Warren? Or was it Maddy's? Julian's? Please God, no! This was exactly how I'd found out that my first husband was cheating on me!

I scrolled down some more, and there were dozens of

them, all obscene. I dialed the sender's number, praying Genie Stacie wouldn't be on the other end of the line.

A male voice kicked in. I almost died. It was Leonardo Cortini's!

With shaky hands I picked up the house phone and dialed all our numbers. The cell phone came alive in my hands after I'd tried Maddy's. I dropped it in horror.

Julian came out of the shower, toweling his head. He stopped. 'What is it?'

Shaking, I shoved the cell phone under his nose.

He stiffened. 'Who sent you this?'

'It's not for me!' I yelled. 'This is *Maddy's* phone! And Leonardo sent it! Julian – he's preying on our daughter!'

'Where is she?'

'She said she was going out with Angelica but now I don't know what to believe! Oh my God, I'm a terrible mother!'

Julian's eyes turned to two slits. 'If he lays one finger on her he's dead meat,' he swore under his breath as he pulled on his jeans and T-shirt, grabbed his car keys and together, forgetting our own unresolved tensions, we climbed into the Jeep.

'Pray we're not too late,' I whispered. 'Pray...'

'It'll be fine. Because I'm going to kill the fucker.'

I glanced over at him, so confident of himself. Even when Ira had his baseball aimed at the side of his head, Julian hadn't faltered.

He drove like a madman all the way past the river and to the hill where Leonardo lived and as his castle came into view Julian slowed down and finally stopped at the bottom. There, we got out of the car and huddled behind a shrub.

I eyed my husband. 'They're in there, I know they are,'

I insisted and that's when I spotted Maddy's scooter just under an olive tree. 'Look!' I pointed and Julian paled. The mere idea of Leonardo touching my daughter made me want to vomit.

'Right. That's good enough for me!' Julian hissed.

Like a commando team, we came out of our hiding place, only to see Maddy bursting through the door and jumping onto her scooter.

'Maddy!' I screamed and she whirled.

We were by her side in a split second. Her hair was tangled and she was in tears. I grabbed her, squeezing her tight. 'Are you OK, sweetheart? Did he hurt you?'

Maddy burst into a new spate of tears. 'Mom, Dad, help!' she sobbed. 'Angelica's in there and he's gone crazy!'

I catapulted myself forward, Maddy behind me, hanging on to my arm.

There was a loud bang to our right as Julian kicked down the front door to see Leonardo – and Angelica in tears, eyes huge.

I rushed to her as Julian strode over to Leonardo and punched him square in the jaw. Just once and it was enough. The jerk fell like a sack of potatoes at his feet.

Then I turned to see a patrol car and a *Carabiniere* officer, Massimo Guarini, a friend of ours, who had somehow appeared out of nowhere and whom we later learned Maddy had called from Angelica's phone. Smart girl.

I drew a blanket over a shivering Angelica as Maddy wrapped her arms around her and we took them both home before Julian went down to the police station to put in a deposition against Leonardo Cortini. On the way I called

Angelica's parents who came to pick her up immediately, crying and vowing to kill Cortini.

'You can try, but I honestly don't think there will be much left of him once he meets his future inmates in jail,' I assured them.

Joey and I cuddled Maddy all evening, reassuring her that Angelica was fine, just a bit shaken like herself. And then, it was time for me to ask the *Dreaded Question*.

'Maddy… what the hell's been going on?'

At that she sniffed. 'Angelica was thrilled by his bad-boy reputation. He was so sexy and out of this world, you know? And then one day he finally talked to her and she couldn't believe he'd chosen her.'

I fought not to roll my eyes. Oh, what young girls would do for a bit of male attention. I remembered myself, pining over Tony Esposito's every breath. If only young girls had the wisdom we old witches have. Then there'd be no danger of any young girl getting hurt.

To them it started out as fun, sure, but how the hell was a fifteen-year-old girl expected to tame an adult male who was not exactly a gentleman? It made my blood boil. Leonardo Cortini had had a beautiful, naïve girl in his hands and had been determined to ruin her.

'But you know how strict Angelica's parents are,' she said, calmer now. 'They always watch her like a hawk and even check her cell phone.'

'So he sent the messages to you.'

She wiped her eyes. 'Yeah. But then he started sending

them to me, too. I told Angelica, but she wouldn't listen. So I stuck to her like glue, making sure she'd never be alone with him. And today—'

'Lucky for her you were there to call for help.'

'I'd forgotten my cell phone at home,' she explained.

Which was lucky for us otherwise we'd have never known.

'He's awful, Mom,' she moaned as I hugged her close, almost breaking her in the process, but she didn't mind.

'Are you sure you're OK? Do you want to see the doctor? A nurse?' *My shrink?* I almost asked her.

'Mom,' she repeated. 'He didn't get to me. Not even to Angelica. I swear.'

My jaw dropped open and I exhaled in relief, spluttering. 'Are you sure?'

She let out a short, bitter laugh despite herself. 'I'm pretty sure of that, Mom. I'm not that stupid. But it was stupid of me to cover up for Angelica. I know that now. I was just trying to live an exciting life, although vicariously, through her.'

Vicariously. That was the longest word I'd ever heard from her. Longer and deeper than any word she had ever uttered. Maybe she wasn't going to be like Marcy or Genie Stacie after all. I gasped in relief again, for a million reasons, and she smiled at me before hugging me back. Really tight.

'I love you, Mom, for wanting to protect me.'

'Mmph,' was all I could say through my clogged windpipe. I could have cleared my throat and said something memorable, something she could have related to her own daughter one day, but decided that I'd said and done enough for now, and was just happy to hold her in my arms.

'We were just two stupid idiots. Angelica thought—'
Maddy wiped her eyes. 'She thought she could control him.
Even Renata thought she could control him.'

My mind did a rewind. 'Renata?'

Maddy nodded. 'She saw them together once and warned
Angelica. She also told me to stay away from him, but he
wasn't interested in me. Not until later, at least. Renata told
us all sorts of stories about him.'

Renata knew?

'Remember that day when Leonardo drove straight onto
her property? He'd gone to tell her to butt out of his story
with Angelica.'

Story? But Angelica was a child. What was wrong with
this guy? Renata had known and had tried to keep it from
me, because she knew I had enough on my plate. She was
trying to protect me, I know, but she shouldn't have.

'It's over and you're both OK,' Joey whispered as she
hugged Maddy who let herself be pampered. Joey, the one
who never got herself into shit situations like this, was good
for Maddy. Joey was a quality girl. And so was Renata. And I
had doubted my best friend. I had thought she was cheating
on her husband when she was only trying to protect my
daughter. Was I a piece of work or what?

'Are you mad, Mom?'

I looked up. 'I'm so mad I'm going to spoil you rotten.
Both of you.'

Angelica had worshipped Genie Stacie, and had tried to
emulate her by having her own impossible crush, and had
almost paid the price. Damn Genie Stacie. Damn Leonardo
Cortini. I wished they would hook up and bugger off
together forever.

Maddy laughed and cried at the same time, then smiled at Joey and patted the bed. 'Get in,' she said and Joey stared at her, wide-eyed.

'Really?'

'Of course. We're family now, aren't we?'

I got to my feet before they could see my tears and tried to remember if I had all the ingredients for a major chocolate cake. Who was I fooling? Of course I did.

I floated down the stairs and sank into a chair at the kitchen table. And then I dialed Julian's number.

'He's in hospital,' came Julian's flat voice. 'With a broken jaw.'

'That's too bad. You should have let *me* finish him off. What did the police say?'

'They actually said *thank you*.'

'I'm sure. That little shit's been on the loose too long.'

'Well, now that they have the evidence they can incriminate him. How's Maddy?'

'She and Joey are huddled under the covers together,' I said.

'You're a great mother, Erica,' he whispered, and I could actually feel him smile.

'I know,' I said with a sigh. 'When are you coming home? I'm making a cake.'

'I'm on my way.'

Next I called Renata.

'*Pronto?*'

'I'm a terrible mother and you're the best friend a woman could have.'

'What?'

'Leonardo. He tried to seduce Angelica—'

'*Oh, mio Dio...*' she moaned.

'She's OK. So is Maddy who was there.'

'I didn't think...'

'No, you didn't think. I had a right to know. You only wanted to spare me some grief, and for that I love you. But you can't keep things from me. OK?'

'OK...'

'Good. Can you go down to the *Carabinieri* and make a statement?'

'He's been arrested?'

'You think we'd let him get away with this bullshit?'

'Thank God...'

'Listen, I'm coming over to pick up your kids. You go to the *Carabinieri* right now. And then get your ass back here. I'm making a cake to celebrate this bastard's downfall, and you're getting the biggest slice.'

A low, bitter laugh. 'I love you, Erica.'

I swallowed. 'Hurry up.' And then I put the phone down.

The filthy bastard finally got a jail sentence the size of a medieval cathedral. He ended up selling most of his properties to pay for the legal fees. Too bad for him. That ought to teach him to try and lure minors to his bed. But little did I know my actions had picked up momentum:

Erica Foxham, politically incorrect marriage blogger, and husband Julian Foxham attack the lover of a friend, read the title in the paper. Oh, I only wished I'd had a swing at him! That the friend was my daughter's and was also a minor was apparently a minor issue. I decided to set the record straight.

Tuscan prince of medieval hamlet caught with his pants down sounded like the perfect title, but I wanted it to say more.

Town pedophile finally gets what he deserves.

I told of how many hearts he'd broken, how many marriage promises he'd sowed and no woman had ever reaped; of how he propositioned them (I'd had the unpleasant experience myself, if you remember), obtained what he'd wanted and abandoned them.

Leonardo Cortini had even shamelessly run for mayor but had never made it. Thanks to secret ballot. To his face, everyone was helpful and sustained him, but only in words. Every time someone went behind the curtains in the voting booth, you could be sure they weren't voting for him.

'Do you know how many years we've been wanting to nail this asshole but just couldn't get to him?' our agent-friend Massimo Guarini had told us. 'We're putting him away for a very long time.'

Amen.

21

Going Global

After things got back to normal, Julian flew to the States – with Genie Stacie – to sort out the legalities while Joey stayed with us where she belonged. The days without Julian went by so slowly, my only contacts with the world being the kids, my dad, Paul and Renata – my lifelines.

'You're going to love Joey,' I told Paul over the phone.

'She sounds adorable. Just think of how she'll benefit from all this. A stable family – a stepmom who actually listens. And cooks!'

I smiled into the mouthpiece. 'Stepmom. Does that sound OK? I keep thinking of bloody Cinderella's stepmom.'

Paul chuckled. 'You'll do fine. You've always been so full of love. And right now Julian needs you more than anything.'

'I know. I miss you, Paulie. When are you coming back? I want to have a special lunch for Joey when they get back. Introduce her to the townspeople. If Julian can get Genie Stacie to agree to her living here I want her to feel at home.'

'She's *already* home with you guys, Erica.'

'Thanks, Paulie…'

I thought about it. Paul was right. It was amazing, the clarity that derived from sharing a problem with a loved one. Paul was such a scatterbrain in his own love life, but in mine he saw everything crystal clear. Julian and I would be Joey's rock. We would all be each other's rock in this family.

'Honey, are you OK?' came my sister's voice over the phone, all the way from Boston. And it wasn't even one a.m. yet.

'Yes, Why?'

'You don't watch your satellite TV much, huh? Do yourself a favor and turn it on, will you?'

'What channel?'

'Any channel. It's all over the news.'

'Is it Julian? Is he OK?' I rasped as my heart jumped into my throat. 'Was there an accident?'

I gripped the phone in naked terror, already seeing myself standing in a horrible black dress in a graveyard. Had his plane crashed? Was I an unwitting widow? Had he been caught in a tsunami? An earthquake? Had someone kidnapped him? Had a bomb dropped on his hotel? Had my nightmares somehow come true after all?

'Oh, he's fine – at least until *you* get your hands on him,' my sister snorted angrily as I fumbled with the remote. I was so nervous I dropped it twice. And, practically on every channel, there he was, my loyal, beautiful husband, with his arms around Genie Stacie's perfect derrière as he practically pushed her into a limousine, so desperate was he to get his hands on her – so desperate was he to touch a thin, beautiful and glamorous woman again (I assumed he hadn't in all these years in Tuscany with me). All this while the ticker tape ran a repeated message as if World War Three was about to begin:

Genie Stacie Grant and Julian Foxham announce their engagement to the press. Love child thrilled to see her parents reunited.

My heart forgot to beat, leaving me bloodless and cold all over. My lungs forgot to breathe, and I think I must have passed out while sitting on the sofa.

'The tabloids and media have described their secret night out like a homecoming,' Judy informed me. 'And you can imagine what kind of homecoming.'

But I was unable to think, unable to even dislike her sick joke. My brain was frozen and my face paralyzed. All that talk about his love and loyalty toward me and the kids – where had that gone? Was it just to keep me good while he sorted himself out for his new life? Apparently so. But he'd lied to me the entire time, and here was the proof. He was supposed to have tried to reason with Genie Stacie into joint custody– not roll around in a limousine with her! How could he *do* this to me, go parading around the world, now flaunting his once presumably clandestine relationship even in front of *cameras*? After all we'd been through? We were a team. Or at least I thought we were. All this time I'd thought he was on my side, that we were inseparable. In love. A family. But now he had this whole new other family: Joey and Genie Stacie.

He was done with us. Genie Stacie and his biological

daughter were his final choice, and he hadn't even bothered to let me know. Was it possible? Was it all falling apart like a deck of cards?

I could've taken anything from anybody, but not this. Not Julian – the man I had trusted enough to try marriage again. The only one who I thought would never hurt me, had done it in one single blow. Twice.

'Erica, are you there?' my sister called. 'Don't be upset, honey – men are all the same, you've always known that.'

Had I? Yeah, I guess I had, only I thought Julian was an exception. Christ, how could I have been so *stupid*?

'Honey, why don't I fly over and we can sit this one out together? We'll go shopping and spend all our husbands' money, OK?'

The truth was I had been wrong to be so sure of Julian. I'd given him my full support regarding Joey. All he had to do was go get himself a lawyer, go through a few hearings and get at least joint custody. Easy. But no, men have to be men. Cheaters. Liars. Dedicated to their own pleasures. Forget the (first) wife and kids. People should be *incarcerated* for cheating. Really, why is it that they went unpunished for such a heinous crime? Betrayal was just as bad as murder, because every time, a little piece of you died.

I could have called Julian (just to tell him what I thought of him) but he beat me to it.

'I'm busy,' I snapped at Maddy who was holding the phone out to me.

She eyed me, up to my elbows in the kitchen sink, with a look of pity on her face. 'Mom – you want my advice? Talk to him. You don't want to upset him.'

I'd had enough of people telling me I didn't want to piss

off the man who had lowered his royal standards (if you'll pardon the pun) to marry a mere mortal like me and then wanted out the minute his starlet appeared. Julian was *not* perfect. Far from it. He was a huge procrastinator, had become too laidback and had adopted this cavalier *domani, domani* (tomorrow, tomorrow) attitude. Well, he certainly didn't waste any time on this. When were people going to understand that and stop venerating him like a bloody god? And now that he'd officially cheated on me, *I* had to talk to *him*?

'Is he still there?' I asked Maddy, then took the phone from her.

'I'm here,' came his deep, low voice. The voice of the man I loved more than any other and who had betrayed me at the drop of a hat.

'Good,' I said, and then hung up on him.

My cell phone rang endlessly for the rest of the day. People wanting to know more. What did I think? Was I surprised? Was it something out of the blue? So I turned it off.

But when I checked my emails later, there was a message from Dad:

Hey kiddo, long time no hear. Give me a call. Dad x

I glanced at my phone. If there was anyone who would understand, it was him.

He answered on the second ring. 'Hey, princess!'

'Hey, Dad, how's it going?'

'Good, good. I'm going fishing tomorrow.'

'Wow. You haven't done that in ages,' I said, glad to distract myself with everyday chitchat.

'Yeah, well, I figured I could use the time off.'

Off from Marcy, was the message, but he let it hang in the ether.

'Who are you going with, the guys?'

'Yeah, minus Bob. He's got the flu.'

I smiled. 'You love your little group, don't you, Dad?'

'Yeah, they're good guys. We all have our problems but the minute we get into the car the fun banter starts and it's like we're on holiday, you know?'

'That's good. I feel the same way with Paul and Renata.'

'Honey?'

'Yes, Dad?'

'I heard.'

'Yeah. I figured as much.'

'Do you want to talk about it, sweetie?'

'No. Yes. What am I supposed to do, Dad? I'm being humiliated, and publicly, too!'

'Erica. Do you love Julian?'

I groaned. 'That's not the point. It's not right to continue loving someone who's hurt you.'

'Isn't it?' he echoed. Meaning that if he could still love Marcy, in his own way, then I could forgive Julian.

'But look what he's done to me. He's got another kid. While I was trying to get pregnant. He asked me for another kid, and I was ready to go through all the necessary steps. No, that's a lie. I *went* through all the necessary steps. And he goes and cheats on me? Am I supposed to accept that, Dad?'

'Did he admit to cheating on you? Because I won't believe it for a single moment. Your husband is a solid man, honey.'

I rubbed my forehead in exhaustion. 'He denies it, but I saw the footage.'

'Maybe you saw what you wanted to see.'

'You think I wanted to see my husband's hands on my rival?'

'She's not your rival, Erica. She's just a poor flake who's trying to get by.'

'By stealing other women's husbands. Did you know that she hired Paul to plan her engagement party?'

'Who's she getting engaged to?'

'To Julian. I'm sure of it. It was a secret, not even Paul knew. And I guess the news of a biological daughter just swayed everything in her favor...'

'Erica, I love you to the moon and back, but you're talking a lot of nonsense. Forget about the news and the tabloids. They feed on lies. Just concentrate on your husband. And talk to him. That's all the advice I can give you.'

I bit my lip. Dear old Dad just didn't understand. He was probably resigned to unconditional forgiveness. 'OK, Dad. We'll see how it goes. I'll keep you posted.'

'You do that.'

'Say hi to Marcy and everyone for me.'

'Will do, hon.'

'Bye. Love you.'

'Love you more, princess.'

I hung up, an enormous wave of tenderness washing over me. Good old Dad. So kind and meek. He'd forgive anyone anything. I must have taken after my mom.

An hour later Renata came over. 'How's it going?' she asked as she sank into a chair at the table. 'I'm glad the two of you managed to patch things up.'

NANCY BARONE

'Patch things up? That's old news. Have you seen the *new* news?' I flicked the remote to the entertainment channel. And, as if on cue, there they were, Julian and Genie Stacie, his hands squeezing her Brazilian butt as he pushed her into that damn limo, over and over again. The speaker's voice rambled on and on about how Julian Foxham, formerly of the Red Sox, had reunited with his one and only love, without even informing his wife.

Renata watched for a bit, then looked at me.

'There must be an explanation,' she finally said.

'Yeah – my husband is in love with another woman who has given him what he wanted most. A daughter.'

'You're not even going to listen to his explanation?'

'Would you?'

'Marco doesn't know any models.'

'I'm serious!'

'Oh, Erica – really. You're going to listen to this garbage?'

'There,' I said, flicking the remote. 'The volume is off. The sight of my husband's hands on Genie Stacie is more than enough. I knew it! Paul told me he was planning her secret engagement party, and that the guy was still married! Don't you see, Renata? It was all just stalling tactics!'

Renata paled. 'I can't believe it. It can't be Julian. I won't believe it.'

'How can you not? It's all over the news.'

'Mom!' Maddy called, coming down the stairs with her cell phone. 'It's Uncle Paul – he wants to talk to you.'

'Thanks,' I said, grabbing her phone like a lifeline.

'Sunshine…' was all he said and I melted. He was the only man who would never break my heart.

'Paulie – this is the end…' I sobbed as Renata rolled her eyes.

'Don't be silly. There's a perfectly good explanation.'

'That's exactly what Renata said, but I don't believe it.'

'I do,' he said simply.

'Of course you do.' Paul had always been head over heels with Julian, calling him *The Man of Our Life*.

'Don't you remember all that he's done for you, Erica? Don't you remember how he was there for you after Ira left you?'

I swallowed. Of course I did. Julian had restored my faith in myself. And in love.

'And don't you remember how he broke into your home to save your life when Ira attacked you with that baseball bat?'

I remembered.

'And don't you remember how he stayed with you and the kids all night after that?'

And the time he carried me home when I had showed up at his office after dark, having walked for miles, getting these blisters on my feet that were so huge I couldn't even put my shoes back on. And the time Ira kidnapped Maddy, how he stayed with me all night. And the time when I showed up on his doorstep in the middle of the night and we… yeah. I remembered it all. I remembered every single word, every single caress that had sent me to heaven and back. I remembered how even his name could make me tingle all over with excitement.

But now things were different. I couldn't trust him anymore and that was that. Eight years, I'd loved this man.

With all my heart, believing that not all men were like my first husband Ira. It turned out that I was wrong.

'Paulie, just tell me. Had there been any gossip about her seeing another man? Is there even a hint of another guy who could possibly be the groom?'

Paul hesitated. 'None. But…'

'And you still believe that another guy she hasn't even been seen with is going to jump out of the woodwork to marry her?'

'Er…'

'Exactly.'

'Sunshine, come on. It can't be him.'

'Well, when you find out who the real groom is, if there is another one, please do let me know.'

Two days and two nights of not sleeping later, while I was conjuring up many scenarios, Julian came through the front door, absolutely drained. He was the last person I wanted to see, and the last things I wanted to hear were his lies.

'Hey,' he said tiredly, hesitating on the threshold as if I'd booby-trapped it. Seven years and my bedroom was once again iffy territory. I couldn't believe I was back here again. I'd had my fill of Ira and deceiving men, but this…

'We need to talk,' he said as he put his bag down.

I gave him my world-famous hairy eyeball and then turned away. Talk? We were past that. *So* past it.

Damn, if only none of this had happened, we'd be hugging and kissing. Never again. I swiped at my eyes. 'I'm not interested, Julian.'

Just then Julian filled the distance between us, taking my face in his hands.

'Erica, it's me. Remember me, Julian, the bloke who tore your clothes off at first sight? The one who loved you right from the moment you fell off that chair in my office?'

I blinked at him. It seemed like he was talking about someone else and not us a million light years ago. Back then everything had seemed so easy from the moment he'd appeared in my life.

'Remember, Erica? I'm still that man. I know what you went through with Ira's betrayal. I was there for you, remember? And you know I would never do that to you, sweetheart. Ever. I'm not like that.'

I looked up at him but couldn't see my delicious British principal of yesteryear, the one who swore eternal love to me. Had we been happy until then? Absolutely. Julian had fulfilled his vows to love and protect and cherish the children and me. To work so we could prosper. But then it had all gone to hell. And now I couldn't look at him without seeing Genie Stacie attached to him.

He reached out and took my arm. I looked down at his hand coolly, so composed. I'd die before I let him know how that footage had made me suffer.

'Do you mind?' I asked.

He let go out of sheer politeness, but I knew he was dying to slam me down onto a chair and read me the riot act. As if I'd been the one away playing with an old flame.

'I think you and I need to discuss a few things, Erica.'

'There's nothing to discuss. Can you let me through to the kitchen now? I have to cook my family dinner.'

'Genie Stacie and I had a huge fight over Joey. She

threatened to take her back to the States and never let me see her again if I didn't get back with her. She then went out drinking. I got a call late at night from a friend of hers in tears, begging me to go retrieve her. What was I supposed to do, leave her drunk in the middle of the road?'

'So you decided to go pick her up with a limousine?'

'It was the hotel's car…'

'And of course you had to put your hands on her butt…'

'I was trying to get her into the car; she was putting up a fight…'

'I don't believe you.'

He looked at me, his eyes red. Whether from fatigue or tears, I didn't know. 'I have never lied to you about a single thing, Erica. And I forgave you for kissing Alberto…' he whispered. 'I believed you. Why can't you believe me when I say that I feel nothing for her?'

'Because this is not the same. Your engagement is all over the news!'

His jaw dropped, but he said nothing. What could he possibly say?

'Just as I thought,' I spat.

'Just a minute, please,' he suddenly said. 'You know what the press is like. She must have said something and they ate it all up.'

'She did, did she? She must have been pretty confident to give out such a statement!'

'Oh God, Erica, not again, please?'

'Oh, so I'm annoying you now, am I?'

Julian groaned and sat down on the bed. I ignored him and left to sleep in the guest bedroom. There was no way I could sleep with him by my side tonight – or ever again.

Not with this hanging between us, and this was something that wasn't going away. A child, I could take, even if the fact reminded me of my own shortcomings in the fertility department. Because, first of all, Joey was adorable and second of all, it happened years before we had met and was really no one's fault. But this humiliation on a global level? Not in a million years.

22

Goodbye

Before I knew it, fall was over and with it all my hopes of motherhood and a happy marriage. Julian and I were barely talking again as he was flying to the States on a regular basis, because how I felt was of no consequence to him.

Sure, he'd tried to explain several times, but all I could hear were lies. The real Julian was long gone. Had been gone for quite a while now. Not only did he not care how I felt, he did nothing to alleviate my pain. We were officially over. It only remained for one of us to actually move out.

He came and went and I didn't even know where. Let him go to New York, L.A., Liechtenstein, for all I cared. Let him go anywhere he wanted. I didn't need to know how he and Genie Stacie were facing parenthood together. I only felt bad because Joey wasn't at fault.

*

The phone call came out of the blue. At first I didn't recognize the muffled moan and thought it was a dirty crank call. You know, where the guy asks you how big your boobs are. I was about to hang up when I heard: 'Erica? Erica?'

Renata? Was she in trouble?

'It's Judy…'

'Judy, what's up? Who was that on the phone just now?'

Silence, then: 'Vince.'

'What's wrong? Is he crying?'

'Erica, you have to come home…'

My heart shrank into a marble at the bottom of my stomach. 'What's wrong?'

'It's Dad… he died this morning.'

One phone call and Renata was there, her kids in tow, to drop me off at the airport and later go pick Maddy up from school and tell her and Warren what had happened.

I had thrown a few things into an overnight case, not sure what I was doing or how long I'd be staying. I swiped at my eyes, refusing to fall apart. *Passport. House keys for when I got back. Toothbrush. Cell phone, even if it didn't work in the US. Wallet.*

'When did it happen?' Renata asked as she passed me some other items she thought I might need and I lobbed them into my bag.

'This morning. I have to go, I have to go. Judy and Vince don't do well in emergencies.'

Renata put a hand on my shoulder. 'Sweetheart, if there's anything—'

I turned to her. 'Please take care of my kids...'

'Of course, you don't even have to mention that...'

'Thank you,' I choked. Dad. *Dear*, dear old Dad...

It was a three-flight ordeal; Siena–Milan, Milan–New York, New York–Boston, for a total of twenty hours including the stopovers. I don't even remember boarding the Milan–New York flight, but as I sat there all strapped in, staring over the sea of heads in front of me, an elderly couple kept turning to look at me worriedly. I must have looked like a real mess. Maybe they even thought I was a terrorist debating at the last moment whether to go ahead with my kamikaze mission.

I pulled out my compact mirror. Nothing new in there, except that I didn't recognize me at all. Even though I had never been a dead ringer for Angelina Jolie, the woman in my mirror looked like an overstuffed scarecrow with deep-sunken eyes.

How had this happened so suddenly? How could Dad just have suddenly died? He hadn't been ill but I should've seen the signs. We all should have. And then I remembered I actually had, during the last family trip/row.

I remembered the humiliation Marcy had put us all through at the table, firing upon everyone and anyone, for no reason at all, and Dad telling her to please calm down.

Which she hadn't. She had, if anything, continued putting him through hell. Marcy had been driving Dad crazy for years, and he was all the weaker for it. Everyone knows that unhappiness will lower your autoimmune system. A lack of serenity and happiness will do that to you. For years my dad had been suffering in silence, missing my real mother, the love of his life.

I remember Dad having that moment when he had appeared to be spaced out. Had he had a stroke and none of us had realized?

Julian. I suddenly realized how much I needed him.

I knew he was still mad at me, but this was bigger than both of us. He would understand and forgive me for not believing him and shutting him out. Or rather, I hoped. Because, although Julian was the greater of the two of us, I had really screwed the pooch this time.

And then I thought about Marcy, and what she must have been going through. Would she be strong enough to uphold the rest of the family, let alone herself?

I pictured my brother Vince in tears, nearly keeling over while Judy made an effort to hold them both up, one on each side of her. Because I wasn't there when it happened. And it was taking me a whole damn day to get back.

'It's never as bad as it seems,' came a soft, strangled voice. I opened my eyes and found a kind, wrinkly face only inches from my own.

'Love comes and goes. The only problem that can't be dealt with is death.'

I stared at the elderly woman who was being so kind to me. And because she had absolutely no idea of what she was talking about. I smiled and nodded, murmuring a thank you, although on the inside I was screaming.

Like the Jews who roamed the land for forty years, so did I the New York terminal looking for my connection, but all the letters on the screen made me so dizzy I thought I would collapse from sheer exhaustion. My mouth felt like someone had forced a bale of hay down my throat and my head felt like someone had been bashing my brains in for hours on end.

'Erica?' came a voice from behind me.

I whirled around and, after a moment of ultra-shock added to my already existing shock, focused on the familiar and yet not so familiar face.

'Ira…?' I breathed. He looked terrible.

'You look amazing, Erica.'

Years of doing my best and he never noticed and now that I looked like shit he comes out and compliments me.

'You're about nine years late,' I said and his brow shot up.

'What?'

'Nothing,' I said hastily.

'Oh. I'm heading for Atlantic City. I'm waiting for… some buddies of mine.'

Yeah, right.

'And you? I heard you were in Italy.'

He'd *heard* it from my lawyer regarding Julian's request to adopt Maddy and Warren seven years ago. But all that didn't matter anymore.

'My dad just died. I'm going home for the funeral.'

We both turned at the sound of a shrill voice – a (would you believe it?) Genie Stacie look-alike.

He looked at her, his eyes wide with lust, then back to me.

The last thing I needed was to meet another one of Ira's lovers. 'That's my flight,' I said, pretending to listen to an overhead announcement. 'Gotta go.'

He nodded, his eyes unfocused, as if he'd been drinking or taking crack. Or perhaps even both. His hair was all gone and his face was sallow and hollow, while a stomach the size of a hot air balloon hung over his belt.

His clothes were shabby and dirty and even his breath was a nightmare. I stepped back, catching a glimpse of rotting brown teeth.

'Say hi to your parents for me,' he said, just to fill the awkward void.

Say hi to my parents? As usual, he hadn't listened to a word I'd said. What about his kids? Should I not say hi to them? You could bet I wouldn't. Imagine, re-exhuming that nightmare for them.

And with that, he turned to face the blonde running to him. She wasn't a day over twenty and certainly not interested in his looks. And then I remembered what Paul had once told me. Ira had become a famous target for hookers to sponge on. I swallowed back the bitter knot in my throat and without looking back, I ran for my gate, the babelic cacophony of the world around me just about to make my head explode.

'Uhm, ma'am?' came a soft voice at my elbow. I turned to look at the thin young man next to me, young enough to be my son, had I had one really young, or old enough to be my toy boy, had I had the strength, stamina and stupidity to believe I could get away with it.

'Yes?' I answered, wiping my eyes.

'It can't be that bad, ma'am. Only family and health are really that important, you know,' he advised me, wiping out half the causes of world sadness. When had people become so empathetic all of a sudden? And moreover, what the hell did this guy know about me? I blew my nose and gave him my best smile to show him he didn't need to worry about me.

As we touched down at Logan International, I had a strong *déjà vu* of Julian, the kids and I flying out of Boston for a new life only seven years ago. Not a long time, really, until you stop and think of how many things can change in seven years. Warren had turned into a man, Maddy was struggling with womanhood, and oh – so was I, even if there were twenty-seven years between us. I convinced myself that I'd manage to navigate all the heartache. Any day now…

Paul came to pick me up at the airport along with Judy's eldest son Tony who gave me the full details of how grandpa had *keeled over* after yet *another* argument with Grandma Marcy. Last month it was her Visa bills, two months ago her cell-phone bill.

Paul glanced over at me. He was always there when I needed him. 'You holding together, Sunshine?' he whispered and I nodded although I was about to fall apart any minute. I couldn't believe I was here, after all these years, in this traffic that seemed like a revved-up, out-of-control movie reel where nothing made sense. I had lived a whole lifetime in Italy in the meantime, but funnily, at the same time it was as if I'd never left. Paul was here; Tony was here. Soon I'd see my aunts Maria, Martina and Monica, my sister Judy, my brother Vince, his wife Sandra, Marcy and the rest of the bunch. Except for (I swallowed back the pain) my *father*.

Dad had gone, all of a sudden, bringing me back to where my home had been, among my family members. I was catapulted years back, to when I was a kid and my Nonna Silvia had died. How lonely and bereft we had been. I thought about how my own kids would take the news, getting home to an empty house if not for Renata's presence. Renata would make sure the kids would be OK.

And Julian. I missed him terribly. Right here in my chest there was a huge Julian-shaped hole that only he could fill. But what was the point of calling him right now, when he was full to the brim with his own problems? I didn't want to burden him with mine. Besides, even if he was here, what could he say that would make me feel better? Certainly not any more of the platitudes that I simply couldn't bear. I would call him after I got to the house, maybe. If I ever did, judging by the way Tony was going on and on about family crises.

'...you know, Auntie Erica?'

'Uh-huh.' I leaned forward to the driver's seat. 'Paul, I love you but can you please slow down? My dad's dead, he's not going anywhere.'

Paul's eyes widened and he searched my face.

Gone. Gone were two pillars of our family. My Nonna Silvia, and now Dad. He had been the glue holding our family together. And since he'd died nothing really mattered anymore.

'Don't cry,' Tony said and as we pulled up in front of my parents' house.

I began to panic. In a minute I would no longer be able

to wake up from this nightmare. In a minute I would have proof that all this was true, and that I would never see my father smiling down at me tenderly ever again.

I can't remember how I made my way through the front door. I barely remember the coffin, the teary faces of distant relatives I'd only seen two or three times in my life. All I remember is my aunts Maria, Martina and Monica embracing me, enveloping me with their familiar support, and somehow the panic subsided.

'That's our girl,' Zia Maria soothed as Zia Martina nodded and Zia Monica dried her eyes. 'Everything's going to be all right.'

I nodded in return, straightened my back and took a deep breath. They had reminded me about my strength so that I could be strong for Marcy and my siblings.

Marcy reached out to kiss me in a gesture of unusual selflessness. 'Poor Erica, what a shock for you,' she sobbed into my coat, and my arms automatically went around her tiny little shoulders.

I shook hands with people, let them hang on to me, hold me, caress my cheek, while all the time I was wondering if Maddy had done her homework, if Warren used a condom with his new girlfriend, how Renata was doing, and if our dog Sookie missed me. My body was here in Boston, but my mind was atop my own Tuscan hill, on Colle d'Oro. And my heart was wherever Julian was.

All that really mattered to me now was the family I had created on my own, far away from the one I'd left behind, and, as awful as it sounded, I was happy to have moved away from Marcy, Judy and Vince. They so reminded me of my past, and all that I had striven to change since then.

Julian had given me the chance to believe in a fresh start. To believe in myself, and that not all was so bad. But I hadn't come such a long way if now I couldn't even manage to pick up the phone and tell my husband my father had died.

I detached myself from the throng and went up to my old room to make the call. There was nothing left of mine in there except for my old phone and my dear old record player, which had turned rusty, as if it would fall apart if I dared to touch it.

With a loud sigh I dialed Julian's number and listened to three rings before his phone conked out completely.

After that I called home. Maddy answered and I could hear Sookie barking outside through the open door. It must have been yet another beautiful day in Tuscany. If I closed my eyes I could go back in time and see the green, unripe wheat gently swaying in the breeze of a summer evening, feeling its warmth on my face, and hear a chugging tractor in the distance. Home. How I so desperately wanted to be there!

'*Pronto?*' my daughter said in perfect Italian, although her voice was low and sad.

'Maddy, it's me.'

I heard her intake of breath before she said, 'Mom! Finally – how are you?' and I wanted to cry at the tenderness in her voice.

'Fine, fine. I'm at Grandma Marcy's.'

'Oh, Mom, I'm so, so sorry…' she whispered.

'I know, thank you, sweetie…'

'How is Grandma taking it? Please give her a hug for me, will you?'

'I will, Maddy. Did you tell Warren yet?'

'I did and he wants to come back but he has an exam tomorrow so I said there was no point and that I'd keep him posted about your return.'

'That's good, sweetie. Thank you.'

'Renata is here. She wants to talk to you. And, Mom...? Hang in there, OK?'

'I will,' I whispered, feeling guilty and at the same time elated I would be going home soon.

There were muffled words and then Renata came on. 'Hey... how are you?'

'I'm fine.' *My dad's the dead one*, I almost said, but luckily stopped myself in time. I'd already freaked the family out with my flippancy.

'We've sent a telegram – everyone in Castellino has. Maddy found the address.'

'Thank you, everybody. And thank you for taking care—' I swallowed. *Of everything that was most precious to me.*

'Stop,' she simply whispered. 'You take as long as you need. OK, sweetie?'

'OK, Renata. Thank you.' And that was all I could muster for the day.

The next day was the day of the funeral.

The house, although full of family members, was very quiet, as everyone found the comfort they needed in silent, passing hugs, caresses and hand squeezes. Grief was a funny thing. It seemed to cover everything like a thick blanket of snow. All the ugliness disappeared under a beautiful white coating of sympathy and togetherness.

As I put on my black dress and the pearls my real mother had left me, I could hear Vince sobbing and Sandra softly shushing him in the next room. Dad had meant different things to different members of the family, but Vince was the one who showed his feelings the most. Dad had been his hero, his rock of kindness.

Squaring my shoulders, I descended the stairs, my fingers caressing the wooden banister that had become smooth over the years. How many times had my dad's hands touched this very banister on his way down? And then I asked myself, out of the blue, just how many times had he been happy? How many days had he been happy in his life? Because that was all that mattered, at the end of the day and at the end of your life. But I already knew the answer: very few, and it was all because he'd lost my mother. And now, the two people who had loved me the most were both gone. And when love is gone, what else is left? Absolutely nothing. Nothing else matters once you've lost someone's love.

I made a note to myself to try and patch things up with Julian when I got home and at least remain on amicable terms, assuming we could ever manage to be there at the same time.

One by one, everyone came downstairs, hanging around in the small kitchen where we used to congregate as kids, waiting for Nonna Silvia to bring dinner and our aunts to bring our laundry and spend some time with us or help us with our homework. And now it was all just a blur.

We went out into the living room, where family friends had already gathered, just as the hearse arrived. As I ducked into the family limousine that would take us to the funeral hall, I glanced up at a taxi pulling up next to me. Before I even recognized him, my heart skipped a couple of beats. Julian unfurled out of the vehicle, haggard and sad, his eyes searching for me.

All around me, there was a sudden hush and a murmur to the effect that, *See? She's not divorcing – there's her husband now*.

'Oh, Julian! You came...' Marcy breathed like Scarlett O'Hara and started to cry. He turned and embraced her as, high over the crowd, our eyes met and held. Marcy clung to him and started to cry really hard, her nose going red and dripping.

Then came Judy who threw herself at him so violently he almost dropped her. Vince pried her out of Julian's arms and shook his hand thoroughly. Vince had always liked Julian. Everybody had always liked him. Because he was a decent guy.

I watched as he weaved his way through the sea of relatives that parted before him. I swallowed. He'd come. He was here.

'Don't screw it up, Erica,' Paul whispered to me as Julian approached and stopped right in front of me, his eyes searching mine.

'You look absolutely gorgeous,' was all I could say as he folded me in his arms, kissing my forehead and instantly filling me with that usual warmth that could only come from his presence.

'Maddy called me. I took the first flight back... I'm so

sorry, sweetheart. I'm so sorry – for everything,' he breathed into my hair.

Or that's what I think he said. For now he was here, and that was enough.

23

The Beginning

It was cold for late December and the trees surrounding the cemetery were like giant burning black arrows shooting up into an anthrax sky.

We had buried my dad three days earlier and at my request to return to the cemetery Judy insisted on accompanying me and Julian while Vince stayed home with Marcy. And now I wanted to share with my husband one of the most important things in my life.

Winter was already a fact and I breathed in the familiar fragrance of Boston just before a snowfall. I slung my arm through his and stuffed my free hand into the new black coat I'd purchased at – you guessed it – Macy's (without Marcy) and headed toward the south side of the cemetery.

'Dad's grave is the other way,' Judy called after us. I stopped amidst the flaming leaves, kicking at them with my feet the way I used to as a girl. 'I'm not going to Dad's grave yet,' I called back, and to Julian who was regarding me quizzically, I smiled and explained, 'I'm taking you to meet my Grandma Silvia.'

We stopped just before her headstone. *Silvia Bettarini, Beloved Mother and Grandmother.*

'You'd have loved her. She was amazing.'

'She was if she was anything like you.'

I turned to look at him and our eyes held. 'I love you so much, sweetheart,' he choked.

He pulled me close for a kiss and I fell against him. I hadn't done that in a long time. 'She would have loved you...' I hiccupped.

'We have so much to talk about...'

'Yes...'

'And when we're done, we'll take the kids on a fantastic trip – anywhere you want.'

'Anywhere?'

'Absolutely.'

'Sounds like heaven,' I said with a smile as a snowflake landed on my nose and Julian kissed it.

We stayed around for a few more days to help with all the paperwork and all the thank you notes until Marcy assured us she'd be OK, and that we should go back to the kids.

It was only on the flight back, while resting my head on Julian's shoulder, that I finally allowed myself to cry. Really cry.

Sweet, soppy Dad. Never a harsh word, never a reproach. Just his mild smiles and weak words of compliance. 'Yes, Marcy. No, Marcy.' And now none of it mattered anymore. I was only sorry that he wouldn't get to meet the two new additions to the family. Joey... and... well... it had been at least six weeks since my period. And I was feeling that same old feeling.

I'd done a pregnancy test in Marcy's en suite bathroom, my hands shaking so badly I had to repeat it three times. How ironic, I'd asked myself, was it that I got pregnant the natural way, during that one night that Julian and I had stopped the hostilities?

Yet I couldn't bring myself to tell Julian just yet because I was afraid that he – I knew it would be a boy – might go away. Just like the last time.

'I forgot to tell you,' Julian said, wrapping an arm around my neck and pulling me in for a kiss. 'As it turns out, you were right about Genie Stacie's crazy engagement plans. There was no other groom.'

'You see? I told you.'

He shook his head. 'It's absolutely bonkers. She had Paul plan everything down to the finest detail. The poor bloke had no idea it was me.'

I looked up at him. 'You mean she was counting her chickens before they hatched?'

He grinned. 'It would appear so.'

'Talk about optimism.' Why was it that some women had the confidence to win men over, the same confidence I lacked toward my own husband? Why had it taken me this long?

'Anyway, enough about that. We're home, sweetheart...'

We stepped into the blinding light of a glorious day outside Siena airport. Yes, finally home. Julian wrapped his arms around me and I hugged him back hard before getting into the Jeep he'd left parked there ages ago. Before Dad had died. I turned to look at him, feeling my mouth widen with a big smile.

'What?' Julian said, somewhat thrown. We'd just come back from my dad's funeral and somehow I couldn't stop the feeling of hope and life that was now bursting inside me once we'd arrived on home soil. 'What's funny?'

'I'll tell you when we get home.'

'Tell me now. I need a laugh.'

'You'll have to wait.'

'Give me a hint at least.'

'Well, let's say I've got a nice Christmas present.'

I wanted to tell him when we were home. And together we would tell our kids Maddy, Warren and Joey.

Joey stayed with us despite Genie Stacie's threats alternating with her pleas to help her 'sort out' Joey and convince her to go home. But Joey was already home, and she knew exactly what she wanted. A solid family. And to enroll in the International University for Foreigners in nearby Perugia. She'd had the choice between living in Perugia or commuting, as it was only fifty kilometers away. But I suspected she needed to be with us, her family. Something she'd always craved.

Maddy was in her fourth year of the Academy of Art and had buckled down for her assignments like the good student that she was. She and Angelica were as close as ever, and together with Joey, they formed a loyal trio.

Warren was in his third year of medicine and although the loss of his grandfather had dealt him a huge blow, he was at the same time overjoyed to have gained a sister who was a baseball freak like him. He was also grateful to have escaped teenage fatherhood. He still dated but was always, he says, very careful.

And the anti-heroine of the story, you may ask? Once Julian had very clearly explained to Genie Stacie once and for all how things were going to work, that is, that she was going to acknowledge that he was happily married to me, and that it was time for her to stop trying to break us up, she had no choice but to bow out. She had also accepted that Joey was free to live in Italy with us and to not pester her every other day about it.

As far as the movie was concerned, Julian was already talking to other producers.

Marcy called once a week when Judy went over there to see her.

My siblings were trying to patch up their relationships, while Paul and Gabriele seemed to have something going, but I didn't hold my breath.

As far as my sweet secret was concerned, I was saving it for the next day, Christmas Eve, the very same day their biological father Ira had walked out on them years ago. Tomorrow night I'd sit them all around the tree and announce that the family was getting bigger. Four children. And a loving husband. How lucky could I get?

Epilogue

'Ciao, *bella*, want a rride?' came the deep voice at my side as I trudged up the dirt road leading to our home with my eternally flat tire.

'You shouldn't be bicycling around in your state, you stubborn American woman.' The man grinned as he lifted my bike into the back of his car and placed his hands on my hips, very intimate and sure of himself. Sure, he was sexy as hell, but what made him think I was going to surrender to him in the middle of a country road as the pale February sun set behind the Tuscan hills? Just because he smelled so great and I knew for a fact he was a really good lover?

'Let me take my damsel in distress home and give her a long, long... foot rub,' Julian coaxed, nuzzling my neck.

'Is that all that's on offer?' I teased and he took my lips in one of his delicious kisses.

He beamed down at me, his eyes twinkling. 'What were you thinking, exactly?'

'Oh, I don't know. I was thinking you could cook one of your specialties.'

'Consider it done. Anything else?'

'Well, maybe later we could relax...'

'Done and done.'

'Ooh, I could get used to being pregnant!'

'Erica Cantelli, I love the hell out of you.'

'Do you, now?'

'I love you and our family and our home and our life. I couldn't be any happier. I just want to wake up every morning so I can start the new day with you.'

'Awh, me too, Julian...'

'Whatever comes our way – locusts, models, chefs, your stepmother – we will always brave the storm, together, forever...'

Any more romance and I wouldn't have felt married to the guy.

Apology

As much as I wish it were real, Castellino is a fictitious town of my own making that sums up everything I love about Tuscany, my home for six years and where my best friends still live today.

Visit my Pinterest page for photos of landscapes and who you think Erica and her tribe should be portrayed by in a movie. I'm thinking Melissa McCarthy! Also, you'll find recipes from this glorious Italian region. And by all means, leave one of your own. We love to eat in Italy!

Acknowledgements

As always, so many people to thank for the making of this book. I can't imagine what it would be like without you all!

Many thanks to my lovely editor Martina Arzu and everyone on Team Aria and Head of Zeus.

And without my brilliant agent Lorella Belli and her agency, I wouldn't be here. So glad to have you all on my side!

Also, thank you to my Tuscan buddy Rolando Bettarini from my university days for all the laughs and everything Tuscan. And showing me how a winery works. Today he owns and runs an award-winning winery called Fattoria di Piazzano near Empoli, Tuscany.

I would have never taken this writing business seriously if it hadn't been for the amazing romance author, my mentor and Fairy Godmother Elizabeth Jennings.

Thank you also to those who have inspired me, helped me, brought me cakes, remembered names and places for me. I can't imagine what this book would have been like without you.

And finally, thank you to my partner in crime, Nick, for being my very own Julian.

About the Author

NANCY BARONE grew up in Canada, but at the age of twelve her family moved to Italy. Catapulted into a world where her only contact with the English language was her old Judy Blume books, Nancy became an avid reader and a die-hard romantic.

Nancy stayed in Italy and, despite being surrounded by handsome Italian men, she married an even more handsome Brit. They now live in Sicily where she teaches English.

Nancy is a member of the Romantic Novelists' Association and a keen supporter of the Women's Fiction Festival at Matera where she meets up with writing friends from all over the globe.